UNKNOWN FATE

"The Beginning"

Dedication

"This book is dedicated to all who have left me a wiser man, and to my lovely wife for all of her love and support."

Love Eric

The Essence

Since the dawn of time, fire has been the essence of light, protection, and destruction. As an ally and savior, it has built the mightiest of citadels, empires, and countries. As an enemy and destroyer, it has consumed everything it touches. It was prophesied in the ancient world, the destruction of Earth, as we know it, would come in the form of fire. But what if fire was the essence we needed to save this world?

During the early 1970's, after segregation, an unlikely bond formed between an African American boy named Billy Smalls and Caucasian girl named Mariah Clover. Though segregation was over, the southern town of Stone Mountain, Georgia held on to many of their racial ideologies. Though their friendship faced many obstacles, Billy and Mariah formed a bond of undying love.

At the center of Stone Mountain's economy, was a nuclear power plant owned by a business tycoon who inherited his father's wealth. Needing to make his own mark on the world, he does whatever it takes to gain more control and power in the world. After him and Billy's paths cross, they are effected by a nuclear disaster that changes the fate of the world. When super human power emerges, evil takes root to destroy all that is good.

In the midst of evil, a hero is born with the power of the sun. Though young, this hero journeys into the unknown to protect and save the world. Will this hero be ready for the world's greatest adversaries, or will everything be consumed by evil?

Chapter 1
The bullied and the beaten

The hands of evil never slept in the small southern town of Stone Mountain, Georgia. The beauty of the small town, was an iconic 3500 feet mountain that stood majestically in the back drop of the town. However, this majestic stone structure had a two -sided history. On one side, the mountain was smooth and firm, but on the opposite side lurked the shadows of a troubled past. Though the civil rights act was passed in the 1960's, this town pushed forward to complete the engraving of three confederate heroes in 1972. The town of Stone Mountain, Georgia struggled to adapt to new ideas and change. Though the country was on the brink of progress, Stone Mountain was slow to embrace change.

In the late spring of 1974, interracial friendships weren't openly accepted in Stone Mountain. However, together a black boy, and a white girl formed a friendship that withstood many obstacles, and ultimately created a fate that saved mankind.

Since head start, Billy and Mariah have been friends. Billy, who is currently the ambitious age of thirteen, has always been an introvert, always staying to himself and not quite fitting in with other kids his age. His dark, mysterious eyes, brittle hair, short and husky frame kept him from being the basketball star. However, in the classroom his brilliance shined, which is why he had the opportunity to attend a predominately white school.

Mariah, who is also at the blooming age of thirteen, was the complete opposite of Billy in the social department. She was outspoken, popular, and sassy. Her skin was milky white, with a soft fragileness to it. Her hair was the mark of her strong Irish heritage. It was fiery red, and long with waves that flowed down her back, like the Red River in Texas. Though her Irish bloodline was strong, her eyes were as blue and clear as the sky. However, her southern drawl was also strong and identifiable when she spoke.

She had a lot of friends and was very popular at Stone Mountain Middle School. Most of her friends were white for the exception of Billy and his friends.

Billy and Mariah's parents were longtime friends. Mariah's aunt took care of Billy, when his parents were out of town on business for the power plant, which powered all of Stone Mountain.

With summertime approaching in a couple of weeks, Billy was ready for his weekend break from Stone Mountain Junior High School. He ran towards the door where Mariah stopped him.

"Hey Billy."

"Yes Mariah," says Billy as he pants out of breath.

"Why are you running?"

"I am trying to get the first seat on the bus."

Mariah giggled as she formed a fist and punched him.

"You are such a square Billy."

Billy smirks, "Whatever."

"Can you take my books for me since you are headed in my direction? I have to drop off my cheerleader uniform."

"Sure thing Mariah," Billy says while taking her books from her.

Mariah warned Billy not to go behind the gym, because bullies hung out in that area. Billy assured her, he could handle himself, and would not let some over-sized bully get in his way.

"See you at the bus, and save a seat for me," says Mariah as she walks away.

"Sure thing."

Billy was a curious boy. Though Mariah warned him, he sneaked a quick peek behind the gym to see if anyone was there. Just as he breathed a sigh of relief, a student passed by and warned him not to go back there. The boy looked at Billy as he took off running in the opposite direction.

Billy walked towards the gym cautiously, while looking in every direction. As he continued his way behind the gym, he had a second thought, and decided to turn around. When he stepped back, he stumbled into Leroy. He was about 6 feet 3 inches tall and weighed two hundred and twenty pounds. He wore his hair in an afro and had a sweat band around it. He was an ornery and intense individual. Leroy and Billy had a history of conflict, which usually involved Leroy beating Billy up each chance he got.

In a deep and husky voice, Leroy asks, "just where do you think you're going?"

Billy was nervous. He stuttered, as he tried to explain to Leroy, he didn't have time for his antics, and would like to pass through towards the school bus. Leroy was shocked and appalled at the way Billy spoke to him.

"I will let you pass," he says, "but first you must pay my toll."

"This is America, the land of the free! Stars and stripes Leroy!"

"Oh yeah? If you don't pay up, I'm going to give you a complementary stumping, and I promise you will see stars," says Leroy as he rolled up the arms of his long sleeve shirt, and cracked his knuckles.

"Let me pass," says Billy loudly!

"I am going to say this one more time, pay up or go down hard."

Billy told Leroy "no" once more.

In anger, he grabbed Billy and threw him against the gym wall, punching and kicking him profusely. Students heard the commotion, and began to gather around and watch the action as Leroy pummeled Billy to the ground. Billy tried to defend himself, but he was no match against Leroy. After Leroy finished beating up Billy, he reached into Billy's pockets and took two dollars, leaving him on the ground in the fetal position with a bloody nose. Leroy laughed at Billy and walked away.

A second later, an infuriated Mariah came to Billy's aide.

"Leroy, get back here," she yells!

Leroy continued to walk away as if he did not hear Mariah.

"Are you alright Billy?"

"Yeah, I am okay."

Billy held his stomach in pain, as he looked towards Leroy's direction.

"Forget that jerk. He's a loser."

Mariah handed Billy her handkerchief, and offered to wipe his nose, but he told her he could take care of himself and stood up. His balance was a little off due to Leroy's punches, but he managed to pull himself together.

"We have a bus to catch Mariah," he says as he walked slowly, but steadily to the bus with his head down.

Mariah looked around and shook her head.

"Why do I even bother? Why aren't the teachers out here? They know students get bullied in this area every day, but they do nothing about it."

"I don't know, and right now, I don't care. I really feel embarrassed and just want to go home."

Billy and Mariah walked toward the bus, as students who witnessed the fight asked Billy, if he was alright. Billy assured them, he was fine, but knew good and well a few minutes ago, they were laughing at him getting his butt kicked.

"Just a few more steps and we will be at the bus," says Mariah.

When Billy and Mariah entered the noisy bus, everyone all of a sudden became quiet, and looked at Billy, as he wobbled to find a seat. One of Billy's classmates, asked him what happened. Then, he started to laugh and tease him.

Mariah told the boy to shut up, as she found a seat for them.

10

She allowed Billy to sit by the window, while he did the usual, and clean his face up before he arrived at home. Then, she handed him his books.

"Thank you for carrying my books Mariah. I was supposed to be carrying yours."

"Don't worry about it Billy. It's the least I can do."

"Billy, why don't your parents do something about Leroy's weekly bashing?"

"My parents are hardly at home, and I can take care of myself," replies Billy.

"You mean more like intensive care, if you keep getting beat up like this."

"Yeah, yeah. It's really none of my parents business. Going to them, to take care of my problems will make me look like a chump. If they did talk to the principal, they would probably write Leroy up and send him back to class. Then, he would really cut my butt, not only one day out of the week, but every day."

"Well, you can't let this go on forever Billy."

"I know, but for now, can we please talk about something else," begs Billy.

Billy continued to stare out of the window in frustration. Mariah watched him from the peripheral of her eyes. She felt bad for Billy. She knew the real reason he continued to take the back way to the bus stop, was to earn Leroy's respect, and stand up for people who were bullied. She hoped he would allow his parents to help him, but knew he wouldn't. Then, she came up with an idea to help cheer him.

11

"So Billy, what do you have planned for the weekend, because I am going to the movies with my parents tonight?"

Billy gave Mariah an empty look.

"Umm…the usual…nothing."

"I have an idea. Would you like to go with us to the movies?"

Billy hesitated for a moment, and replied he couldn't go.

Mariah looked hurt and questioned why, but Billy shrugged his shoulders and told her, he didn't want to intrude. Mariah shook her head, and insisted he go.

After listening to Mariah's constant reasoning for why he should go with them to the movies, he agreed.

"Well, since you're begging me to go, I guess I have no other choice."

Mariah gently nudged Billy on his shoulder and thanked him.

Just as he laughed, the bus hit a bump in the road forcing Mariah to grab onto Billy. As they stared at each other for a split second, the bus came to an abrupt stop at a long dirt road. The driver looked at Billy and told him rudely to get off. As Billy walked by the bus driver, he called him *piñata boy*.

Billy looked at him angrily, and told him to put a cork in it as he exited the bus.

As the bus drove away, Mariah yelled out of the window for Billy to be ready at seven o'clock. He gave her a thumbs up.

While Billy walked down the warm, dusty road, he thought of a lie to tell his parents to explain his bloody nose, dirty hair, and ripped shirt.

When he entered the front door of his house, he called out for his parents.

When no one answered, he ran to the bathroom and cleaned up quickly. He then plopped onto the couch looking around at the empty room and sighed.

"They left me again," he says to himself.

Just as he begun to think about another lonely weekend without his parents, he heard a familiar voice.

"Billy, is that you?"

Billy turned around and smiled as Mrs. Anderson stood in the doorway.

Mrs. Anderson is Mariah's aunt. Her real name was Patty, but everyone called her Mrs. Anderson. She and Mariah's mom were sisters, though Mrs. Anderson was much older. Her hair had a mixture of red hair with gray streaks. She wore her hair in a bun, or pinned up most of the time. She also had a pleasant smile and always wore a dress and an apron. Her husband died during World War II. She was very young back then, and had high hopes of having children. After her husband's death, she never remarried. She dedicated most of her time to the Civil Rights movement and affirmative action. Before long, her child bearing years were gone and she was childless.

She and Billy's parents were close. She met Billy's parents during a freedom march in Birmingham, Alabama to end segregation in schools. In many ways, had it not been for her, they would not have their careers at the power plant.

Once Billy was born, she offered to help raise him, because they were so busy with their careers at the power plant. This is how Billy and Mariah became close friends.

Billy jumped up and hugged Mrs. Anderson.

"Where's mom and dad," he asks?

"They had an emergency meeting with the counsel today and had to leave. They will be back Monday. What is wrong with your nose boy? Did you fall?"

Billy shook his head in agreement with Mrs. Anderson's comment. Then, he hung his head down in disappointment.

"What's the matter Billy?"

"Of lately, since they have this new position, it seems like my parents are never home."

Mrs. Anderson explained, his parents took this new position in order to provide a better life for him. His dad was an excellent chemist, and his mom was one of the plant's top sales persons. She also reminded him, they are a big part of the affirmative action bill that was passed.

"I appreciate all they are doing, I just miss them a lot Mrs. Anderson."

"It's okay son, and I am sure they miss you too."

She smiled and gave Billy a hug. He could smell the scent of apples on her and immediately began to feel better. He knew she was baking, and hoped she made an apple pie.

He smiled and began to tell her about his invitation to the movies with Mariah.

"May I please go to the movies?"

"Well, I don't see why not. What time will you be leaving?"

"About seven o'clock."

"Okay, but I want to speak with my sister, and make sure it is okay for you to go with them. I know Mariah, and she can sometimes leap forward and ask later."

"Yes ma'am."

Just as Billy went to his room to get ready, the telephone rang. Mrs. Anderson answered the telephone, and with a pleasant tone spoke to her niece. Mariah called to confirm the time with Billy, and tell him they were going out to dinner first. Mrs. Anderson told Mariah, she would past the message on, and asked to speak with her sister Sarah.

After they laughed for a while, and talked about Billy joining them for the night, Mrs. Anderson told her sister, she would see her soon and ended the call.

Billy stood in the mirror and stared at his chest. He had old and new bruises on his body. He began to question why, he allowed himself to get into fights at school.

"This not fair. I go to school, I do my homework, and I get straight A's. I do all of this hard work, and Leroy beats the stew out of me each week. All I want is his respect."

Billy wanted to tell his parents about the fights, but they were hardly around. He did not want his father to think he was weak. He wanted his father to be proud of him. He tried to hold back the tears, but the pain and anguish were too great for his heart.

As he stood in the mirror, he wiped tears of sadness away, and smiled as thoughts of Mariah entered his head. He was really looking forward to going out with her and her parents tonight.

While Mariah was waiting for her parents to get dress, there was a knock on the door. Mariah ran to the door to see who was there. Through the peep hole, she saw her friend Zola on the other end. Mariah hesitated, but then opened the door.

"It's about time you opened the damn door," says Zola.

"Watch your mouth. My parents are upstairs."

"It's my mouth and I will say whatever I want."

"Zola, how did you get over here?"

"I walked," replies Zola.

"You walked! Why did you do that? You live two miles away!"

"I walked over to see what you were doing this afternoon."

"Why didn't you call instead?"

"Because someone was on the phone, smart ass."

"More like fat ass if we are talking about you," says Mariah jokingly.

"Are you calling me fat?"

"Well, if the clothes don't fit."

"Okay, Mariah I am just jiving about calling you that."

"Do you want to come upstairs with me, while I finish get ready to go out with my parents? We are going to dinner and a movie."

"Really? What movie are you guys going to see?"

"We are going to see a movie called, *Check In*."

"*Check In*? Isn't that a suspense movie?"

"Yeah, it is about a rich married couple, who is staying at this really nice hotel, and they are murdered. Two famous detectives are assigned to their case."

"Can I go with you and your family? My mom and dad are going to see a race tonight at the tracks, and that is a total drag."

"Of course. I am sure my parents have enough room for one more friend."

"One more friend?"

"Oh yeah, I almost forgot to tell you Billy Smalls is going with us."

"Small Bill? He can't go with us, Mariah," exclaim Zola!

"Why not Zola?"

"For starters, he is weird, and creepy, and a Negro. My dad told me not to trust Negroes."

Mariah looked at Zola in disgust.

"First of all Zola, his name is Billy Smalls, not *Small Bill*. Secondly, he has been my friend a lot longer than you have, and if you don't like it, then go to the race track with your racist parents!"

Zola stared at Mariah in disbelief. She could not believe, Mariah was choosing to take Billy to the movies over her.

"Out of all of my friends, you have always been the first to mention Billy's skin color."

"That's because, I am not afraid to speak up. He is dumb and looks like a little fat monkey."

They both argued back and forth about Billy, and his parents. Zola commented, that his parents got a job at the nuclear power plant, because of affirmative action. She claimed her parents were fired from the power plant to give Billy's parents a job. Once Zola started to state she hates all of "*those people*," Mariah told her to leave and never come back.

"You would end our friendship over some stupid nigger," asks Zola?

"You ended this friendship all by yourself, so take your fat ass home, to your bigot ass parents. Maybe you'll finally lose some weight in the process," says Mariah!

"Nigger lover," shouts Zola!

Mariah slammed the door in her face. A few seconds later, her father came downstairs. Mariah explained to her father what happened, between her and Zola. He shook his head in disbelief, and hugged his little girl, as she trembled with anger.

"We do not promote racism, and we will not allow racist slurs or derogatory comments in our home."

He assured Mariah she did the right thing, and asked if she wanted to cancel tonight, and be alone.

"No way daddy. Canceling tonight would defeat the purpose."

Charles left the room to speak with Sarah. Mariah tried to eavesdrop on what they were saying, but she could barely hear a single word. She heard her father talking about Zola and her parents. Charles stated, he did not want Zola coming back to their home again. Sarah was in agreement.

When they came back in the room, Charles sat beside Mariah, and told her how proud he was of her for standing up to Zola. He then shared a story with her.

"It was about 14 years ago. Your mother and I were in a small diner on a date, when this black couple walked in. The young man had on a cap and gown, and was ready to celebrate his graduation, when these two intoxicated white men insulted and threatened them. The couple clearly wanted no part of the racial comments being made to them, so they got up to leave. One of the white men called them the "N" word and shoved both of them into the door. Just as the other white guy picked up a wooden chair to strike the black man in his back, I quickly jumped out of my seat to snatch it from him. A fight broke out between me and the other guys. In the end, the cops showed up and arrested the black man."

"No way daddy they started it," shouts Mariah!

 "I know sweetie, but that's how the world worked back then. Your mother and I both had first-hand experience with racism. Even though, I confessed to starting the fight,

Fred still had to do thirty days in jail."

"Fred! You mean Billy's dad?"

"That's right Mariah."

"Wow," smiles Mariah!

Charles embraced Mariah tightly and told her to finish getting ready, so they could get Billy.

Within a few minutes, a black sedan pulled up at Billy's house. Billy ran to the door as Mariah approached.

"Hi Auntie," she says, as she runs up and hugs Mrs. Anderson.

"Hi sweetie, how are you?"

"I am okay," says Mariah.

"What happened Mariah, and why were you guys late," questions Billy?

"It's nothing Billy. Come on and let's go have some fun," says Mariah.

Billy looked at Mariah and then at Mrs. Anderson. She nodded at them both and told them to have a blast. They both ran out of the house to the car, while Mrs. Anderson stood on the front porch and waved at her sister and brother-in-law.

Later on, they arrived in town, where they were greeted by one of Charles' friend, the town sheriff. Everyone greeted Sheriff Lanksford, as he and Charles made jokes towards each other and laughed.

Billy noticed Mariah was blushing, as she watched her dad talk with the sheriff.

"Hey Mariah, what's with the look?"

"What are you talking about Billy?"

Mariah drew her lips in for a second, and smiled as if she was caught in the middle of a crime. She motioned for Billy to come closer, as she whispered in his ear.

"Isn't he dreamy?"

"Who, the sheriff? If you're telling me you have the hots for him Mariah, that's disgusting."

"What are you kids whispering about," ask Charles?

Billy attempted to blurt out Mariah's romantic interest, but she quickly placed her hands over his mouth. Then, she elbowed him in his ribs and laughed.

"Where are we going for dinner daddy," she asks?

"It's Billy's choice tonight," says Charles.

"How about Spacely's Star Dust," comments Mariah?

"Spacely's Star Dust? What's that," asks Billy?

"You don't get out enough, do you Billy? Spacely's is the best burger joint in town. They have seasoned fries and creamy milkshakes, which are really out of this world, and on the weekends they play live music," says Mariah.

"Groovy! Let's go there!"

"Yay!" shouts Mariah with excitement.

21

When they arrived at Spacely's, Billy was wowed by what he saw. It was decorated like the galaxy. The walls had planets and stars on them, the seats were made from stones that looked like meteor rocks, and the windows were glowing with neon green lights around them.

As they all took their seats, the sound of rock music filled the air. The waitress walked up to them, and greeted them by name. The Clovers were regulars, but she didn't know Billy. Once Mariah introduced him, she made him feel welcomed.

Mariah's mom and dad told Billy, he was their guest of honor, and could order anything he wanted from the menu. Billy pulled out some money to hand them, but Charles told him to put it back in his pocket.

With excitement and hunger, Billy ordered a Jupiter Burger, Saturn Onion Rings of Fire, and a Milky Way Shake. Mariah and her parents ordered their usual.

While they waited for their food, Charles and Sarah left the table to go dance. Mariah asked Billy if he wanted to cut a rug, but he declined.

"Come on Billy. It's not like I am asking you to marry me or something."

Billy hesitated for a moment, but then gave in to Mariah's wishes.

They all danced until, their food arrived at their table. When Billy sat down in front of his plate, he was in awe.

"Sweet Jesus! That's a big cheeseburger. I can't even fit my hands around it," he says!

After they left Spacely's, they walked over to the movie theater. Charles asked Billy and Mariah to find the best seats. When they passed by the restrooms, Billy told Mariah to go and find the seats, while he used the bathroom. To his surprise, he saw Leroy coming out of a stall. While Leroy was washing his hands, he saw Billy out of the corner of his eyes. With a vengeful smile, he turned towards Billy and approached him.

"Well, well, well. Look at that, Mr. Clean is as sharp as a tack," jokes Leroy.

"What do you want?"

"Well, since you asked, I thought you might be able to spare a brother some change."

"I don't have any more money. You took what I had earlier today," says Billy.

Leroy angrily grabbed Billy by his shirt.

"I know you have more money, and you better give it up now! Or I'm gonna mop the floor with you!"

"I don't have any more money!"

"Well that's too bad fat boy, because it looks like I'm gonna have to beat it out of you! Again!"

Billy shouts, "Let me go," as he knees Leroy in the stomach.

Billy momentarily broke free, but Leroy grabbed Billy by the arm, and threatened to knock him out. Just then, Charles entered the bathroom. Leroy quickly moved away from Billy, and looked as if nothing happened. He turned towards the door to walk out. Before he left, he gave Billy a sinister glare, to warn him, this was not over.

"What is going on Billy?"

"Nothing Sir, I'm fine."

"Did he want to fight with you son?"

"It's all right Mr. Clover, he is one of the goons at school. I handled it."

"Ok, but if you need to talk, I am here for you. I use to be bullied at your age, because I wore glasses and braces. This bully took my lunch money every day until, I had enough and stood up to him."

"What happened when you stood up to him?"

"He beat me up, but I won his respect."

Billy looked at Charles and smiled, because he could relate and understood the message. They left the restroom and entered the movie theater, to join Mariah and Sarah. Billy and Mariah shared a bucket of popcorn. During the movie, Billy and Mariah accidently touch hands, while reaching for popcorn. They blushed and quickly withdrew their hands from one another.

After the movie, Billy and Mariah stared at the stars, while riding back to Billy's house. Mr. Clover pulled his wife close to him, as Sinatra softly played in the background. The mood was right for love. Billy slowly slid closer to Mariah. He couldn't stop thinking about how soft Mariah's hands felt in the bucket of popcorn. Mariah gazed out of the window, not noticing how close Billy sat next to her. He touched her hand making her jump nervously. Her reaction startled him and made him jump as well.

"Y'all alright back there," asks Charles?

In unison they replied they were fine. They began to talk about the movie and Spacely's. Billy told them he had a blast and thanked them for the invitation.

Mr. Clover pulled into the drive way of Billy's house, where Mrs. Anderson left the porch light on. When he walked on the porch, Mrs. Anderson opened to the door to let him in.

"Mrs. Anderson, were you standing at the door the whole time?"

"Of course not, I do have a life you know. Did you have a good time?"

"Yes ma'am. We went to this cool restaurant called Spacely's and to the movies."

"Spacely's?"

"It's a burger joint Mrs. Anderson."

"Oh, okay. Well it is time for bed Billy."

"Yes ma'am."

As Billy walked away, he turned around to ask Mrs. Anderson a question.

"Mrs. Anderson, can I go fishing with Terrence and Hartwell tomorrow morning?"

"The last time you went fishing with those Einstein's, they capsized the boat. While you three argued about who caught the biggest fish, all of the fish you originally caught swam away. Y'all had to swim from the middle of the lake. Thank goodness you boys can swim. Meanwhile, you caught a cold."

Billy scratched his head and laughed.

"But, I guess it is alright with me if you go. Just be careful."

"Thank you. I will make sure to catch a big catfish for dinner."

"Sounds great Billy, goodnight."

"Goodnight, Mrs. Anderson."

As Billy laid in bed, he thought about Mariah. He thought about her soft hands, and her beautiful ocean blue eyes, as he drifted off to sleep. Unbeknownst to him, Mariah was laying in her bed, thinking of him as well, as she drifted off to sleep.

The next morning, Billy woke up to the smell of bacon, eggs, and sausage. He was excited about hanging out with his good friends, Terrence and Hartwell at One Mile Lake.

Terrence and Hartwell were fraternal twins. In appearances, both brothers were light brown skin with a slender build, and hazel brown eyes. Their hair was curly and dusty brown. Both of them were extroverts, and loved to have a good time by joking and laughing with each other. That is what made Billy and them close. He thought of them as brothers.

When Billy arrived, they shoved off from the embankment, and paddled to the middle of the lake. Billy told his friends what happened last night with Mariah. Terrence and Hartwell mocked Billy and Mariah, by blowing kisses to one another as he told his story. Billy became embarrassed and started to fuss with them. Terrence fishing rod wiggled. Terrence thought he caught a whopper of a fish. He asked for help, so all three grabbed hold of the rod and pulled, until the fishing line snapped which made them fall in the lake. The boys all laughed, when they found out Terrence hooked his rod to the capsized boat they sank last year. At least the boat didn't capsize and sink this time. Despite all three getting wet, Billy was the only one who caught two twenty pound cat fish, and two brims that day. He gave the two brothers a brim a piece.

Needless to say, he and Mrs. Anderson ate very well that night.

The next day was Sunday, so Billy did his usual. He went to Sunday school and church with Mrs. Anderson.

After church, they went to the park to feed the ducks, and then to dinner at the Clover's House. Later that afternoon, when they got home, Billy noticed a black car parked in the yard. He asked Mrs. Anderson if they were expecting company, but she looked at him and shook her head smiling.

When Billy and Mrs. Anderson walked through the front door, his mom and dad were standing in the doorway of the kitchen.

"Mom, Dad," shouts Billy as he runs towards them for a hug!

"Hi baby. We missed you so much," says Mrs. Smalls.

"We sure did," says Mr. Smalls.

"I thought you both weren't coming home until tomorrow?"

"The convention concluded early, so we rushed home. We just arrived a few minutes ago, and wanted to surprise you."

"Whose black car is in the back?"

"It's ours son."

"Really," shouts Billy!

"We traded our crate on wheels in for a brand new Lincoln," says Mr. Smalls.

"Wow! That's a groovy car!"

Billy's mom asked him about his weekend. He proceeded to tell her about his outing with Mariah and her parents. Then, he told them about fishing, going to church, and studying.

When he mentioned studying, his dad chimed in and asked him about school.

With confidence, Billy told them he had straight "A's".

They were amazed with Billy's confidence. He also mentioned, he was invited to go out with Mariah and her parents again. They both said it was okay for him to go. Billy felt a rush of happiness, and kissed them both on their cheeks. Mr. Smalls asked for Billy's report card, so he ran to his room to get it.

While Billy was upstairs, Mrs. Anderson felt like, this would be a perfect opportunity to speak with the Smalls in private. She told them, she felt as if Billy was having problems with some of the students at school, and would not talk about it. They asked, if she knew what it was about. She commented that she thought Billy was being bullied.

When Billy returned with his report card, they quickly changed the subject. Billy handed his parent his report card, and held his hands out.

They were very pleased with his grades.

"This is outstanding Billy, right on," says Mr. Smalls!

He reached in his wallet and pulled out a five dollar bill to hand Billy. They promised him one dollar for each "A" he made on his report card.

Mr. Smalls asked Billy, about this past Friday.

"I already told you about my Friday, I went out with Mariah and her parents," says Billy.

Mr. Smalls clarified his question, and ask Billy about his day at school. Billy became nervous.

"It was the usual Friday Dad. I was dealing with teachers, testing, and the village idiots. You know how it is."

"Village idiots," says Mr. Smalls, "Patty thinks you were in a fight. Is that true?"

"Yes," says Billy, "but I didn't start it."

"What happened son," asks Fred?

"I don't want to talk about it."

As Billy pouted and looked away, his parents starred at him in amazement at his reaction. He felt their glares and continued to hold firm, but he finally cracked and told them about Leroy.

"I was walking to my bus, when this jerk by the name of Leroy kicked my butt, took my money and my dignity. I hope you're satisfied!"

Billy was so upset, he stormed away to his room. Mr. Smalls called out for him to come back, but all he heard was Billy's room door slam shut.

"I'm sorry for causing such an up roar," says Mrs. Anderson.

"It's all right Patty, you did the right thing. Sometimes Billy holds it all inside."

"You know I love Billy like one of my own. I just don't want to see him get hurt," she says.

Mrs. Anderson asked if they needed anything else. The Smalls thanked her, and assured her, they would handle Billy. Mrs. Anderson spoke out to Billy telling him goodnight, but he did not respond. She hugged Mrs. Smalls on her way out and left.

Fred looked at his wife in disbelief of Billy's behavior.

"Helen, I am going up to talk with Billy."

"I am coming too," she says.

"I think I should talk to him alone Helen. This is something a woman would not understand. Maybe I can get through to him without your help."

"That's fine, but we are going to pay the school a visit tomorrow. I can't believe Principal Peabody condones this type of behavior!"

Fred embraced his wife and gave her a kiss. She told him to tell Billy she love him and good night. He smiled at her and nodded his head.

Fred went to Billy's room to have a man to man talk with him. Helen, locked up and went to bed.

The next morning, the Smalls went to school to have a

conference with Principal Peabody. Determined and ready, they walked into the office like they were on a mission. The secretary asked them to stop, but they ignored her. They marched into Principle Peabody's office, surprising him out of his chair.

"Mr. & Mrs. Smalls, what is the meaning of this?"

"Do you want me to call the police," asks his secretary?

"No. That will not be necessary. Please close my door," says Mr. Peabody.

"Please have a seat Mr. and Mrs. Smalls, and tell me what is going on."

"Our son is being bullied," exclaims Mrs. Smalls!

"This past Friday, my son was harassed and assaulted on school grounds!"

Principal Peabody looked shocked, and asked them to explain to him what happened. He also called his secretary, to summon Leroy Jackson to the office.

While the Smalls were in the principal's office, Leroy was in the boy's bathroom threatening to put a student into the toilet, unless he gave up his lunch money. Then, Leroy told him not to tell anyone, or he would permanently damage his face. He made the student clean up before he went back to class. As he counted his stolen money, he heard his name on the school's intercom.

"Leroy Jackson, please report to the principal's office."

"Shoot! What does old rotten face Peabody want now," says Leroy.

Leroy straightened up his clothes, and slowly made his way to the Principals office.

Fifteen minutes had past, and the Smalls family had already explained to the principal what happened to Billy. They grew more and more impatient waiting for Leroy to join them.

"Are you sure Leroy is here today," ask Mr. Smalls.

"Yes," says Principal Peabody. "I saw him in the hallway this morning."

Leroy entered into Mr. Peabody's office, and stopped at the door when he saw Billy and his parents.

"Peabody, what do you want man? Can't you see I am trying to get an education," says Leroy?

Mr. Peabody stood up from his chair, and with a stern voice, he demanded Leroy to address him as Principal Peabody.

Leroy laughed and called him Principal Pee.

"That's enough Leroy. You need to come in and have a seat. Now!"

Leroy glanced at Billy and took a seat across the room.

Mr. Peabody proceeded to question Leroy, and asked if he and Billy were engaged in altercation last Friday.

"Yes," replies Leroy.

"Why," asked Principal Peabody?

"I don't like his sorry fat butt."

Mr. Smalls was appalled by Leroy's behavior.

"You don't like him? What gives you the right to hit my son? He has never done anything to you?"

"Yes he did," says Leroy, "he was born…and you two were wrong for giving birth to him. After all, he swung at me first. All I did was talk smack to him."

"He's lying," says Billy, "he swung at me first. I was merely trying to protect myself after he hit me."

"It's my word against yours," replies Leroy.

"Speaking of your word against his word. Before you walked into my office, I had called a few students to my office, who witnessed what you did last Friday. They all told me you started the fight. Judging by your body language, I believe them."

"Slander, and I will see to it that my dad sues this school."

"Careful Leroy, this is not cops and robbers. This is an institution for higher education."

"I didn't start this fight, but I promise you I will finish it!"

The Smalls became irate, and started arguing with Leroy. As they feuded back and forth, there was a knock on the door. It was the secretary with the student of whom Leroy just threatened to put in the toilet. He told Mr. Peabody what transpired a few minutes ago. Leroy denied everything the student said, but his body language gave him away. Principal Peabody excused the Smalls and the student. He wanted to speak with Leroy alone.

A few minutes later, Leroy exited the office shouting and swearing.

Mr. Peabody called the Smalls back into his office, and apologized for what happened. He told them Leroy was suspended for five days, and a parent and principal conference will be scheduled before he can return. With some confidence and reassurance, the Smalls thanked him for his assistance and left. Billy went to class.

When he arrived at class, his teacher asked him why he was late. Billy told the teacher he was in the principal's office. He gave the written excuse to the teacher which explained the situation, then quietly took his seat next to Mariah. When the teacher turned her head to write on the chalkboard, Mariah asked Billy what happened. He told her he would explain later.

After class, Billy told Mariah what happened in Mr. Peabody's office. Mariah was pleased with the results.

"Serves that jerk right for messing with you and the other students."

"I agree."

"I wish he would have been suspended for the rest of the school term. It is so silly to bring him back on the last day of school. Besides, you know what bullies like him do the last day of school."

"Yeah I know. He looked as if, he wanted to fight me right then. You should have seen the hate in his eyes Mariah."

"What are you going to do?"

"I don't know…pretend to be sick that day."

Mariah could see the worry and torment on Billy's face.

"Maybe you should tell your parents what might happen if Leroy comes back."

"I think they did enough. After all, I didn't want them involved in the first place. This is my fight."

"He is strong Billy. You can't do this alone."

Billy sighed at what Mariah said. He knew she was right, and he would need help. As they sat in silence for a few seconds, Mariah suddenly jumped up, and declared she had an idea that would help Billy.

"I have an idea that will help you Billy, but you may not like it."

While Mariah told Billy her plan, he listened carefully to her. In agreement they gave each other a high five.

A week had past, and Leroy was back in the principal's office with his father. Leroy's father was a very intimidating person. He was built like a wall of muscle, and had a very dark face that was always covered in motor oil. Looking at him, you could see he worked hard, and lived hard. He was infuriated about missing work.

"Leroy, this is the last day of school. I had enough of your mess. If I hear you caused some more stupid stuff, I will swell both of your eyes so badly, you will need a magnifying glass to see out of it. Do you understand me?" says his father with a stern voice.

"Yes sir."

"I'm supposed to be fixing on cars today, but instead I am bringing you to school like a five year old."

"Sorry dad,"

"Shut your mouth, and not another word until we talk with Peabody."

They sat in the front office waiting for Mr. Peabody to call them inside. As they walked into his office, Leroy cursed. His dad slapped him over the head and told him to mind his manners.

After an hour's long conference with Mr. Peabody, Leroy was cleared to go back class. Before he left the principal's office, his dad gave him the look of death. He summoned Leroy over to him.

He softly grabbed Leroy and pulled him close, like he was going to hug him. When no one was looking, he held Leroy firm and tight while he whispered in his ear.

"Stay out of trouble, and I will stay out of your hide."

Leroy left Principal Peabody's office feeling weak and powerless to his father. He knew his father was upset about missing work. A minute later, Leroy entered math class, and took a seat. Students looked at him as he walked in. Some of them fearfully straightened up in their seats.

The teacher welcomed Leroy back, and addressed the students about it being the last day of school. She told them to open their text book, and gave them work to do.

Leroy was furious. He told the teacher, it made no sense for them to do work on the last day of school. Students looked at the teacher to see what her response would be. She told Leroy a mind was a terrible thing to waste, and she would not let that happen in her class.

When she turned towards the chalk board to write an equation, Leroy released a loud and disgusting belch. The students were in an uproar with laughter. It was as if, watching Leroy was the best entertainment they had all week.

The teacher looked at Leroy and pointed towards the door for him to leave.

Leroy stood up, and passed gas as he took his bow. Students clapped and laughed as he exited class.

Unknown to his teacher and fellow students, he reacted that way on purpose. He wanted to get out of class so he could prepare for his revenge on Billy.

He ran and hid amongst the bushes behind the gym and waited for Billy. Angrily he pounded his fist into his palm, and he glared towards the sidewalk.

"Billy, Billy, Billy," he says, "you will feel my wrath."

A few hours later the bell rung and students happily left the school building talking about their summer vacations.

While talks of the summer took place, violence also filled the air as students fought to settle old scores. Billy and Mariah watched from a distance, as teachers franticly tried to contain the fights.

Billy and Mariah discussed their plan one more time.

"Billy, this plan has to work," says Mariah.

"It will work, because I'm sick and tired of getting beaten up by that brute. Leroy will be passed to the ninth grade, because he is an athlete. If I don't put an end to this carnage, not only I will have to worry about Leroy, but other students will have to deal with him as well. My idea has to work."

"You know Leroy is waiting behind the gym?"

"Well, let's find out, shall we Mariah?"

As they walked behind the gym, Billy winked at Hartwell. He nodded with approval.

"We are almost behind the gym Billy," says Mariah.

They passed some bushes, Leroy leaped out from behind and knocked Billy to the ground.

"Are you ok Mariah," shouts Billy!

Leroy cocked his fist back, and struck Billy in his face knocking him to the ground again. Billy stood up, and Leroy struck him in the face again. Billy covered his face from the relentless onslaught from Leroy. Passing students watched in horror, as Leroy pummeled Billy to the ground. Billy gasped for air, but every time he took a breather, Leroy knocked the wind out of him.

Mariah leaped onto Leroy's back.

"Leave him alone you animal," she cries!

"Get off of my back you heifer," shouts Leroy!

He grabbed Mariah by her hair, and flipped her over onto the ground. The wind left her body, as Leroy smirked at Billy. He was incensed by Leroy's actions...

"Leave her alone dammit," cries Billy!

He wildly charged into Leroy, pushing him into a thorny bush. Then he leaped in after him. The both of them were scratched up, but at that point, Billy didn't care. He started to swing like a wild lunatic, hitting Leroy with everything he had.

Leroy finally gained his ground and punched Billy in the groin area. Billy's eyes stretched wide open as he gasped for air. Holding his groin, he fell into Leroy.

"Get off of me you punk," says Leroy as he shoves Billy away.

"Do you think you can beat me?" says Leroy as he continues to hit Billy.

"Someone help him," says a student.

"Yeah, well come on and get your asses whipped," shouts Leroy!

Thinking he had Billy down for the count, he kicked Billy in his stomach. Billy cried out in pain as Leroy laughed, and kicked him again in the stomach.

Out of nowhere, Hartwell jumped on Leroy and knocked him to the ground. Leroy punched Hartwell in the face.

Just as Leroy was about to strike Hartwell again, Terrence grabbed him from behind, and held onto him. Five other students helped Terrence contain Leroy. Billy and Mariah were helped to their feet by other students.

With a bloody noise, ripped black t-shirt, and dirty blue jeans, Billy walked up to Leroy and stared at him in anger.

"How does it feel to be over powered?"

Leroy struggled to break free of his captivity, but he was at the mercy of a gang of students, who were all fed up with his bullying.

"You have fought and stolen from us. Now we are going to take back what you have taken from us...our pride."

Billy was so angry, he could barely see straight. He tightly clenched his fist, and drew it back. Just as he was about to strike Leroy, Mariah stood in his way of victory.

"Wait, Billy! Don't do this, he is not worth it!"

She turned around and faced Leroy. As he looked up at Mariah, he licked his lips with a perverted smirk on his face.

Suddenly out of the blue, she quickly drew back her fist and struck Leroy in his face. Then, she started to kicking him over, and over again in his groin area while cursing at him. It took Billy and two other students to restrain Mariah.

"Don't you ever look at me like that again, and don't ever touch me, you filthy piece of crap!"

It took Mariah a while to settle down, but once she did, she took a look at the dress she wore. Like being shocked with a glass of ice cold water in her face, she turned white.

"Oh my God, look what you have done to my dress," she screams!

Filled with the rage of a charging bull, she broke free and jumped on Leroy again hitting him wildly in his chest.

Billy and Terrence restrain her again, but students who saw this started to laugh in amusement.

"Look at you now Leroy. You have terrorized us for years. You thought we were weak, but now you are the weak one," says Billy.

Leroy was grunting and squirming in pain.

"Look at how many of you it took to take me down. You are all punks. You couldn't handle me one on one, so you had to ask all of your little loser friends for help. That makes you a coward Billy," he says.

"You know what Leroy. You are right. Maybe I can't beat you one on one, but a very wise person told me, it's not always the strongest that wins, but the smartest. And we all know how stupid you are."

Leroy looked at Billy in defeat, as Billy walked away towards Mariah.

"Wait," cries one of the students who were holding Leroy down.

"What do you want us to do with him?"

"I am finished with him. Do whatever you want to do to him. I don't care," says Billy.

"This isn't over Billy Smalls," shouts Leroy!
Billy turned around and faced his nemesis.

"It's over Leroy, because if you ever come after me or my friends again, you will be sorry."

Finally, all of the students Leroy tortured over the years got their revenge. As Billy walked away from the fight with a sense of satisfaction, he heard Leroy's scream in the distance. He knew Leroy was right. He would have to deal with him next school year. For now, it was over. He wouldn't have to face Leroy for the rest of the summer. Billy met up with Mariah, Terrence, and Hartwell. Together they all proudly walked onto the bus.

Chapter 2

Summer time

The next day, Billy and Mariah were at her house saying their farewells to each other for the summer. It was an exciting time for them. Mariah was going to New York to visit her family, and Billy was going to spend the summer on his aunt and uncle's farm.

"Hey Mariah, don't forget to bring me back the Statue of Liberty," says Billy.

"I will see if I can fit her in my purse. Have fun at your aunt and uncle's house."

Mariah touched Billy's belly and smiled.

"You better not eat too much. You always tell me how great of a cook your aunt is."

"Stop touching my stomach," says Billy playfully, "I'm pregnant."

Mariah nudged Billy with her arms, almost knocking him off balance.

Mrs. Anderson pulled up at the Clover's house, just as Mariah's father came to the porch to tell her it was time to go to the airport. Billy stood up, and walked towards the car as she hurried back inside, and waved at him from the door.

"Bye Mariah, see you in a couple of months."

"See you soon Billy."

Mariah giggled and smiled with excitement. She had never been to New York before, so she was really looking forward to her trip. As she rode to the airport with her parents, she asked them dozens of questions about New York.

Her dad explained, New York City had a lot of malls, restaurants, parks, and historical museums. As she listened to him, she gazed out the window and imagined herself in New York wearing the latest fashion.

She would be staying with her dad's sister and brother-in-law. They asked Mariah if she wanted to visit them for the summer. She jumped at this opportunity, though she knew she would miss Billy, Hartwell, and Terrence. They all promised to write each other over the summer break.

At the airport, Mariah and her parents quickly ran to her gate.

Mariah's mom, Sarah, was extremely emotional and held onto Mariah for a long time.

"Mom, you're smothering me," she says.

"I am sorry sweetie. I am just going to really miss you," says Sarah.

Charles reminded her how emotional her mother could be.

As they watched Mariah go through her gate to get on the plane, Sarah started to cough frantically.

"Are you okay," ask Charles?

"Yes dear," replies Sarah, "something is in my throat."

Sarah turned away and looked down into her handkerchief as Charles waved to Mariah; who smiled from ear to ear, because she had a window seat. There was a small amount of blood in it. She quickly placed her handkerchief inside her purse, and walked over to her husband to wave to Mariah.

Meanwhile, Billy was heading to his aunt and uncles farm. They lived about 30 minutes north of Stone Mountain close to the Appalachian chain.

When they arrived, Billy jumped out of the car and took a deep breath of fresh farm air. There were hundreds of acres of fields filled with corn, tomatoes, sugar cane, tobacco, and watermelon. They also had a lot of farm animals.

"Dad, I have died and gone to hog heaven."

"Billy, grab your bags and get a grip," says Fred, "you act as if you have never seen my brother's farm before."

They looked around for Fred's brother Joe. He honked the car horn, wondering where everyone was.

Billy tapped his father on the shoulder and pointed in the direction of a tall, dark and husky man coming towards them from in the corn field. He had a slight limp.

Joseph Smalls, often called Joe by most, was a proud and hardworking man. He inherited the family farm, after Fred decided to move and go to college. He worked from sun up to sun down in the fields to keep his family legacy alive.

Fred extended his hand out to his brother, but Joe grabbed his baby brother and gave him a big bear hug. He made his way towards Helen, twirling her around, and then Billy of whom he could barely get his arms around.

"Well, Well, sonny boy. Looks like you have grown since last year," says Joe.

"I did Uncle Joe, and look forward to growing more before the summer is done," says Billy as he rubs his stomach.

"All he kept talking about was visiting you and Joy on the farm this summer," says Helen.

"Well sonny boy, the wait is over and I hope you will enjoy yourself," replies Joe.

"Believe me Uncle Joe I will."

"Where is Joy," ask Helen?

"She went into town, but she will be back soon."

"Well then, on that note, we best be on our way," says Fred.

Joe begged them to stay a little longer, but Fred explained to him they had a conference the next day.

"It's bad enough living in Stone Mountain, if you know what I mean," says Fred.

"Yeah I know what you mean. Times haven't changed that much," says Fred as he nods in agreement.

"We will be back in two weeks to check on you guys," says Fred. "Maybe I'll challenge you in a bar-b-que cook off."

"You're on little brother," says Joe.

They embraced one more time, and said their goodbyes to

Billy, as they reminded him to stay out of trouble. Billy asked his uncle if it was okay to invite a couple of friends over tomorrow. Joe agreed and told Billy to have them come around six in the morning, because everyone in the house is an early bird.

After they left, Joe looked over at Billy and asked him if he knew how to pick a watermelon. Billy told him he did, so Joe asked him to go over and pick a good one. He told him to yell out if he saw a snake.

As Joe walked away, Billy made his way to the watermelon field.

When Billy entered the watermelon field, he was in awe of how big they were. He thought to himself they must be a hundred pounds each.

Billy stooped down to grab the largest watermelon he could find.

"You're coming with me," he says.

Billy grabbed hold to the watermelon, and jerked at the vine, until it gave way. He stumbled with the oversize melon.

"Shoot," he says, "this is a big one. Maybe I should roll it."

Billy made his way towards the house with his conquest. In the distance, he heard a familiar voice and saw a familiar face. It was his Aunt Joy.

Joyce Smalls, best known as Joy, was an older woman, but fit and firm with broad shoulders. She had a warm smile, yet fierce eyes. Her grey hair was always pulled back, but it was long and straight due to her Native American heritage.

She walked over to Billy and gave him a big hug.

"How is my number one nephew," asks Joy?

"I am fine auntie and yourself," replies Billy.

"I am great, especially now that my favorite nephew is here."

"Ghee, thanks Auntie."

"I saw your mom and dad as I was coming home. We spoke for a few minutes, but they told me they were in a hurry to get home. It seems they are always in a hurry."

"I know what you mean."

Billy held his head down for a moment, but then refocused his attention on the gigantic watermelon he battled with and tried to lift it. Aunt Joy grabbed one end and helped him carry it into the house.

"For heaven's sake, where is that uncle of yours," asks Joy?

"He is in the cornfield."

She went to the screen door of their house and called out to Joe, asking him how much longer he would be. He told her he would be there in a few.

Joe asked Billy to help his aunt get the rest of the groceries out of the car. He jumped up to see what she brought back from the A&P.

As he helped his aunt with the groceries, a green apple fell from the bag. He reached down to pick it up and began to look inside the bags. Joy saw him peeping through the groceries and smiled.

"I am going to make an apple pie tonight."

With delighted eyes, Billy grabbed his aunt by the waist and gave her a big hug. He was so elated, he told her he died and went to apple pie heaven.

When Joe entered the house, he walked over to Joy and gave her a kiss on the cheek. He handed her the corn, and went to the chicken coup to pick eggs for breakfast in the morning. Joy warned him not to get lost in the fields, because dinner would be ready in a few hours.

Billy bragged about Joy making him an apple pie. Joe smiled sarcastically and rubbed his stomach.

"I wish someone would make me an apple pie," he jokes.

"I made you a deep dish Georgia peach pie the other day, and you ate the whole thing," says Joy.

"I am a growing boy."

"More like a growing pain."

Joe winks at Billy and says, "It's all right Joyce I still love you."

"And I love you too Joseph," she replies.

Billy asked if he could go with Joe to get some eggs. Joy agreed and reminded them to be back in time for dinner. Joe assured her they would be back before dinner.

When he and Billy arrived at the chicken coop, there were a lot of chickens, but only one rooster. Billy asked his uncle why there was only one male chicken.

"A man doesn't share his women, and neither do roosters," says Joe.

Billy looked confused, but agreed with what Joe said.

"I have something to show you in the barn," says Joe.

"What's in there?"

"Sweet Jesus you ask a lot of questions son. You'll see."

After Billy and Joe collected eggs, they walked over to a bright red barn.

Joe opened the door, letting the light into the dark barn. It smelled like hay and manure. Joe turned on the lights and told Billy he had a surprise.

"Kane, come out here and meet Billy," says Joe.

In one of the stalls, emerged a black and shiny horse.

"Oh wow, Uncle Joe. He's a mustang!"

"You betcha kid-o. He is a true American dream. I won him at the county fair a year ago. He is only four years old."

"Can I take him out for a ride," ask Billy?

Joe looked at Billy with a smile and said, "We will take Kane out for a ride. He is a fast horse and doesn't know you quite yet."

Together, they saddled the horse. When they mounted Kane, Billy was in the back and Joe was in the front. Joe gave a light kick and whistle, which summoned Kane to take off into the fields.

They rode from field to field as Joe gave Billy a tour of the farm. Billy held on to his uncle, and looked up towards the big country sky. There were millions of stars twinkling above their heads. He thought about Mariah for a brief moment, wondering if she could see the same stars in New York City.

Just as he and his uncle turned left, Kane came to a stop.

"Dang nab-bit," says Joe.

"What is it," ask Billy?

"Your aunt is going to kill us. We're late for dinner."

With a slight kick to Kane's right side, and a whistle in the air, Joe told Billy to hold on as they took off towards the barn.

They grabbed the basket of eggs, and ran towards the house. Joy was already on the porch with her hands on her waist.

"What happened to you guys? Dinner was finished thirty minutes ago."

"We lost track of time Joy," says Joe as he hands her the eggs and gives her a big kiss on the lips.

She blushed and told them to wash their hands before dinner.

Joe looked at his nephew and winked. Then, she told them

to take their muddy boots off, after riding Kane, if they wanted a piece of pie.

After they sat down and said grace, Billy's mouth fell open. Joy cooked sautéed spinach with bacon and onions, mashed potatoes, and porter house steaks.

"Do y'all eat like this every night," he asks?

"Of course not son, sometimes Joy fry up some pork chops."

Billy and Joe ate until they could barely move. Joy's apple pie was amazing and to top it off, Billy had his pie with a glass of milk.

"Thank you Aunt Joy," says Billy.

"You are welcome sweetie."

They all cleaned up the dishes and went outside to sit on the screened in porch.

Joe pulled out his harmonica, and began to play, as Billy told them about school. He even told them about Leroy, and what happened on the last day of school. Joy was concerned, but Joe was proud.

"That boy really must have pushed your buttons," says Joe.

"Leroy bullied us since we were kids. It was time we taught him a lesson, so I stood up for myself and the others."

Joy still expressed her disapproval of fighting at school, but Joe defended Billy and told him it was important to stand up for his self. He winked at Billy to let him know he understood.

"Well, I am going to turn in," says Joe.

"It's only eight o'clock," says Billy.

"The early bird always catches the worm, and it's going to be a busy day tomorrow. We have to crop tobacco, and I have some guys coming in the morning to help."

"May I help tomorrow?"

"If you want, but I have to warn you, cropping tobacco isn't easy. You have to watch out for worms and snakes."

"Joe, it's going to be over one hundred degrees tomorrow," says Joy worried.

"It's not going to be hot in the morning Aunt Joy. May I please help since my friends are going to be here? They can help, too."

Joy looked at Billy's face and couldn't resist. She smiled at his tenacity.

"Okay, but you must be back in the house before noon."

They all prepared for bed. Joe told Billy they must wake up at five o'clock in the morning. Billy looked nervous at first, but agreed. He jumped into his bed, and thought about his next exciting adventure on the farm. His bed was extremely comfortable. Before long, Billy was fast asleep.

The next day, Joy was up bright and early. She woke Billy for breakfast.

Billy walked to the bathroom and was greeted by his uncle, already dressed in his overalls.

"Good morning Billy. Are you ready to crop some

tobacco," he asks?

"Well," replies Billy in hesitation, as his stomach rumbled and he rubbed his eyes.

"A good wash and breakfast will brighten your sleepy face, and if not, the sun will," replies Joe laughing.

Billy smiled back.

After getting dressed, Billy sat at the table with his aunt and uncle. He was in awe. Joy cooked his favorites.

"Wow. Blueberry pancakes and bacon," says Billy.

Just as Billy started to stuff his face with a pancake, there was a knock on the door.

"Who is it," ask Joe?

Then a faint and soft spoken voice called out, "Sam."

Sam worked with Joe for a long time. They fought in the Vietnam War together. He was a big strong country boy, who was always serious about everything. He loved to wear flannel shirts and green jeans. He was also a real handy man. He could fix anything with an engine.

Sam came in while everyone was eating. Joy offered him breakfast, but he refused.

"Sam I want to re-introduce you to my nephew Billy," says Joe.

"What's happening Billy?"

"It is nice to make your acquaintance again."

Sam was baffled by Billy's excellent vocabulary. He repeated what Billy said a few times, and then jumped as if the light bulb came on in his head.

"Oh yeah, you are Fred's kid. It is great to meet your acquaintance as well. Oh, and Joe, one of the tractors have a flat tire."

Joe and Sam went outside to change the tires on the tractor. He mentioned Billy was going to help them. Sam looked Billy up and down and nodded. Then, Joe told him the Wilson brothers were coming to help as well.

"Oh no, not them," replies Sam.

"They aren't that bad Sam."

"Speak for yourself. Last year, the youngest one stuck ears of corn into your tractor's exhaust pipe to see if they could make popcorn, and when I cranked it up, BOOM! The motor blew."

Billy started to laugh. Joe looked at Sam and smiled, too. He then told Billy to finish his breakfast and be ready in fifteen minutes.

Billy finished his breakfast, then gave his aunt a kiss and left. He ran towards Joe and told him he was ready to go.

"We are still waiting on a few more people. Where is everyone Sam? Can you please go into the house and call your cousins?"

Just as Sam turned to walk towards the house, they all heard a loud banging sound coming down the dirt road.

"Hey Uncle Joe a red truck is pulling up in the yard," says Billy.

"Finally the Wilson brothers are here. Derrick, Jimmy, and Vance," says Sam.

The Wilson brothers were young and playful. Derrick Wilson was the oldest of the three. He kept the other two in line. Jimmy, the middle child was the more reserved brother. Vance was the youngest and the most rebellious and carefree of them all. He was always in the middle of the action.

The brothers always looked up to Joe, Fred, and Sam as big brothers. They didn't have steady paying jobs, so every now and then Joe called them for help.

"How are you guys doing," ask Joe?

"We are doing fine, and how are you doing," asks Jimmy?

"You guys are late," replies Sam.

"We apologize. Vance was out last night with some random chick. He didn't get home with the truck until five this morning," says Jimmy elbowing his baby brother in the ribs.

"Yeah guys, I am sorry for being late, but you know I'm smooth with the ladies. Chicks dig this."

"Yeah, sure. They dig you alright. Dig you a grave and urinate on it, after they found you jiving around with another chick," says Jimmy sarcastically.

55

"Anyway, Jimmy, when was the last time you were with a girl," asks Vance?

"I am saving myself for the right girl. Someone who is sweet as a glass of iced tea," says Jimmy.

"Ok boys save the romance and comedy show for another day," says Derrick pulling his brothers back to reality.

"That sounds good to me, but before we get to work, I want to introduce my nephew Billy," says Joe.

"It's a pleasure to meet you all," says Billy.

"Yeah, you're Fred's boy. Wow you have grown," says Derrick?

"Yes sir," replies Billy with smile.

Derrick shook Billy's hand, and then introduced him to his brothers.

"Give me five, little nephew," says Vance extending his palm.

Billy looked at Vance with confusion, because he didn't understand his gesture.

"Despite us being white Billy, every one of us grew up together in the same neighborhood. So we are like blood brothers," says Derrick.

Billy looked at Derrick and nodded his head.

"Ok guys, who is ready to crop and collect," asks Joe!

"We all are," says Sam.

"Ok then. Let's go," says Joe!

Just as they turned toward the field, they all heard a faint screeching noise coming closer as a cloud of dust followed. It sounded like the tires on a rusty tricycle.

"What in tar-nation is that," ask Vance?

They all squinted their eyes as an old black mingled up car emerged from the settling dust.

"That car looks familiar," says Billy.

Soon after the car door swung open, out jumped Terrence and Hartwell. After they jumped out of the car, the door slammed shut and sped off. Billy smiled and ran over to his two best friends.

"Thanks for coming guys!"

"Well, we didn't really have anyone to play tricks on, so when you invited us over, we asked our mom if she would bring us," says Terrence.

"If we stayed one more day with her, she would have killed us. Didn't she seem a little hurried when she dropped us off, Billy," ask Hartwell?

"Now that you mention it, she did. What did you do," ask Billy?

"You know us. It was the usual… rubber snakes in the laundry basket, eating half of her chocolate cake and decorating the empty space with paper and frosting. Oh and setting her Jackson Five wigs on fire," says Hartwell laughing.

As the three of them continued to laugh and talk, Joe cleared his throat and waited for an introduction.

"Everyone, I would like for you to meet my best friends. Terrence and Hartwell," says Billy.

"Nice to meet you all," says Terrence.

Joe extended his hand and gave them both a hearty hand shake.

"Nice to meet you boys," says Joe, "I have heard so much about you two from Billy."

"Whatever he has told you sir, we are ten times funnier," says Hartwell.

Sam looked at both of them and smiled.

"So boys, have you ever cropped tobacco," ask Joe as he looks at Sam and winks?

"We have watched our uncles and cousins crop tobacco, but we never have," says Terrence.

"Well there's always a first time for everything," says Hartwell.

"Sure, as long as we can stay for dinner," says Terrence.

Hartwell looked at Terrence and punched him in the arm. The two of them went back and forth joking with each other, while everyone else prepared to go into the field.

Joe drove up on his tractor and blew the horn. Everyone loaded onto the trailer for the exception of Hartwell and Terrence.

Joe pulled off, and left them behind. When they saw the tractor moving, they ran after it.

Terrence and Hartwell caught up with them a half mile down the dirt road. When they arrived at the field, Joe and Sam explained the art of cropping tobacco. For hours they slaved in the relentless sun.

As a team, Terrence, Hartwell, and Billy chopped the tobacco by the root. Then, they carried it to the barn where Joe and Sam strung it to a piece of wood and hung it up to dry. They worked until lunch time. Joe and Sam came back with ham sandwiches and sweet tea.

"How's everyone doing," ask Joe?

"We are doing fine Mr. Joe," says Derrick.

"God oh mighty it is hot out there. Thank you for the refreshments," says Jimmy.

"You said it bro. I felt like a monkey was about to jump on my back," replies Vance.

"How are you holding up Billy, Terrence, and Hartwell," ask Joe with concern?

"I thought it would be rough, but it's not really that bad," says Billy.

Terrence and Hartwell agreed.

"Are you ready to head back to the house and relax," replies Joe?

"No sir! I want to help, and I am not even tired," says Billy anxiously.

"Speak for yourself Billy. I'd like to go rest at the big house. I'm pooped. No more late nights for me," says Vance.

Joe looked at Vance and shook his head smiling at his sense of humor.

"Please let me help," ask Billy.

"Okay, but only for one more hour," says Joe, "I am not going to let your aunt deprive me of dinner tonight, because you're sick from the heat."

"So that's how it is, huh, Joe," jokes Vance.

Joe's face became stern as he puffed out his chest attempting to reassure the guys he wear the pants in the house. They all looked at him with eyebrows raised and smirked.

For the next few hours and thirty minutes, everyone worked hard and made up for lost time. They exceeded their goal, which made Joe very happy.

As the day ended, Sam and the Wilson brothers went home to rest up for the next day of adventure on the farm. Joe, Billy, Terrence, and Hartwell headed towards the house to clean up for a fantastic dinner Joy prepared.

They all sat at the table and ate like kings. They had meat loaf, mashed potatoes, green beans, and pound cake. Joe told Terrence and Hartwell, they could come back the next day, as long as it was alright with their mother. They became excited and thanked Joe.

After Terrence and Hartwell's mother picked them up, Billy

spoke to his parents on the telephone, and told them about the great time he was having. Then, he told his aunt and uncle good night and went to bed. He fell asleep to a quiet and peaceful night.

The next day everyone showed up and ready to work. Terrence came by himself because Hartwell was sick.

"Wow it is hotter today than yesterday," says Derrick.

"Yeah brother, I thought I saw a lake in the fields, but it was only a merrige in the fields," replies Vance.

"A what," ask Derrick?

"A merrige," says Vance confidently.

Derrick looked at his brother with a blank stare on his face.

"Don't you mean a *mirage*," he says?

"Yeah. That is what I just said."

"Okay guys, enough with jokes, and back to work," says Joe.

They all teamed up in the fields to crop tobacco. Lunch came and went quickly. By mid-noon, they were done for the day. Joe asked Billy if he could pick some muscadine grapes. Billy agreed and asked Terrence to go with him.

As the two of them walked down the dirt road towards the house, they reminisced on school and all of the fun they had. Billy stopped all of a sudden.

"Do you hear that," he says.

"Hear what," replies Terrence?

"A rattling sound."

"Do you think that is a rattlesnake?"

"I think so, it sounds really close Terrence!"

"I think it is coming from the bushes ahead. We need to step back slowly," whispers Billy nervously.

They slowly inched back from the bushes. Terrence screamed out for Billy to look out. Billy jumped and screamed as Terrence began to laugh hysterically.

"What is so funny," replies Billy?

"Catch," says Terrence.

He pulled something out of his pockets and threw it in Billy's direction.

"Of all the dirty tricks Terrence…a rattlesnake's tail," replies Billy angrily.

"You should have seen the look on your face."

"I would have expected this from Hartwell, but not you Terrence. One day your jokes and pranks will hurt someone."

"Come on Billy, you take life way too seriously. It was just a joke."

"Yeah, yeah, I bet."

Billy and Terrence arrived at the house to get two huge

baskets, so they could pick grapes. He told Terrence he was going to start picking the fruits. Terrence agreed to join him, after he called his mother.

When Billy arrived at the make shift grape stand, he was impressed by the amount of grapes hanging from the vines. He tasted one of the grapes, and smacked his lips from the sweet, juiciness of it. Billy noticed it was getting close to sunset, so he picked the best grapes he could find. As he continued to pick and eat the grapes, he noticed an unusual smell. He also heard a rattling sound, and thought Terrence might be nearby.

"Terrence, quit fooling around," he says!

As Billy continued to tell Terrence to stop playing, he noticed the rattling sound got closer and closer. Billy looked around in panic. When he saw a rattle snake slowly crawling down a vine, fear gripped him and placed him at its mercy.

Billy slowly stepped back, one foot after the other. When he heard Terrence calling his name, he softly cried out for him to get help.

Terrence continued to yell Billy's name, until he faintly heard Billy whisper to get help.

"Billy I can barely hear you. Why are you whispering?"

"I don't have time to explain. Please find Aunt Joy or Uncle Joe, and tell them to bring the shot gun," whispers Billy!

"Shot gun," shouts Terrence!

"Yes, and hurry."

Terrence heard the faint sound of a snake's rattle. He felt inside his pockets and noticed his rattlesnake's tail was still there. When he realized Billy was in real danger, he panicked and ran towards the house.

"I'll be back," he says.

Billy continued to slowly step back, as he kept his eyes on the snake. Suddenly, he tripped over a vine and screamed as he fell to the damp ground. The snake fell out of the tangled vines above, and slowly began to slither towards Billy. Only a mere few feet away, the snake started to coil. Billy knew he was in serious danger, because rattlesnakes are known to strike their targets once they begin to coil. Petrified with fear, Billy closed his eyes at the mercy of the snake, and waited to meet his fate. Suddenly, the sound of thunder filled the air, along with the smell of gun powder. When Billy opened his eyes, he saw the headless snake squirming on the ground.

"Billy are you all right," shouts Joy!

Billy exhaled with a sigh of relief.

"Yes ma'am. You saved me."

Terrence came from behind Joy, and he ran towards his friend with a wooden pellet he found on the ground.

"Billy are you okay? Were you bitten?"

"No Terrence. Thanks to you and Aunt Joy I am no longer reptile bait."

"Well, you know me, Super T. It's all in a day's work," says Terrence.

"You do realize you're an idiot," says Billy laughing at
Terrence.

"No, I am a hero."

Soon after, Joe and the Wilson brothers pulled up in the
truck as it quickly came to a stop.

"I heard a gunshot! What happened," ask Joe?

With excitement in his voice Terrence explained to them
what happened. He made sure to embellish his part on
saving Billy from the hands of a gigantic rattlesnake.

"And you shot it, Terrence," ask Joe?

"Um, not really," says Terrence scratching his head looking
up at the sky.

"Aunt Joy shot the snake," replies Billy, "she is the true
hero."

"Billy are you ok? You weren't bit were you," ask Joe?

"I'm fine Uncle Joe."

"We are all okay," says Joy.

"Thank God. Joyce Smalls, you are one remarkable
woman," says Joe as he hugs his wife.

Jimmy walked over to the snake, and looked down at it
scratching his head.

"That sure is a pretty big snake. It must be six or seven feet
long. Do you mind if we take it off your hands Mr. Joe?"

"You fellas are more than welcome to take it," replies Joe!

"Well I have dibs on the rattler," replies Terrence.

"Hartwell would like it."

"Cut the rattle off Terrence, and throw the rest in the back of our truck. We're having rattler stew tonight boys," says Derrick.

Terrence cringed at the sound of snake stew.

"Yuck, don't you guys eat real food? The thought of a snake swimming around in brown gravy make my stomach turn."

"Better than those cow patties your mom makes," says Vance.

"Watch your tongue Vance," replies Terrence.

While Terrence and Vance did their usual joking match, Billy looked as if he was still in a daze.

"Uncle Joe, I've been having a string of bad luck lately," says Billy.

"Really son? Like what?"

"I didn't tell anyone, but earlier I was moving a rope to the other side of the fence when Big Red, your bull, dragged me about ten feet in the mud."

"Something must have spooked him. Red is a very mild mannered bull, who usually runs from you, not the other way around."

"Also, last night after I feel asleep, I woke up in the middle of the night to an owl setting in my window. Its eyes shimmered in darkness as it stared directly at me."

Everyone stopped talking and looked at Billy with concern. Even Vance and Terrence stopped joking with each other and stared.

"It's all a coincidence son."

"Your uncle is right," says Joy.

"I hope the both of you are right," replies Billy, "this snake incident was the final straw for me. I have this very bad feeling something is about to happen."

Unfortunately for Billy, these three ominous signs were the preludes to a summer that eventually changed his life.

Later on that week, Billy's aunt and uncle frantically woke him up in tears. His parents were involved in a tragic car accident while returning from their conference. Their tire blew out causing their brand new car to flip over and crash. Unfortunately, Fred and Helen Smalls did not survive.

While Joe and Joy told Billy the news, tears of rage and pain flowed from his eyes. Joe held him close to his chest and told him it was going to be okay. But for Billy, it would never be okay again. His world changed forever.

Chapter 3

Death and the illusions of love

The death of Billy's parents devastated him. He didn't sleep for two days straight and barely ate anything. The smile he once had, was replaced with depression and despair. His family and friends tried desperately to console him, but his pain overwhelmed all of their efforts.

Terrence called often to check on Billy, but Joe and Joy told him Billy did not want to speak to anyone. He sympathized for his friend and wanted to do anything he could for him.

The next day Terrence asked a neighbor to take him to visit Billy. He also brought sodas and a sweet potato pie his mom baked.

"Please thank your mother for the pie and sodas," says Joe.

"I will. How are you and Mrs. Joy holding up," he asks?

"We've had better days, son. It's been pretty hard around here knowing I will never get to see my brother and sister-in-law again."

"I know this does not sound very comforting right now, but they will always be with you," says Terrence.

Joe thought about what Terrence said. With a smile and a heavy heart, he asked Terrence to pray for them.

"Is Billy still locked up in his room," ask Terrence?

"I'm afraid so. He comes out here and there, but he has isolated himself for last two days," says Joe.

"Poor guy. I feel really bad for him."

"We left food at the door for him, but he won't eat or talk to anyone. You, Hartwell and Mariah are his best friends, and he will need all of your support to get him through this."

"Has Mariah called?"

"No, not yet, but I am sure she knows. Her parents called just after I told Patty what happened. I am sure they told her."

Terrence stared down the hallway towards Billy's room and sighed.

"I am going to check on Billy," he replies.

Joe patted Terrence on his head and told him, he didn't think that was good idea, because Billy was not in the best of moods.

Terrence knew Joe was trying to spare his feelings and Billy's pride, but he felt that best friends should be there for each other through the best and the worst of times. He told Joe he would be fine, so Joe motioned for him to go and see Billy.

As Terrence approached Billy's room door, he took a deep breath and knocked. Billy did not answer. He knocked again, but there was no answer. He called out to Billy letting him know he was entering the room.

When Terrence opened Billy's door, he saw torn pillows and blankets around the room. Billy sat on the edge of his bed unresponsive, and depressed as he looked out of the window watching the rain.

Terrence didn't know what to say to his best friend, so with a joyful voice and a smile he greeted Billy.

"Hey Billy, do you want to play football," he asked?

Billy's face was as still as rocks. He responded to Terrence with silence.

"Hartwell had some errands to run, so he couldn't come with me. He told me to let you know he was praying for you. If you come over to my house to play football you'll get to see him. You know how funny he can be when he plays football. It's like watching Big Bird play tennis."

Terrence started to laugh at his joke in hopes, Billy would do the same, but he glanced past Terrence and continued to look out of the window.

"It's a lousy day to play football," replies Billy softly, "it's raining outside."

"Nonsense Billy, we've played football in rainy weather before. Besides, the rain will stop by this afternoon," says Terrence.

"Yeah, and I have a better idea."

"What's that," asks Terrence with anticipation.

"Why don't you get the heck out of my room and leave me alone," shouts Billy slamming his fist down into his bed!

Terrence was shocked by Billy's outburst, and took a few steps back.

"I am truly sorry. I thought playing football with us would make you feel better."

70

"Feel better," replies Billy sarcastically, "you can't make me feel better! No one can!"

Joe heard the commotion and opened the door to Billy's room. He asked if everything was alright. Billy was crying as he looked at his uncle, and told him he did not want to see anyone, and wanted to be left alone.

Joe looked at Terrence and shook his head. Terrence turned toward the door and walk away. Before he left, he told Billy to call him if he needed to talk. He left the room and apologized to Joe for making Billy upset. Joe assured him Billy didn't mean what he said, and told him to come back when he feels better. Terrence walked towards the car that patiently waited for him. With his head hung low, he got in and they drove off.

Joe walked back into Billy's room and sat on the bed beside him. He placed his arms around Billy's shoulder.

"Billy I am going to give you a word of advice. You shouldn't push your family and friends away. I know you are hurting badly, but please don't shut us out. Everyone who knew my brother and sister, your father and mother, are hurting. When your father and I lost our parents, we stood together and leaned on each other. We also prayed and asked God for strength. God is a true redeemer, and will not put more on your heart than it can bear."

Joe held his nephew firmly and hugged him. Billy looked at his uncle with hurt and disappointment.

"Why," he asked, "why did God take my parents away from me?"

"No one knows son, but we shouldn't question God's decisions. He knows best, and you must believe that."

Billy turned from his uncle and stared out of the window again, as Joe patted him on his leg.

"Billy, I hope you know that we are the last bloodline of the Smalls family. You are the only living legacy left of our family. Therefore you are the hope of your parents and me."

"My parents died for no reason. The car accident was senseless. A blown tire costed them their lives. They never should have bought that stupid car."

"Billy, your parents didn't die in vain. They contributed a lot to the civil rights movement, and battled racism from every corner. They received numerous death threats for most of their lives, and kept you at a distance to protect you. Do you think they wanted to spend so much time away from you? Of course not, they trusted Mrs. Anderson to help take care of you, because she supported their efforts and loved them. They persevered so you, and so many others in Stone Mountain could have a fair opportunity in life! Your parents were heroes in all of our eyes! That's what our family did for centuries. Your grandparents were share croppers, who later inherited this very farm we live on. They raised your dad and me, to stand up for what we believed in. Therefore, we cannot give up on our futures, because we are in pain. Giving up on life would be like spitting on their graves."

Billy sat still for a moment and thought about what his uncle said. He felt hurt and embarrassed about how he treated Terrence. He also thought about how proud he should be of his parents, instead of blaming the world for their deaths.

After Joe left the room, he continued to stare out of the window as the tears fell down his face. He cried so much he eyes were swollen. His aunt came in with some hot tea, and told him to drink it so he can feel a little better. Billy did as he was told, and soon fell asleep.

Visitors came and went that afternoon. Mrs. Anderson and the Clovers came by to visit. They asked about Billy, but Joe told them he wasn't up to having company.

Mr. and Mrs. Clover told him Mariah would be coming home the next day. To his surprise, Mariah told her parents she needed to be there for Billy, because his parents were like her parents as well. Joe was a bit relieved given the circumstances, so he rushed to Billy's room to tell him the great news. When he opened the door, he saw Billy sleeping soundly. He softly closed the door and left. Unbeknownst to Joe, Billy opened his eyes after he left. He was up the entire time, yet he was paralyzed with emotional pain. He knew the next day, his parent's funeral was going to take place, and it would be the last time he would lay eyes on them. He buried his sorrows into a damp pillow as he softly cried the entire night. For a brief moment, he wished it was his funeral, too.

Early the next morning Joe went into Billy's room to check in on him, but he wasn't there. He was sitting on the front porch staring at the last remaining stars, before the sun brightened up the morning sky. Joe slowly walked behind Billy and touched his shoulder.

"Are you okay son?"

"I just wanted some fresh air. This is so hard Uncle Joe. It hurts like no pain I have ever felt before. I can't even see straight. I feel so alone."

"Son, you are not alone. I know it's not going to be easy, but we will get through this as a family."

They embraced one another, as the sun peeked through the clouds and shined down on them.

"Come and eat Billy, I know you are hungry," says Joe with a smile?

"Yes Sir," says Billy.

"I also found out from the Clovers that Mariah will be home today."

"She shouldn't have done that. She should have stayed in New York."

"Billy you know Mariah is like family to us. She would want to be here. She even told her parent, we are all family."

"That sounds just like her. Always thinking about others," replies Billy with a gentle smile on his face.

"Billy, I think you and Mariah would be a nice item together."

"All right Uncle it time to eat," interrupts Billy.

"Seriously Billy, you guys would be great for one another," says Joe.

"Breakfast time Uncle," says Billy grabbing his uncle by the arm and dragging him inside.

After breakfast, they all prepared for the funeral. Family and friends gathered at their house just as it started to rain. As they got inside their cars, Billy looked around at everyone dressed in black. He looked for Mrs. Anderson and the Clover family, but there was no sign of them.

When they arrived at church, close to a hundred cars and trucks were parked outside.

When the family processional began, the sounds of slow and solemn music filled the tiny church. Tears began to flow from Billy and Joe's eyes as sorrow crept into their hearts. Billy fell to the floor with overwhelming grief, as Joe attempted to hold him up. Joy assisted Joe, along with some church ushers and helped him to his seat.

Behind them sat the Clovers, Mrs. Anderson, Terrence, and Hartwell. Sitting directly behind Billy was Mariah. She leaned forward and touched his shoulder to let him know she was there for him. Billy felt her warmth and felt encouraged.

"I will always be here for you no matter where I am," she whispers.

After the funeral, Mariah was allowed to stay with Billy for several days, hoping she might be able to lift his spirits.

Her first night there, was spent trying to understand how Billy felt. When he talked, she listened and when he didn't she sat quietly by his side. When he finally fell asleep, she went to the guestroom and did the same. For the first time since the death of his parents, Billy slept peacefully.

The next morning Billy asked his uncle, if he and Mariah could go horseback riding. When Joe agreed, Mariah jumped for joy. They both rode for hours, enjoying each other's company as Joe and Joy watched from a distance. After they disappeared in the fields, Joe told Joy, he was going to check on them and make sure they were okay.

"Joe, they are having fun. Leave those two kids alone," says Joy.

"I wanted to give Kane to Billy."

Joy looked at Joe with astonishment. She knew Kane was his pride and joy.

"You are going to give Kane to Billy? Are you sure?"

"Yes, if he can master him. Billy just lost his parents; now we are the only parents he has left. He is like the son we never had. I want him to know how special he is to us."

Joe jumped into his pick-up truck and drove to the stables. He mounted Kane with another horse in tow and rode off to find Billy and Mariah.

Joe spotted them under an apple tree. He rode over to them and smiled.

"Billy! I have a surprise for you," he says.

"What is it Uncle Joe?"

"I want you to have Kane. That is if you can ride, and take care of him," says Joe nervously.

Billy shook his head in disbelief, but once the shock wore off, he quickly jumped to his feet and hugged his uncle.

76

"Thank you Uncle Joe. Can I try to ride him now?"

Joe nodded in approval. Billy attempted to mount Kane as he bucked back and forth, almost throwing Billy off. Billy continued to try, but each time, Kane refused to let Billy mount him. Joe and Mariah looked at each other in amazement at Billy's determination. Before long, the sun started to set. Joe yarned tiredly as he watched Billy's countless attempts.

"We should call it a day," he says.

"No Uncle Joe. I can't give up now."

Billy looked at Kane and sighed. He calmly stroked Kane's mane and asked him for permission to ride him.

Kane stomped his right hoof in the ground, as his head went up and down. Cautiously Billy climbed onto Kane's back. He gently rubbed Kane's side to say thank you. Then, he whistled in the wind, and Kane took off. Billy smiled as he rode around thanking his uncle. Kane now belonged to Billy, and together they forged a new bond.

Billy, Mariah, and Joe rode back to the stables and returned to the house for dinner. After dinner everyone headed to the porch for more fun and relaxation. Joe congratulated Billy again for taming Kane as he told Joy what happened.

"And that's how the west was won," says Joe as he ended his story like he was explaining a movie.

After Joy and Joe retired for the night, Billy and Mariah sat on the porch and stared into space.

"Do you think there is life on other planets Billy?"

"I don't think so. If they did exist, wouldn't they have tried to take over the Earth by now?"

"Yeah, or control our thoughts with their minds. They may be living amongst us now Billy, as super humans."

Billy looked at Mariah and smiled. They talked a little while longer about aliens and super humans, until Mariah yawned and told Billy she was about to go to bed. Billy grabbed her by the hand and thanked her for everything. He told her, he had a special surprise for her the next day. Excited and exhausted, Mariah smiled and told him she would see him in the morning.

The next day, flew by quickly. Billy and Mariah watched cartoons and played games most of the day.

Later on that evening, Billy coaxed Mariah into sneaking out with him to the stables. Quietly they mounted Kane, and rode out to the lake located on the edge of the farm. There was a small boat anchored to a tree.

Billy turned on his flashlight to check the boat for snakes. Then, he helped Mariah into the boat and gave it a push from the shore. As he jumped into the boat, it almost capsized which made Mariah laugh as she helped him in.

"Come on you goof," says Mariah.

"This is the best view on the farm to see stars," says Billy with a smile.

As they gazed towards the heavens and saw billions of stars, Mariah shivered as the wind blew from the lake.

"I brought a blanket if you need one," replies Billy.

"Thank you Billy. Aren't you a gentleman," says Mariah in a pretend Southern voice.

"You're welcome my lady."

Billy glanced over at Mariah and could see the excitement in her eyes.

"Wow Billy. It is so beautiful out here. I have never seen the stars like this before. They are reflecting off of the water."

"That is not all Mariah."

Billy pointed towards the darkness and Mariah's eyes followed. In the distance hundreds of fire flies reflected off of the lake. As they came closer to the boat, Mariah and Billy's eyes lit up. Billy felt nervous, but he really did like Mariah, more than she knew. As they gazed at the lights, he thought about ways to express how he felt.

"You know Mariah, the fireflies represent the stars and we represent the moon and sun."

"Really, you must be the moon Billy, because you are dark and mysterious. There is a lot to you I don't know."

"Well, I know you are the sun, because you have brightened up my cloudy days."

Mariah blushed and told Billy to stop flattering her.

"Mariah, at my parent's funeral, I heard you whisper, that you would always be there for me. Did you really mean it?"

"Of course, you are my friend and I am always there for my friends."

Though Billy expected Mariah to call him more than a friend, he smiled, so she would not see his disappointment.

"Is something wrong Billy?"

"I just thought we were, you know, a little more than friends."

Mariah became nervous at Billy's forward response. She did not want to hurt him, or lose a friend, but she felt he needed to hear how she felt.

"Billy, we have been friends since we were babies. I haven't really considered us being more. Besides, we have our whole lives ahead of us for love, and heartbreak."

With that statement, Billy felt a chill through his bones as Mariah's words cut straight through him. He felt there was no need to lick his wounds, so he changed the subject and talked about school.

After an hour on the lake, Billy and Mariah sneaked back into the house.

"Do you think Mr. Smalls will let us ride Kane tomorrow," asks Mariah?

"Of course he will. Kane belongs to me now," says Billy with a smile.

With a smile, Mariah thanked Billy and wished him a goodnight. She hoped Billy wasn't upset about her response to his question.

Billy wished Mariah a goodnight as well. He was disappointed Mariah didn't feel the way he felt, but was still grateful to have her as a friend.

The next day, after breakfast, Joe allowed Mariah and Billy to take Kane out for a ride.

"Can we go fishing," ask Mariah?

"Of course, but is this how you wish to finish your last day here," replies Billy?

"Absolutely, and besides, you know I will be back," says Mariah.

Billy and Mariah gathered fishing supplies and rode back to the lake. As they approached the lake, nervous tension mounted in Billy's stomach as he remembered last night. Billy helped Mariah down from Kane, and grabbed the fishing equipment they brought with them.

With the fishing supplies in hand, they stepped into the small boat. For hours they sat quietly, until suddenly they felt a pull on their lines. Before they knew it, each of them had three fish a piece.

The sun started to set, and as the day drew to a close, they mounted Kane and hurried back home. Joe and Joy were outside grilling some food. They argued back and forth about the amount of meat Joe grilled, while Billy and Mariah laughed at them both.

Joe and Joy thanked Mariah for being there, and said the cookout was in her honor. She blushed and told them, they didn't have to do that for her.

They both hugged Mariah as she looked at Billy and smiled. Once the food was finished, everyone filled their face with barbeque and turned in for the night.

The next morning, Billy and Mariah woke up early and sat out on the porch. Billy was sad to see Mariah go. When her parents pulled up, Mariah told him he could visit her anytime. He promised he would, as long as it was alright with his aunt and uncle. Billy thanked Mariah for being his best friend when he needed her the most. She assured Billy, he would have done the same thing if her parents died.

Mariah's parents and Billy's new parents shared some small talk about the weather and the farming business. Joe and Joy thanked them for allowing Mariah to spend some time with Billy. Mr. and Mrs. Clover asked Billy if he was feeling better, which he replied he was.

"Your father was like a brother to me Billy. If you ever need anything, and I mean anything at all, we will do whatever we can to help," he says.

Billy smiled and looked at Mariah with assurance.

"Thank you Mr. and Mrs. Clover," he replies. .

They all agreed Billy would visit Mariah, and stay with them a week from day. After they said their goodbyes, the Clovers left, leaving a trail of dust in the distance.

"She's a nice girl," says Joe.

"Yes she is Uncle Joe."

"Last night I couldn't sleep, so I went out deer hunting. On my way back to the house, I saw the both of you in the rowboat on the lake."

Billy shifted his eyes away from his uncle and looked towards the fields.

"Hey Uncle Joe, did you get lucky and kill a deer?"

"No, and I hope you didn't get lucky either. What were you kids doing out there so late?"

"I wanted to surprise Mariah, so I took her out to the lake and that's all. Nothing else happened."

Joe looked at Billy and rubbed his chin with suspicion. He squinted his eyes in curiosity.

"I watched the both of you, and I am just going to come out and ask. Do you have feelings for her?"

Billy's eyes widened with surprise at his uncle's straight forward question.

"I guess so," says Billy hesitantly.

"Did you tell her how you felt?"

"Kind of," says Billy.

"What did she say?"

"She said she wanted to be friends and nothing more."

Joe looked at Billy and shook his head.

"Listen son, women want to be chased."

"Chased," says Billy, "we have been running around playing since we were kids."

Joe looked at Billy, and let out a hearty laugh that echoed in the air.

"She wants you to woo her, not run her away."

"Huh?"

"Didn't you get in the row boat last night?"

"Yes Sir. It was really nice out, and there was a full moon above our heads."

"Did she kiss you?"

"No Sir. I was a total gentleman," says Billy.

Joe shook his head and laughed at Billy's innocence.

"Well, I see I am going to have to teach you how to woo a girl," says Joe.

"But she only wants to be my friend. I cannot make her want more than that. Mariah likes her freedom."

"She is a very pretty girl Billy, and girls like her don't stay single forever. Trust me, I know these things."

As promised, Billy was allowed to stay at the Clovers. On the way there, Billy asked his uncle to stop at the florist so he could pick up some flowers for Mrs. Clover and Mariah. As he entered the flower shop, Zola spotted him in the store looking at daisies. A sinister smile grew on her face as she approached him.

"Hey roach face," she says!

"Zola, what do you want?"

"I am so sorry to hear about your parents."

"Thanks Zola," says Billy in confusion.

"No," says Zola. "Thank you, because if your parents had not died, my parents would still be unemployed right now."

Billy's eyes grew dark with anger.

"If you were a man, I would punch you right now," he says.

"If you were a man, and not an ape, I would like to see you try it," shouts Zola!

"I don't have time for your petty taunts. I am on my way to see Mariah."

"You took my best friend from me, and I will never forgive you for that monkey boy!"

"What? You're paranoid. I didn't cause the demise of your friendship with Mariah."

Zola stared at Billy viciously, but Billy stood his ground to show her he was not intimidated.

"It is Billy. It's all your fault."

"What do you mean?"

Zola told Billy about the night he went to the movies with Mariah and her family. She told him she came over to visit Mariah, but they had an argument about him. She explained to Billy she didn't think it was right for Mariah and her family to take him to the movies out of pity.

"Why would they feel sorry for me," says Billy.

"Because you are black, and your parents were never around," says Zola.

"That is not true. They invited me to stay a few days with them. That is why I am on my way to their house right now."

"Do you think this is genuine Billy? All they wanted to do is show the world they care about *your* kind. You know niggers and stuff. You are nothing more than a charity case for them."

"I care about Mariah," says Billy holding the daisies firmly in his hands.

"Really, and are those flowers your way of showing her how you feel about her? If you told Mariah you had the hots for her, she would laugh in your face and say you two were friends and nothing more," says Zola.

"You listen to me very carefully Zola; stay away from Mariah and me. You are a horrible person and a horrible friend," says Billy.

Billy and Zola both stared at each other as if either one of them could burn a hole through the other.

Zola smiled at Billy, and gracefully walked out of the flower shop.

Billy was disgusted after hearing what Zola said. Her words had hurt, and with each second, Billy's heart grew darker. He questioned why Mariah never told him about her and Zola's argument. He questioned their friendship and the bond their families shared.

As Billy's heart filled with anger and hurt, he dropped the daisies he had, and stormed out of the flower shop to the truck.

"What is wrong with you son," ask Joe?

"I can't believe they kept this from me," says Billy shaking his head.

"Keep what, and who is they," ask Joe with a confused expression on his face?

"Mariah," says Billy, "I want to go home."

Joe pulled off in the truck and headed home. As they passed through the town and headed back to the farm, Billy looked out of the window like his heart was ripped out. He told Joe what happened on the way home. His uncle urged him to call Mariah and talk about it, but Billy refused.

Joe told Joy what happened, so she called the Clovers and told them Billy wasn't feeling up to his visit.

After watching Billy mope around the farm for days, Joe became tired of watching his self-inflicted pain. He decided to let Billy know how he felt about Zola's comments.

"Billy, I think you are overreacting."

"Uncle Joe, the Clovers betrayed my trust that night we went to the movies. They took me out because of pity."

"Billy I don't think it's true. I think Zola said it to make you mad with Mariah."

"It is all true, and that is why I do not want to see or speak to Mariah."

After Billy didn't show up at the Clovers, Mariah continued to call Billy out of concern. Every time Joy answered, Billy told her to tell Mariah he was busy. Joy was tired of lying to Mariah, and told Billy she was not going to do so anymore.

When Mariah called him again, he finally answered.

"I am not speaking to you ever again, so stop calling me," he demands!

Mariah was totally appalled by Billy's behavior. She wondered what was going on, and why he was so cold to her.

"I will never trust you again Mariah!"

"Why Billy," she pleads?

Billy hung the telephone up and walked away from it as it rang again. He knew it was her calling him back.

Mariah couldn't understand how, or why Billy treated her this way. She needed her best friend badly, and he told her to never call him again.

When Mariah got back from staying with Billy, she found out, her mother was diagnosed with stage four lung cancer. The doctors did everything they could, but nothing worked. She had six weeks to live at best.

Mariah struggled to stay strong for her mom, and spend as much time as she possibly could with her.

Her parents thought having Billy spend some time with them, would make it easier for Mariah, but when he did not show up or called she became concerned.

After Billy told her to stop calling, she focused all of her energy on spending as much time as she could with her mother.

As weeks passed by, it became very difficult on Mariah and her dad. Sarah was in a lot of pain and kept coughing up blood. The doctors gave her morphine to help with the pain, but it didn't always work.

On Sarah's final days, Mariah stayed by her side, holding her hand. Sarah asked, for her jewelry box. Inside of the box were diamond earrings, pearl necklaces, and a ruby ring. Sarah told Mariah, they were all hers. Underneath the insert of the box, was a separate compartment Sarah opened. Inside of it, was a pendant, which had been a family heirloom for over a century. She told Mariah it originally belonged to her great-great-great grandmother who came to this country from Ireland. Mariah quietly sobbed, as her mother shared this story with her. The pendant had rubies embedded into it, with a dark emerald in the middle. She gave the pendant to Mariah. She told Mariah one day, she would pass this pendant to her daughter, and the tradition would continue.

"I'm so sorry," says Sarah.

"Why are apologizing," ask Mariah.

Sarah touched Mariah's hair.

"I'm so sorry. I will not be there to brush your hair at night, or kiss you good night…to give you advice or be there for your prom… graduation… to see you off to college…your wedding day, or the birth of your first child."

A rush of fear and pain swept over Mariah, as she listened to her mother's words.

"Mom," she says, "don't talk like this. All I care about is having you in my life."

Mariah laid her head on Sarah's lap, as Sarah caressed her head.

"I want you to be strong, and look after your father. You both will need one another. You both will face many challenges, but I know you two will overcome, any obstacle. Stay together, stay stronger my darling Mariah. I will always love you," says Sarah.

"I love you too mom," replies Mariah with a redden face.

Suddenly, Sarah stopped caressing Mariah's head, and her breathing became shallow.

"Mom," she ask?

Sarah didn't answer back. Mariah held her head up and glanced at her mother, who looked like she was asleep. She called her name over and over again, but there was no response.

The entire time Sarah and Mariah were talking, her dad was in kitchen waiting. Sarah asked him to give her and Mariah some time. When he heard Mariah crying, he ran into the room, and saw her on knees at his wife's bed. He saw the peaceful expression on Sarah's face, and knew she was gone.

On the day of Sarah's funeral, mostly everyone in town showed up. Mariah glanced over the huge crowd looking for Billy to see if he was there, but there was no sign of him. She asked Mrs. Anderson if she heard from Billy. She did, but did not want to get into it at the moment.

Later on, after the service, Mariah and her aunt had a chance to talk.

"I didn't see Billy there," says Mrs. Anderson, "but there were a lot of people around, and he has been having a very difficult time grieving over his parent's death. He is so angry with everyone."

"I came all the way from New York when his parents died. Why couldn't he put his differences aside and stand by my side when I need him," exclaims Mariah!

"Would you like for me to speak with him?"

"Frankly Aunt Patty, I don't care anymore," she says, "as far as I am concerned, Billy and I are through. We are no longer friends."

As Mariah grieved in front of her Aunt Patty, her anger toward Billy grew. She felt like he abandoned her when she needed him the most.

On that unfortunate day, Billy and Mariah's friendship came to a bitter end. The summer that brought them together tore them apart in the end.

Chapter 4

Urban school stars

"Finally, finally, I am back in my element. It's back to school," says Billy with a smile on his face.

"I thought your aunt and uncle were going to send you to the high school closer to their farm," replies Terrence.

"They were, but Aunt Joy felt it would be better if I surrounded myself with familiar faces and friends."

"Well we are glad to have you back man," says Terrence.

"And I am happy to be back," replies Billy enthusiastically.

"Wow, man. I have never seen anyone so happy about going to school," replies Terrence.

"Word, man. I was just thinking about how school drives me crazy. I'd rather be in Mr. Joe's tobacco field or scooping up hog poop," says Hartwell.

"Right on brother," says Terrence as he gives Hartwell a high five.

"Well I wasn't expecting too much enthusiasm about school from you two zeros anyway," replies Billy.

"Hey I resent that," says Terrence.

"Yeah, me too," replies Hartwell.

"Whatever guys, besides I need to go to class," says Billy as he takes off quickly.

Terrence and Hartwell were surprised at Billy's rude

attitude. They both took off in his direction asking him to wait up. When they caught up with him, Billy continued to walk away.

"Hey, Billy, why didn't you wait for us? Do you even know where our first class is located," ask Terrence?

"Yeah. Maybe we should stick together," replies Hartwell.

"Sure. I guess you two would look smarter standing next to me…a pure genius," replies Billy.

Hartwell and Terrence looked at each other and burst into laughter.

"Dude, you are wearing a light blue button down shirt and pink pants with a green scarf around your neck, does it look like we enjoy standing next to you," ask Terrence?

"Yeah, you look like a chunky black version of Fred from Scooby Doo," replies Hartwell.

"Whatever. This is the preppy look," replies Billy.

"Seriously Billy, this is the dump me in the trash can look. They have these rituals in high school, where the upper classmen finds the freakiest of freshmen and dump them in the dumpster behind the school."

"Rituals, really," says Billy with a sarcastic tone.

Terrence jumped into the conversation to explain to Billy; it was not a joke.

"I'm telling you Billy, Hartwell is right. Be careful and trust no one."

With a nonchalant look, Billy says, "On that note, I will see you both in biology class."

As Billy walked away, Hartwell and Terrence looked at him with concern. Again they were both shocked at Billy's snobby comments, and his reaction to ritual they warned him about.

"Hartwell, it seems as though Billy has changed overnight."

"Yeah I see what you mean, but I'm not digging his vibe at all."

The two of them decided they would stick together, but keep an eye on Billy as well.

Meanwhile, Billy was happily marching along, and looking for his class when he saw two girls he didn't expected to see together.

"Well, well, well, look at those hot pants Mariah," says Zola as she points at Billy.

Billy was going to continue to walk to class and ignore Zola, but he decided he would rather return the favor.

"With all that brown you are wearing today Zola, one might think you are a colored girl."

Zola was surprised at Billy's boldness.

"Why you good for nothing monkey," shouts Zola!

As Zola fixed her next choice of words to lay into Billy, Mariah stopped her.

"Let it go Zola," she says.

Billy crosses his arms and says, "Why thank you Mariah, but I don't need your assistance."

"I wasn't helping you. I just don't want to waste my energy watching you two argue."

Billy rolls his eyes and says, "Well excuse me for upsetting the high and mighty Princess Mariah."

"Grow up Billy," says Mariah.

"Maybe you should grow up and stop telling lies."

"Lies, what are you talking about Billy. I have always been honest with you. What lies are you talking about?"

Zola saw where the conversation between Mariah and Billy was headed. So she seized the opportunity manipulate the situation.

"Wait just one minute chunky. Mariah was there for you when you lost your parents. It's more than I can say for you," says Zola.

Billy felt the cold sting of Zola's words on his brow, and dropped his head in guilt.

"Zola, that is enough," says Mariah.

"It hurts doesn't it Billy," says Zola.

Mariah looked at Billy and then turned to walk away.

"Come on Zola."

"Even now you are protecting him?"

"I don't need protection, or pity. Forget you both," says Billy as he walks away.

"You're so insensitive Billy," says Mariah.

Billy stopped and quickly turned around to face Mariah.

"You are no better than that bigot of a friend of yours."

Enraged, Mariah drew her right hand and slapped Billy. Students passing by saw what she did, and started to laugh. Zola pulled Mariah by the hand and dragged her away.

A few minutes later, Zola asks Mariah if she slapped Billy because she was defending her, or he compared her to her racist friend.

Mariah looked at Zola with tears in her eyes and told her to let it go.

Embarrassed, Billy rubbed his face and ran to the language arts building as students laughed at what they witnessed between him, Mariah, and Zola. Zola did more than hurt his pride. She had also hurt his feelings. He knew, he was wrong for not being there for Mariah, when her mom died. Hearing Zola say it just reconfirmed his guilt.

After a few minutes of gathering himself, Billy walked out of the building. He pulled out his schedule, and campus map as he looked to find his first class. As he stared at the paper in confusion, a student with dark course hair and a medium build approached him.

"Excuse me, are you lost," asks the student?

"Yes. I cannot find my way to the Walter Edison Building."

"Luckily for you, I am heading in that general direction."

The student handed his fist to Billy for him to pound as a symbol of friendship. Then, he introduced himself as Paul. He asked Billy, if he was a transfer student? Billy told him, he was a freshman.

"I am a senior," says Paul.

On the way to class, Billy tried to make small talk with Paul. He was so thrilled to be making friends with an upper classmen.

As they were headed in the direction of the buildings on the other side of school, Paul saw one of his friends.

"There you are Paulie," says the student.

"Rolen, what's happening," says Paul?

"Nothing much man. How's it going," says Rolen?

"I was just checking out some of the new hot mamas around, if you dig," says Paul.

Rolen looked towards Billy as if he was waiting for Paul to introduce him.

"Rolen, this is Billy," says Paul.

"What's happening Billy," replies Rolen.

"It's a pleasure to meet you Rolen," he says.

"I am showing Billy around campus, he has a class in the W.E.B. building," says Paul.

"You must be a transfer student," says Rolen.

"Something like that. I transferred straight from Junior High," says Billy with a smile on his face.

Paul and Rolen both looked at each other and gave a nod. Then, before Billy could even figure out what was about to happen, Paul grabbed his arms and held them behind his back. Billy was kicking and screaming for them to stop, but Rolen grabbed his legs and held them. They both carried Billy to the back of the building, where a crowd of students awaited the main event. Students were laughing and screaming as Paul and Rolen carried Billy to the large green dumpster. They cheered and screamed for Paul and Rolen to throw him in. Billy begged in tears for them to put him down.

"No, please don't," begs Billy, "I thought we were cool," he says.

"How dumb can you be? You are a fat, pathetic freshman. We were never cool," says Paul.

"Especially in those pants," says Rolen laughing.

"Dump him! Dump him! Dump him," chants the crowd!

Rolen looked at Billy and thought about how pathetic he looked.

"I am going to enjoy this, because you deserve it, you will thank us," he says.

He and Paul lifted Billy high above their heads and threw him into the garbage. The crowd cheered and laughed as Billy flew into the dumpster. Once they closed the lid on

Billy, the bell rung and everyone scattered to class.

Minutes went by as Billy struggled to free himself from the dumpster, but the lid was too heavy and the dumpster was too deep. He screamed for help, but everyone was in class. He began to cry in the darkness. He felt like this was karma, because he did not listen to Terrence and Hartwell when they said to stick together. His attitude towards them was horrible. When he thought all hope was gone, he heard two familiar voices calling his name.

"I am in here," he shouts!

"Coming man," says Hartwell as they rush towards the dumpster.

"We were in class and heard about the freshmen ritual being completed," says Terrence.

"And when we didn't see you in class, we were worried and told the teacher we had to go to the bathroom," says Hartwell.

Together, Hartwell and Terrence pulled Billy out of the dumpster. Billy took one look at his outfit and sighed at his appearance. He was covered in food and filth as gnats surrounded him.

"I am going to get those guys," he says.

"You might want go to the office and report what just happened," says Hartwell.

"I am not a wuss, and besides, I have to get to class."

"Billy, you have eggs, ketchup and mustard all over you,"

replies Hartwell.

"Yeah, and you smell bro," says Terrence.

"I'll clean up in the bathroom and put my gym clothes on. Thanks guys," says Billy as he walks away in a hurry.

Hartwell and Terrence looked at Billy and shook their heads. They knew this was just the beginning for Billy, and his life in high school.

When Billy made it to his next class, some of the students heard what happened, and began to laugh at him while covering their noses.

The teacher commented on how awful he smelled and asked him what happened. The students became quiet as Billy's told her, he fell in the cafeteria and knocked over a few trays of food. His teacher did not buy his lie. She told Billy he needed to go to the principal's office. Billy agreed and began to pack his things up to leave class. As soon as he made a move to get out of the tiny green desk he was in, it collapsed with him in it. The students burst into an uproar, as the teacher attempted to help Billy out of the broken desk. She tried to get the class back under control, but it was too much for her to handle. She sent nine students to the principal's office along with Billy.

After a long an extremely frustrating day at school, Billy was dealt yet another devastating blow. He saw Leroy and Mariah talking. She was smiling and twirling her hair as they talked.

Hartwell saw Billy waiting for his ride and ran over to him.

"I heard Leroy has been making passes at Mariah all day,

100

and it seems to be working. Zola is pissed off about it. Also, did you hear about the nuclear plant shutting down," says Hartwell.

"Dear Lord Hartwell, slow down. Did you just say the plant is closing down?"

"Yeah, that's what I heard."

"If this is true Hartwell, this marks the end of an era in Stone Mountain and a lot of people are going to become unemployed," says Billy.

"I know. If the plant shuts down, my parents along with half of the town will lose their jobs," says Hartwell.

Billy thought about the town without Vega Powers. He also thought about how his parents dedicated their lives to the plant.

After Terrence and Hartwell got on their bus, Billy sat in silence thinking about what the future may bring to the town of Stone Mountain.

Chapter 5
The flight of love

Three years and a season had passed, and life progressed for the better. Billy and his friends were on the verge of graduation, he enjoyed living on the farm with his aunt and uncle, and his grades were exceptional. He hardly had a care in the world.

It was early one morning when Joy knocked on Billy's door.

"Billy wake up, it's time for school," she says.

Billy woke up abruptly as if someone stole the last minutes of a great dream.

"Good morning auntie. Is it six, thirty already?"

"Yes it is, and your breakfast is on the table."

"Thank you."

Billy got out of bed sluggishly to get ready for school.

As he entered the kitchen, Joy greeted him with a smile and a cup of coffee. He suddenly perked up, because he was never allowed to drink coffee, though he begged mostly every morning. As he sat at the table with his aunt, she proceeded to talk to him about the prom.

"You know the prom is coming up in a week," she says.

"I know," says Billy with a sigh.

"Joe has a lot of suits and a few tuxedos in the closet you

know."

"Ok," said Billy nervously as if he knew where this conversation was going.

"You are more than welcome to wear any of them."

"Thank you ma'am, but I am not going to the prom."

"Why not?"

"Let's see. I don't have a date or a vehicle to drive."

"Nonsense Billy, you can drive the pickup, or the other car your parents left you."

"I guess you have a point."

Joy smiled and nodded at Billy.

"Now as far as your date situation, you can go to the prom stag," replies Joy.

"Aunt Joy, are you kidding? It is bad to show up to an occasion like this without a date. I will look like a loser."

"Billy you will have fun. You really should go."

"Auntie, did you go to your prom by yourself," asks Billy?

"No, I went with your great cousin Greg," replies Joy jokingly.

Billy raised his eyebrows curiously and looked at his aunt.

"Are you jiving me?"

Joy blushed as she confessed to going to her prom with Joe.

"Ha! See what I am talking about? You had a date. If I go alone, I will look like a joke."

"What about Terrence and Hartwell? Do they have dates?"

"They both have dates."

"What about Mariah?"

Billy drew his mouth tightly together. He looked at his aunt with disgust.

"Don't even mention her name Aunt Joy."

"Come on Billy, you need to let bye-gones be bye-gones."

"She lied to me Auntie."

Joy sighed and shook her head at Billy.

"I maybe old, but I know a lot about females, and Mariah still wants to be your friend. She did not tell you about Zola because she wanted to protect you. And here you are holding a grudge for almost four years."

"I rather not talk about this," says Billy as he looks toward the front door plotting his escape.

"She is still upset with you, because she cares about you, and you are still upset with her, because you still care about her."

"None of this matters because she is dating Leroy," says Billy.

"Billy, do you still think about Mariah?"

"Auntie, please change the subject."

"Well, do you?"

"Every now and then I think about her."

"Okay, then tell her," replies Joy.

Billy pulled his hands away from Joy to look at his watch.

"I better be off to school," he says.

"Okay, but we will talk about this later Billy."

"Yes ma'am," says Billy as he grabs the car keys and heads for the door.

"I all most forgot, Terrence called earlier this morning. He wanted to know if you could pick him up on the way to school," replies Joy.

"Sure. Thank you Auntie."

About thirty minutes later, Billy arrived at Terrence's home to pick him up for school.

"What's happening Billy," says Terrence.

"Nothing much bro."

"Thanks for picking me up. Hartwell needed the car this morning and left early."

"No problem."

"You know, I am trying to get ready for the prom," says Terrence.

"You're kidding," says Billy sarcastically.

Terrence looked at Billy and continued to talk.

"Anyway…my old man wanted me to wear Uncle Seymour's black tuxedo."

"So, what's wrong with that?"

"My uncle has hemorrhoids."

"Ah man, that is just plain nasty," laughs Billy.

"You're right. I told my dad he couldn't pay me enough money to wear that tux," says Terrence.

"I agree man."

"So, what are you wearing to the prom, Billy?"

"I don't know if I am going."

"Come on Billy, you have to go. You only get one senior prom in a lifetime."

"I will think about it."

"I heard Mariah and Leroy are going through some problems," says Terrence.

"So," replies Billy with an attitude.

"So, you can run interference and get Mariah back."

"She can stay with Leroy for all I care. Besides, she was never mine because we were never a couple."

"Yeah, but you two used to be so close. I know you still

have feelings for her Billy. Everyone knows that."

"I have no interest in her," says Billy with an attitude.

"All I am saying, you better make a move soon before it is too late. Life is too short."

"Yeah right," replies Billy.

"Billy, I have never seen you give up on anyone you care about. You and Mariah are meant to be, but I don't understand why you both threw away a friendship. Is it because of pride? Look, before you answer, I get that she lied to you, but she did it to protect your feelings. To be honest with you Billy, she really didn't do anything wrong."

"Pride? That's a load of hog wash and you know it," says Billy angrily.

"Billy, she isn't perfect, and neither are you."

Terrence looked in Billy's direction to read his facial expression.

"Have you ever told a white lie to Mariah before," he asks?

"Why are you defending her?"

"Just answer the question Billy."

"Okay, I did tell her a white lie once, but it was with good reason."

"What is the reason?"

"I don't want to get into it, but just know I did what I did to protect her."

"That is my point man. You did it to protect her, just like she did for you."

Billy sighed as Terrence continued to shed light on the way he has been behaving towards Mariah.

"You have to let this anger and resentment go or you may lose Mariah forever."

"You sound like my aunt this morning. Are you guys drinking the same coffee or something?"

"I am happy to hear someone, other than myself, agrees."

"Finally, we are at school," says Billy as he rush into a parking space.

"By the way, Hartwell and I received an acceptance letter to Central University," says Terrence.

"That's great news. I am happy for you both," replies Billy.

They stepped out of the car and proceeded to get their book bags.

"Thanks for the talk Terrence. I will talk to Mariah," says Billy, "and I am proud of you and Hartwell. You guys aren't as sharp as a bowling ball after all."

Terrence rolled his eyes at Billy and punched him playfully in the stomach. He smiled at Billy, because he got through to him.

"Wow man. You really are going to speak to Mariah. Be smooth though. Mariah is a very tough nut to crack. It will not be easy," says Terrence.

"Believe me, I know. Do you remember when Mariah invited us over to her house to eat some sugar cookie she baked back in Junior High," asks Billy?

"Yeah I remember. They were terrible cookies. It tasted like clay."

"Well? I told her they were delicious, and you guys loved them. I never told her how bad Hartwell's stomach ached after eating them, or that my throat was on fire from the cayenne pepper she used instead of cinnamon. That was the little white lie I told to spare her feelings."

"Okay you have a point not telling her about that one. She would have killed us all."

They both laughed.

Billy thanked Terrence for the advice and told him he would meet up with him and Hartwell at lunch.

After buying lunch for Terrence and Hartwell to congratulate them for getting into college, Billy went outside to look for Mariah. She was sitting underneath a tree reading a college catalog. He was about to turn around and walk away, but he was determined not to back down. He took a deep breath and began to slowly walk over to the bench she was sitting on. He thought to himself, this is his moment of truth. It was time to break the years of silence.

Billy walked up to Mariah and smiled.

 "Hi," he says.

She kept on reading as if Billy was not there.

"Hey Mariah, nice weather we are having," he says.

"You have some nerve Billy," she replies.

Mariah turned her back to Billy and continued to read her catalog. Billy was ready to run away, but he remained smooth as Terrence had advised him to do, and proceeded to confess his sins.

"I wanted to see how you were doing Mariah? I also wanted to apologize for what I said, and did to you all those years ago. I hurt and disappointed you to an unimaginable scale. I was stupid and immature, and don't blame you for being upset with me. This rift between us is my fault."

Mariah stood up and confronted Billy. She was so close, he could smell the peppermint on her breath.

"You make me sick Billy! How dare you approach me with this after all of these years?"

She slapped Billy in the face and called him a jerk. He held his face where she had hit him and sighed.

"I deserved that and even more. I just hope you can find it in your heart to forgive me," he says.

As Billy turned and walked away, Mariah began to speak to him.

"When we were kids, I stood up for you when nobody else would. I stood by you when your parents died. I was in New York City having the time of my life Billy, and left the minute my parents told me what happened. After all I did, you had the nerve to call me immature."

"You're right Mariah. I shouldn't have treated you so badly."

"Most of all, when my mother died, you never visited or came to the funeral. You left me alone to deal with my grief. I thought no one would have understood what I was going through more than you would have. I depended on you to be there for me, but you abandoned me Billy! How could you do that to a friend?"

"Wait Mariah, I came to the funeral. I sat in the back of the church where no one could see me. You had on a white sun dress with a white daisy in your hair, because you never liked wearing black. It brought back so many painful memories of my parent's funeral, I froze. When I saw the pain on your face, I knew I wouldn't be strong enough for you, so I left before it was over."

Mariah rolled her eyes at Billy and called him a liar. Tears flowed down her face, because Billy actually came to her mother's funeral.

Before long, Leroy saw Billy and Mariah talking. He saw Mariah's face and how upset she looked, so he ran towards them and shoved Billy.

"Smalls, what the hell are you doing to my girl," he says!

"This doesn't concern you Leroy."

"Like hell it doesn't. She belongs to me now."

Billy ignored Leroy's comment and continued to express his feelings to Mariah.

"Mariah please forgive me for pushing you away, but I was

at your mother's funeral," says Billy.

Leroy grew impatient with Billy and shoved him again. When Billy pushed him back, he threw a punch to Billy's right cheek and knocked him to the ground.

"Stop it you two," shouts Mariah!

Billy stumbled to his feet and apologized.

"Come on Leroy, let's go," replies Mariah.

"Mariah, I want to be your friend again," begs Billy.

Mariah stopped for a second and sighed. She saw the sincerity in Billy's face.

"I had better not see you near my girl again, or I will crush you like the old days," warns Leroy.

Mariah told Leroy to stop, and they left Billy under the tree, holding his bruised face and his bruised pride in his hands.

Billy felt the cold sting of Mariah, but also felt relieved. He saw the look on her face and knew she believed him.

He thought about what his Aunt Joy said about people hurting more, when they care more.

He slowly walked over to his books on the ground, and picked them up.

Meanwhile, Mariah dragged Leroy by the hand to a quiet spot behind the gym.

"What was that," she says bitterly!

"What was what," replies Leroy innocently?

"You slugged Billy."

"Well, it looks like you did the same thing babe."

"That jerk had it coming from me for years, but not you."

"True, but he had it coming from me too."

"Why is that?"

"Because of what he did to me in Junior High."

"How many times have I told you to stop living in the past?"

"More than I can count."

"Violence only brings more violence, and you are much smarter than that, Leroy."

"Well I am so sick and tired of you telling how to live my life."

"Well I am sick and tired of you thinking you can beat up whomever you want. Look, I know your father abused you for many years, but you have to stop this vicious cycle. Otherwise, it will be passed on, and you are so much better than that."

"I was looking for you Mariah, because I have good news. I have a four year scholarship to play football," replies Leroy.

Mariah jumped into his arms and congratulated him with a hug. As she hugged him, she noticed Leroy trying to pull back. She released him and saw a couple girls walking by who in turn stole Leroy's attention. When she questioned him about it, he denied looking at them. She and Leroy have been having problems, because Leroy wanted to take their relationship to the next level. Mariah was not ready to be intimate with him, and told him she needed time. They argued often, because she caught him cheating on her many times. Every time she vowed to leave him, he would come back to her begging for forgiveness. Mariah was becoming tired of his excuses.

As she walked away from Leroy, he kept calling her name asking her to come back, but she continued to leave.

After school, Billy visited Mr. Clover. He apologized for not visiting after his wife's death. Mr. Clover shook his hands and thanked him.

"I knew you were dealing with the loss of your parents back then, just as I was dealing with the loss of Sarah," says Mr. Clover

They sat for a little longer and talked about how things were going in their lives. Billy told Mr. Clover he apologized to Mariah, but she was still very bitter towards him. Mr. Clover told Billy he would talk to Mariah. Billy thanked him, and told him he had to go. Before he left, he pulled a letter out of his pocket and asked Mr. Clover to give it to Mariah. Mr. Clover agreed and told Billy to visit anytime. Billy left, but wondered how Mariah would react to his letter.

Later on that night, Billy told his aunt and uncle what happen with Mariah and Mr. Clover. He also apologized for how he treated everyone after his parent's died. Joe and Joy told him there was nothing to apologize for, and how proud they were of him.

Meanwhile, after another verbal confrontation with Leroy, Mariah ran up to her room and slammed the door. Mr. Clover came to her room and asked if she was okay. She denied that anything was wrong, but Mr. Clover could tell she and Leroy had another argument.

Once Mariah calmed down, Mr. Clover came back to her room with warm chocolate chip cookies and milk. He proceeded to tell Mariah he had a visitor. She saw the letter on her bed he left her, began to get upset again. Mr. Clover explained what Billy told him, and that he forgave him. He kissed her on the head and left the cookies on her night stand. She picked up the letter and stared it. She was infuriated Billy spoke with her dad. She picked up a cookie and decided to give Billy a chance by reading his letter. As she read each page of Billy's letter, she began to laugh and call him crazy.

"My Dearest and best friend Mariah, (well I hope we can be best friends again)

I have been the fattest, stupidest, smartest, dumb ass in the world. I don't know how to begin to ask for your forgiveness. So let me get started with the beginning. When I was in kindergarten, there was this fiery red curly haired white girl named Mariah who used to beat the little boys up in class for not allowing her to sit down before they did.

As we grew older, we began to learn more about each other. I still remember you hate pickles on your burger, and your favorite color is pink. You like sunsets, horseback riding, and walks around the lake. I can go on and on, but that would take me all day. When Zola told me about the argument you had the night of the movies, she said you only

115

wanted to be my friend because I was black. Deep down inside I should have known better, but I didn't allow myself to remember what we shared. The worst part of all was watching you suffer and knowing I was partially responsible for your pain. Mariah, we are all that we have in this world. I miss my parents each and every day, and I know you feel the same about your mom. Though I miss them all, I have missed you just as much.

You and I are meant to be together Mariah, as friends, and one day, maybe more. There is no one on this earth who can make me feel the way you do. If you consider being my friend again, I will never disappoint you, and I will never leave your side."

As Mariah read Billy's letter, she noticed water marks on the last page. She saw a part of Billy she never knew existed. Tears fell from her eyes, as she allowed her feelings for Billy to take root and grow. That night, she made it up in her mind she was going to forgive Billy.

Chapter 6
The Son of Darkness

It was a cool and unusual autumn afternoon in the city of Barcelona, Spain. The entire country prayed and braced for the health and welfare of their beloved scientist and industrial tycoon Coronado Vega. Coronado was known for his scientific contributions to nuclear energy in the early 1940's.

Through the years he battled the death of his wife and daughter, until his health took a turn for the worst with cancer. When his doctor told him there was nothing more they could do, he felt the time had come for him to tie up some loose ends.

Classical music, Coronado's favorite genre, filled the Vega mansion. Vinares, Coronado's nephew, watched over him as he watched the final moments of his uncle's life.

Vinares was young with a large frame, but a gentle heart. He's been watching over his uncle along with Belmont, a long time fateful servant of the Vegas. Belmont was an older Spaniard, around the same age as Coronado, who lived in the mansion with his wife Silvia, the head maid, and his teenage daughter Maria.

All of Coronado's closest and dearest friends came to his bed side as tears fell from their eyes. Weakly, he extended his hands into the air and called out for his son. When Vinares told him his son was not there, he fell into silence.

"Tio, please drink some water," replies Vinares.

"I am fine Vinares, I just want my son. It has been so many years since I have seen him. Isn't he preparing for graduation and then college," asks Coronado.

"Yes, Tio, and hopefully he will be walking through the door any minute."

Just then, Belmont walked into the room and announced that a black helicopter landed on the premises.

"It must be Francisco," replies Vinares.

"My son, my only child is finally home. Silvia, bring him to me quickly," says Coronado!

Silvia left the room with her daughter Maria to go and greet Coronado's son.

As Maria and Silvia stared from the large bay window, a tall and slender built young man with long black hair approached.

Maria asked her mother about Francisco and wanted to know how old he was. She was intrigued by him and thought he was handsome. Her mother warned her not to shame her father and their family by making a move on Francisco. She assured her she wouldn't, but kept her fingers crossed behind her back.

When Francisco approached the door, Maria opened it with a warm smile on her face.

"Excuse me ladies, I am here to see my father," he replies.

"Are you Francisco," asks Maria?

"Yes I am," he replies.

"You have grown so much since I saw you last," replies Sylvia.

Sylvia gave Francisco a hug and quickly walked him towards his father's room.

"It has been a long time, since I have been home," says Francisco walking briskly behind Silvia, "I was seven when my father sent me to boarding school in Japan."

"That is a long time to be away from home," says Maria.

"Yes, it is," he says.

About halfway to Coronado's room, Vinares greeted his cousin with a hug.

"Forgive me Mr. Vega. I thought you would be waiting for us in the room," ask Silvia?

"It's quite all right Silvia. Coronado insist I bring Francisco to him immediately."

Maria and Silvia left.

"Vinares, I have not seen you in years."

"Yes, it has been a long time Primo."

Francisco and Vinares continued to talk as they walked towards Coronado's room. Francisco felt strange and unfamiliar in his family home.

"I have forgotten this place. It is gigantic."

"Yes, it takes some getting used to, but I am certain you will settle in just fine," says Vinares.

When Francisco and Vinares entered Coronado's room, Belmont greeted them.

"Master Francisco. It is great to see you," he says.

"Likewise Belmont," says Francisco as he moved towards his father.

"Francisco, come here son. I have so much to tell you in so little time," says Coronado as he coughs.

Vinares and Belmont saw the longing connection between father and son, and decided to give them some time alone.

"Father I have missed you," says Francisco.

"So have I," says Coronado as he coughs into his handkerchief wheezing and taking deep breaths.

"Are you in pain?"

"Son, the doctors have done everything they could. My cancer has returned with a vengeance, and there is nothing else to be done."

"Surely they can do more?"

"No, they can't."

"I should have been here for you," replies Francisco.

Coronado looked at his son as he held his head down in remorse. Coronado started to cough again, and as his hand fell from his face, Francisco saw blood in his handkerchief.

"Son I wasn't there for you after your mother died. I loved you and your mother so much, and when she lost our daughter in a car accident, I couldn't bare the pain. I couldn't allow you to see me go through the darkest days of my life, so I felt sending you to school in Japan would have given you an opportunity I couldn't at the time."

"Father you did the best you could. You were building a legacy for me, and making a name for yourself."

"I hope you can forgive me son?"

Francisco looked at his father and nodded.

"All is forgiven," he says.

Francisco told Coronado about high school and his grades. He told him he spoke fluent Japanese which made Coronado proud.

"Francisco, as you know, you are my only child, and when I am no longer here, you will be the heir to my estate."

"Your estate is not important right now," says Francisco and then summons for Belmont to bring his father a glass of water.

Belmont and Vinares entered the room with water. Francisco took it from them and then abruptly turned them both away.

"Son, I never taught you life's lessons. I struggled for many years as a scientist before I gained the respect and admiration of my country. Please remember that in life, you have to earn respect before it is given to you. You didn't have to treat Belmont or Vinares the way you just did."

"Yes Sir," replies Francisco.

"Take care of your love ones, because they will take care of you, and above all, manners and respect will take you places where money can't."

"I won't forget father," says Francisco as he stares at the wall.

Coronado reached out for his son to take his hand. Francisco hesitated for a few seconds, but gently touched his dad's hands.

"I only wish I could live to see you grow into the fine young man you will become one day. You will have a family of your own, and unfortunately I will not be there."

"Father, I will make you proud," says Francisco.

As Francisco stared into his father's eyes with determination, his father stared into his with regret and surrender. He eyes closed shut and his grip loosened from Francisco's hand.

"Father, father, wake up father," shouts Francisco!

He called out for Belmont and Vinares to enter the room. They both quickly rushed in.

"What is it," ask Vinares?

"He is gone," says Francisco.

Belmont walked over to Coronado's body and checked for a pulse. He shook his head as he covered Coronado's face with the satin sheets he laid in. He looked at Francisco's broken expression and felt sorry for the Vega family.

Vinares walked towards his cousin and placed his hands on

his shoulder.

"Belmont, please escort Francisco to his room," he says.

"No," says Francisco harshly, "I want to stay with my father."

"As you wish Francisco," says Vinares as he motions for Belmont to walk to the other side of the room.

"What is it Master Vinares," asks Belmont?

"I need you to hold off on calling the undertaker," says Vinares in a whispering voice. "Call Sonya, our publicist, and tell her to schedule a press conference, as soon as possible."

"The publicist," replies Belmont surprisingly?

"Yes," says Vinares.

"With all due respect, Master Coronado did not want his death made a spectacle," replies Belmont.

Vinares had quickly cut Belmont off.

"This is what Francisco wants," he says.

"I understand, but it is not about the Young Master's wishes, it is about a dying man's last wish," replies Belmont.

Just as Belmont's and Vinares' voice levels rose, Francisco overheard parts of their conversation and intervened.

"Excuse me gentlemen, but Vinares is right," says Francisco.

"What," replies Belmont?

"Are you hard of hearing old man? My father's body is supposed to be cremated. Now that is his final wish," says Francisco.

"Old man," utters Belmont, "this is not right. I must contest your decision Francisco. You are still a little boy and do not know what you are saying."

"Contest? What right have you to contest anything? I am the heir to this estate, and my first decision is to have a press conference announcing my father's death and my resurrection. He will be cremated, do you understand."

Belmont gasped at Francisco's declaration and rebutted his statement.

"Your father wanted to be remembered as a humble and noble man. He wanted to have a traditional Spanish funeral with a parade throughout the streets of Barcelona, followed by a memorial and mass at the cathedral. He then wanted to be buried at the cemetery on the hill," argues Belmont!

"Belmont, I am not going to get into an argument with you. I am his son and this is my decision," says Francisco impatiently!

"Master Francisco, your father and I were best friends. He is a war hero and the people will want to pay their respects to him one last time. Please reconsider," begs Belmont.

"There will be no parades in honor of my father. And if you wish to see him, his ashes will be on the mantel piece above the fireplace," says Francisco.

Francisco's words were cold and cruel. Belmont was surprised at how quickly he and Vinares behavior changed. He couldn't believe what Francisco just told him.

"I can't believe what you are doing! You never loved your father. You only loved his money and power!"

Francisco laughed and waved Belmont off as he passed by him towards the door. Just as he was about to exit the room, he faced Belmont and told him he was fired. Belmont's face turned red as he begged for Francisco to reconsider.

"I have changed your diapers when you were a baby. I looked after you, cooked and cleaned for this family most of my life," replies Belmont.

"Look you old fool, my mother raised me, not you, and after she died, my father shipped me off to the first school he could. He did not write, call, or visit. He left me to raise myself! If you were the best friend you said you were to my father, you could have spoken up for me to stay. You were never more than a servant to this family!"

"You Monster," shouts Belmont!

Vinares, grabbed Belmont by the arms and proceeded to escort him out. As Belmont tried to pull away, he fell to the floor. Vinares laughed as he struggled to get up.

Belmont walked out of the room, as other servants watched in disbelief of what they heard outside of Coronado's room door. He wished them well with their new Master, and warned them of the darkness ahead.

Meanwhile, Vinares and Francisco left his father's chambers and entered the study. They began to speak of plans they made months ago.

Vinares, stayed in Coronado's favor to keep Francisco abreast of his condition. Once he died, they made preparations to reinvent his father's legacy.

"Vinares, in two days, I want you to dispose of Belmont. No one threatens or challenges me and lives to tell the story," says Francisco.

"Consider it done. Did you bring the scrolls?"

"Of course I did. Do you think I would come half way around the globe without it?"

"I can't believe you finally have the scrolls from the House of Honzo. How did you obtain it," asks Vinares with enthusiasm?

"I went in and asked them if I could borrow it you idiot! How do you think I got it?"

"Have you mastered the hidden techniques within the scrolls?"

"Hold this sheet of paper Vinares and watch carefully."

Francisco gave Vinares a sheet of paper. He held out his hands in deep concentration. Suddenly, a sharpening force of energy brushed against the paper cutting it without touching it. Vinares' mouth opened in awe as the paper fell from his hand.

"I hope that answers your question, and don't ever challenge me again, or you'll live to regret it," says Francisco bitterly.

"It won't happen again," replies Vinares.

"I will make you proud father. The plants closed down in America will be reopened. I shall take your legacy and forge my own. With the energy plants back in operation, and my continued involvement in organized crime, the world will bow at my feet, or pay with their lives. High school is for children, and I am not a child."

Francisco stood in the window as a storm gathered in the distance. Darkness consumed the room as he pre-destined the unknown fate of the world.

Chapter 7
Homecoming

Seventeen years passed since graduation from Stone Mountain High. Billy and his wife returned to Stone Mountain six months earlier for the re-opening of the nuclear plant. The reemergence of Vega Powers took the world by storm, as most of its plants were operational again around the globe. With Billy's degrees in chemical engineering and energy conservation, as well as his experience as a nuclear physicist, he was hired as the Chief Engineer and plant manager.

Over the years, Francisco and Vinares became more ambitious as successful plants re-opened across the world. Francisco did as he promised and changed the Vega legacy. Every action done in the name of the Vega family was one of deceit, power, and fear. He and Vinares were two of the most ruthless men in the business world.

Billy's first order of business as Chief Engineer was to meet with Francisco and discuss the safety issues of the plant.

Meanwhile, Francisco and Vinares were passing through Stone Mountain on their way to Atlanta; they decided to meet with Billy.

Matt and Scott were two of Billy's employees. They were hired by Billy after the plant re-opened.

As they walked towards the office area, they noticed two tall gentlemen dressed in black suits. One was slender with his hair pulled into a pony tail and wore a black trench coat. The other man was large with a slightly slumped shoulder.

"Is the FBI here to investigate something," ask Scott?

"No nimrod they are our bosses. Did you really pass the pee test before being hired Scott," jokes Matt?

"Our bosses," says Scott with a clueless look on his face.

"Mr. Vega," replies Matt.

"Oh yeah, I knew that. You meant Mr. Vega, as in Vega Powers. Who is that giant walking with him," asks Scott?

"That is his cousin and personal bodyguard Vinares Vega. Alfred is escorting them around until Billy arrives."

Scott and Matt continued to walk to their areas, and talk about why they think the Vegas were there. A memo was sent to all plant employees explaining there was a convention in Atlanta, and they might have visitors throughout the week. He also mentioned that Mr. Francisco Vega may be among the visitors.

"They are here for a safety assessment of the plant as well as the convention. I sure hope Billy can convince Mr. Vega to give us more funding for the plant," says Matt.

"Yeah me too. These rich folk can be pretty tight pocketed."

Alfred and the Vegas approached Scott and Matt. They both straightened their postures and smiled.

"Matt, something came up on the other side of the plant I need to look at. Would you please show the Vegas to Billy's office," ask Alfred?

"It would be an honor and pleasure. Nice to meet you Mr. Vega," says Matt.

129

Matt accompanied Francisco and Vinares to Billy's office. He also expressed his gratitude to them for re-opening the plant. When they arrived at the office, Billy opened the door with a smile and greeted them. Francisco walked in, while Vinares sat outside of the door.

"Mr. Vega, I know you are a busy man and I appreciate your time," says Billy.

"My secretary told me you have something urgent to discuss with me Mr. Smalls. My time is very valuable, so what is it," replies Francisco?

"We discovered small cracks on the exterior of the reactor Mr. Vega."

"That's strange, because we didn't notice any cracks on the reactor during the walk through," replies Francisco.

"The cracks are located on the back of the reactor. Here are some pictures I took," replies Billy.

"I would like to see the defect in person," says Francisco.

"It's too dangerous Mr. Vega. We have made numerous repairs on the reactor, but it seems more and more cracks are emerging."

"What is causing these cracks Mr. Smalls?"

"It could be a multitude of reasons such as moisture, the elements, wear and tear, a weak foundation, or combination of all."

"According to my records, these reactors are the strongest and steadiest structures assembled."

"And I agree if it was forty or fifty years ago."

"Ok, so what can I do?"

"We need funding to make the necessary repairs or even build a new reactor?"

"As Chief Engineer Mr. Smalls, it is your responsibility to ensure the safety of everyone," says Francisco.

"Yes Mr. Vega and I take my job very seriously. I have already shut this plant down six times because of structural damages."

"Six times," shouts Francisco!

"This plant could go into meltdown at any time, if we do not make the necessary repairs," replies Billy.

"Melt down," says Francisco?

"Yes Mr. Vega," replies Billy.

"I will not give any more money to this plant, I have given millions already."

"Then millions will die if we do not fix these safety issues. Mr. Vega, I am not trying to start any trouble or upset you. I only want what is best for Stone Mountain and Vega Powers. Safety is paramount. The last thing we want is another Chernobyl. I promise we will get the job done, but we need the finances to do it."

"All right Mr. Smalls. Your materials will be here tonight. Do whatever it takes to get the reactor fix," says Francisco.

"Thank you Mr. Vega," replies Billy.

Francisco told Billy he would be checking on the progress of the project while he was in Atlanta. Billy said he would love for him to do so. As Francisco stood up to leave Billy's office, he invited him to lunch. Billy's eyes grew wide with surprise, as he gladly accepted and thanked Francisco for his time.

Alfred, came to Billy's office and escorted Francisco out. Then he came back to ask Billy, how the meeting went. Billy told Alfred the meeting went well, and Francisco wasn't as bad as people made him out to be. Alfred congratulated Billy on getting the funds to fix the reactor, but warned him about Francisco. He told Billy to do everything in his power to ensure the repairs are flawless, because if anything went wrong, the blame would all be on him.

Alfred was a veteran at Vega Powers. He worked with Billy's parents when they were alive, and knew Billy since he was a kid. After the plant closed down, Billy decided he was going to college for chemical engineering, in hopes to one day return to Stone Mountain and bring the nuclear plant back to life. When he was offered the job as Chief Engineer, he immediately reached out to Alfred and offered him the position as his second in command. He valued Alfred's opinion and heeded his warning about Francisco.

"Alfred, the supplies will be here tonight, so I will need you to be here for the first and second shifts to do thermal scans on the reactor every hour," replies Billy.

"Twenty four hours a day, seven days a week," asks Alfred?

"Yes. You and I will rotate third shift at the beginning of every week until the job is done. Mr. Vega will be checking on us, so everyone has to be on their toes," replies Billy.

"You know we have over eighty people working here. That is a lot of overtime and man power," says Alfred.

"We got the funding approved, and we have over a dozen employees with construction experience. Everyone will jump at this opportunity to fix the reactor. Mr. Vega wants the reactor repaired as soon as possible, and I gave him my word it will happen."

"I can't believe it. How did you get him to do it?"

"I showed him my legs," replies Billy laughing.

"Those chicken legs? I am shocked he didn't reclose the plant after seeing those things," says Alfred.

"I told him if we didn't get the necessary funds, we would be putting millions of people at risk for a nuclear disaster."

"I could not have said it better," says Alfred, "I will take over the second and third shift tonight. Go home, kiss that lovely wife of yours and get some rest."

"I need to be here when the materials arrive."

"You have been working nonstop for two weeks Billy. I can handle it, and besides, I have been doing this type of work since you were in diapers," says Alfred.

"Okay. I am going home, but if anything happens call me."

After Alfred agreed, Billy picked up his belongings and left. As he walked towards the exit, he saw Matt and Scott. He told them about funding, and how they will all have additional assigned duties. Matt and Scott high fived one another while Billy shared in their joy. They joked around with Billy for a while and went back to work.

Once Billy sat in his car, he yawned and rubbed his weary eyes. He ran his hands through his hair and realized he needed a haircut. He heard about a new barbershop in town, and thought he should give it a try.

When he pulled up at the barbershop, the sign read *T & H Barbers*. As Billy walked in, to his surprise, he was greeted by his childhood best friends.

"Billy," replies Hartwell!

"What's up buddy? How have you been," ask Terrence?

Billy smiled and hugged them both.

"I've been great. I didn't know you two were back in town. I heard the buzz about a new barbershop, but thought it was owned by some guys from Atlanta."

"Yeah, well we did not know you were back in town too," replies Hartwell.

"Yeah, we came back a few months ago, after the plant re-opened. I am the Chief Engineer there," says Billy.

"Wow Billy that is great! We were happy the plant re-opened, but had no idea you were involved."

Billy walked around the shop with delight and started to laugh.

"I can't believe you two own this barber shop. Maybe I should go somewhere else and get a haircut. The thought of you two cutting hair makes me nervous."

"Whatever Billy boy! That peanut head of yours need a weed whacker. Maybe we should call a landscaper to mow that mane of yours," jokes Terrence.

"Yeah, you might break our clippers. Your head looks so bad, this first cut should be on us," laughs Hartwell.

Terrence looked at Hartwell and shook his head.

"There you go, giving out free cuts again."

"This is my store too Terrence, and besides, he is our friend."

"I know that dummy, and he is entitled to a free haircut, but not the other ten people you gave free cuts to since we opened."

As Terrence and Hartwell continued with their normal sibling rivalry, the television in the barber shop chimed with a special news report. They all paused as Francisco Vega's face came across the screen. He was having a press conference with the town council.

"Man, what gives with all the black. It's like he is going to a funeral or something. He gives me the creeps," says Hartwell.

"I read an article about him. It said he knows martial arts, and he is the second richest man in the world," replies Terrence.

"Yeah, I just had a meeting with him," replies Billy.

"Really, what was he like," ask Terrence?

"Cold and stern from what I see, but he seems fair," replies
135

Billy.

"I am getting bad vibes from watching Mr. Vega on television. Something about him doesn't seem right," says Hartwell.

"Come and sit in my chair Billy," says Terrence.

Billy sat in the chair in front of Terrence. He told Terrence to shave off his afro and give him a low and smooth haircut. Terrence was shocked Billy wanted to cut off his afro. He tried to talk him out of it, but Billy said he wanted to surprise his wife.

"How many years have you been married Billy," ask Hartwell?

"Five years," replies Billy.

"Wow! And no kids," replies Terrence.

"Yeah, I thought for sure you would be first to drop a few mini-me's," says Hartwell.

"Not yet, but some day," replies Billy with a smile on his face.

"Hold on a minute Billy, why didn't we get invited to the wedding," says Hartwell.

"It was a spontaneous thing. We woke up and decided to tie the knot, so we eloped," says Billy.

"Well good for you two. You both deserve each other. Now, as for me, I am a bachelor. I'm too much of a "chick magnet" to settle down," says Terrence.

"More like womanizer," says Hartwell.

"Are you married Hartwell?" ask Billy.

"No. I am waiting for the right one," says Hartwell.

"Man you sound like a sissy," says Terrence.

"Terrence, ever since you lost Ashley, you have changed into a player. She really hurt you bad bro," says Hartwell.

Terrence was annoyed by Hartwell's' comment. He took a deep breath and told Billy about his one true love, Ashley who cheated on him. Billy felt bad for his friend and apologized for asking.

After Terrence was finished with Billy's hair. He looked in the mirror and smiled. He ran his hands over his smooth, low cut mane and smiled. He told Terrence and Hartwell he was staying at his parent's house and invited them over for a bar-b-que and basketball on his next day off. They took him up on the offer and walked him out. When they saw Billy's car, their mouths opened in awe.

"Hey man, nice car," says Terrence!

"Thanks," says Billy as he smiles and opens the door to his brand new Chevy Corvette.

"This is nothing like the old car you drove in high school that belonged to your parents. Don't get me wrong, that was a nice car, too."

"Yeah, do you still have that car Billy," asks Hartwell?

"Absolutely! Now, remember guys, anytime you want to come over, you are always welcome."

Billy entered the car and drove away blowing the horn at his friends. As Billy left the town limits, he headed towards home, he laughed to himself as thoughts of Terrence and Hartwell owning a barbershop came to mind.

Thirty minutes later Billy arrived home. As he entered with a dozen daisies he hid behind his back, he called out to his beautiful wife and friend of so many years.

"Mariah, I am home baby," he says ecstatically.

With a smile and a warm glow, Mariah ran to her husband and kissed him gingerly on the lips.

"Wow what a sweet kiss. And a wet one," says Billy.

"I know. I just ate some watermelon before you arrived home. Thanks for my daisies honey," replies Mariah as she snatches them from behind Billy's back.

Though older, Mariah's skin was still smooth with a milky white glow to it. Her freckles were barely visible, and she had a medium frame with a curvy shape.

"Mariah, your hair," says Billy?

"Well, what do you think," she says as she prances around and models her new blonde hair color.

"I love it! They say blondes have more fun. What do you think about my hair?"

"It looks great! You finally cut that rug off."

Billy rubbed his head and laughed. He and Mariah joked with each other and ran around the kitchen playfully.

"Come here so I can eat you up," says Billy picking her up and twirling her around.

"Put me down, and get away," laughs Mariah!

"I won't put you down unless dinner is ready."

"Well then, king of beast, there is a pot roast with your name on it."

"Yum! So how was work today?"

"Well, I had a student vomit on my new shoes, and I had a parent- teacher conference. How was work for you today?"

"Work was great. We received the funds to repair the reactor."

"That's wonderful news. I saw your boss on television."

"Yeah. He is going to be in Atlanta for a few days. Everyone is talking about it."

"Do you want to invite him over for dinner," ask Mariah?

"He wouldn't come if we did invite him. I don't think Mr. Vega is the family dinner type of guy. Also, I am going to be working evening shifts for the next couple of days with him."

"What did you just say," questions Mariah furiously?

"Baby, in order to get the necessary repairs done I have to supervise this operation like my life depends on it."

"Why can't you get Alfred or someone else to oversee the repairs?"

"Alfred is working tonight, so I agreed to work the next couple of nights."

"Billy, we need to talk," says Mariah as she looks at him in frustration.

"We are talking," says Billy with an innocent look on his face.

Mariah sat at the table barely touching her food, after hearing that Billy will be spending more time at the plant.

"This house is old and needs repairs, we hardly spend time together, and we were supposed to work on getting pregnant."

"I have one guy coming in the morning to finish the roof, another is helping me paint the kitchen, bathroom and living room. We can work on a family when the plant is finished."

Mariah's comments made Billy nervous. His focus was almost, always on work, and every time Mariah brought up the subject of kids, he would shy away from it. However, tonight was as if, Mariah caught him off guard with her comments, making it hard for him to avoid the conversation.

"How about today Billy? I went to the doctor to get a checkup, and he says that the best time to try is when I am ovulating."

Billy looked at Mariah with an empty expression on his face.

"Are you serious?"

"I am ovulating now Billy," says Mariah impatiently.

Billy's eyes mimicked the eyes of an old man without his glasses. He could not figure his wife out, and why she was talking about this right now. He pounded his hands on the table and made Mariah jump.

"Come on Mariah, we are eating. Why are you bringing this up at the dinner table?"

"Nothing is wrong with me talking about children. What's wrong with you?"

Mariah fell silent and looked away from Billy. Billy grew more nervous with each minute, until he snapped.

"What do you mean what's wrong with me? Are you saying we can't have kids, because of me Mariah? Are you implying I have a low sperm count or something?"

Mariah picked up her tea and took a sip trying not to look Billy in the eyes.

"Baby, all I am asking is for you to get examined," she replies.

"Oh boy here we go again. Mariah, I am perfectly fine. My little warriors are always ready to battle."

"And how do you know this Billy?"

Mariah's comment made Billy uncomfortable. Every time he tried to change the topic, Mariah chimed back in on having a child. Truth be told, Billy was nervous because they have been trying for two years. The doctor could not find any reason Mariah could not have children, which left Billy as the constant in this equation of reproduction. He felt that maybe if they continued to try, it would eventually happen for them, but the more they tried, the more they were disappointed.

Billy looked at his wife, of whom he has loved most of his life.

"Ok Mariah, I will schedule an appointment with Dr. Thompson."

"Thank you, sweetheart."

Suddenly, they heard the doorbell rang. Billy jumped up grumbling about it being too late for visitors.

"Who is it," he asks?

"A woman you better respect."

Billy saw Mrs. Anderson's heavy framed silhouette through the frosted glass door, and opened the door immediately with a smile on his face. Mrs. Anderson frowned at Billy and greeted him by grabbing his ear.

"Ouch Auntie! Please let go of my ear. Why are you upset," ask Billy as he tries to squirm away from her grip.

"You know why I am here. You killed my babies," exclaims Mrs. Anderson!

Mariah looked at her aunt in shock, and then glanced over at Billy for answers. Billy shrugged his shoulders in confusion as Mrs. Anderson continued to talk.

"Your husband, Mr. Eco Killer forgot to water my plants," replies Mrs. Anderson.

Mariah took a deep breath of relief. She was convinced

Mrs. Anderson over heard her and Billy's conversation.

"I am so sorry Mrs. Anderson. I forgot that your trip to L.A. was last week. Did you have a good time," replies Billy?

"Don't change the subject. You forgot to water my plants, and now my lilies are dead."

"Mrs. Anderson, I will buy you more plants. As many as you want," says Billy.

"I had those peace lilies for over twelve years. They are irreplaceable."

Mrs. Anderson sat at the table and picked up a roll to eat. She noticed the food still sitting in the plates and became concerned.

"Is everything alright in here? You kids barely touched your food," she says.

Mrs. Anderson looked at Billy and Mariah's face. She could sense tension in the air, but Mariah and Billy both looked at her and shook their heads. Their silence gave her the answer she needed so she stood up and left.

"I will forgive you Billy, under one condition," she says.

"Anything, you just name it."

"I want you to plant me an acre of corn and squash," she replies.

"What? Do you know how long that is going to take," asks Billy?

"You are young, and full of energy," she replies, "it will

take you no time at all if you use your uncle's old tractor."

"When do you want me to start," ask Billy?

Mrs. Anderson smiled at him, and told him to start the next day. Billy almost freaked out, because he had to work two shifts each day for a week at the plant. He asked Mrs. Anderson to compromise by allowing him to plant her vegetables the next week. She agreed, and warned Billy not to forget. On her way, out she complimented Mariah's hair, and mentioned that one of their church members had a baby.

Billy and Mariah fell silent again. Mrs. Anderson noticed the tension in the room, and saw it as her exit.

"Well, I must be going now. You two need to work on, whatever needs working on here. Fix it," she says.

Billy and Mariah watched their aunt drive away, when the kitchen phone rung. Mariah ran inside to answer it.

When Billy entered the kitchen, he saw Mariah in tears.

"Mariah, what's wrong?"

"It's Terrence."

"Oh I meant to tell you, I saw him and Hartwell earlier. They own a barber shop. Was that him on the phone? I'm surprise he remembered the old number. Is he trying to play a prank on us?"

Mariah shook her head and continued to cry. She told Billy that Terrence was in a car accident.

"Oh, no," says Billy, "is he at the hospital?"

144

Billy looked into Mariah's eyes. She told him Terrance died.

Billy sat down and began to cry. Mariah felt his pain, but needed to be strong for him. She sat beside him and held his hand. She told him, she was there for him, and he wasn't alone. Billy held on to her, as if she was the only person he had left in the world. That night, she sung an old hymn as Billy laid his head on her lap. She quietly wept for her old friend, and the child she may never have.

Chapter 8
Next Generation Meeting

A few weeks after Terrence's death, Billy and Mariah continued to suffer a string of bad news. Hartwell decided to quit the barbershop business and leave. He couldn't stand the thought of running the barber shop alone. Billy also found out he had a low sperm count, which devastated him and Mariah. They could not conceive children. To make matters worse, Billy was working around the clock at the plant, and had another lunch meeting scheduled, with Mr. Vega to discuss the progress of the repairs.

"Mariah, I am on my way to have lunch with Mr. Vega," says Billy.

"Wait," she says running towards the door.

Billy stood in the door frame emotionless. He barely ate since Terrence's death, and he barely slept because of work. Mariah touched his shoulder gently, and asked him if he was alright. He nodded and said he was okay, but just a little stressed. Mariah gave him some words of comfort, and told him she loved him. He smiled a little, and kissed her before he left.

About an hour and half later, Billy arrived at an Italian restaurant for his meeting with Francisco. He was very anxious, as he sat in a private booth, and sipped ice water as he anticipated Francisco's arrival. When Francisco and Vinares arrived, he stood up and straightened his tie.

"Good afternoon Mr. Vega," says Billy as he stood to shake

Francisco and Vinares' hands.

"I hope you are enjoying the sights of Stone Mountain," he says.

"It's a very quaint and wholesome town," replies Francisco.

The server came over to their table to take their drink orders. Francisco ordered a whiskey on ice, and Vinares ordered a gin and tonic.

"Let's get down to business. How much progress have you and your team made on the reactors?"

"We have repaired about ninety-five percent of them Mr. Vega."

"I am very impressed," he says.

Billy opened his briefcase, and pulled out a thick black leather binder. He handed it over to Francisco.

"What is this," asks Francisco?

"Here are the financial reports, and inspections that were completed so far," says Billy.

Francisco looked at the report summary, and raised an eyebrow. He looked up at Billy in astonishment.

"Mr. Smalls you have saved me millions," he replies, "I am impressed. You utilized the employees and equipment that was already in the plant to speed things along and reduce cost."

"I thought it would have taken three or more weeks to complete this project, but we will be done in thirteen days," says Billy.

As the server approached the table, Vinares frowned at her.

"It's about time you brought our damn drinks," he snaps.

The server was shocked at Vinares' reaction and tried to apologize. He belittled her continuously until, she was in tears.

"Vinares, stop this nonsense. She said she was sorry," says Francisco.

The young server placed their drinks on the table, and apologized again before she left in a hurry.

"Mr. Smalls, do you drink?" ask Francisco.

"Sometimes," replies Billy.

Francisco motioned for the server to come back. She walked towards them in hesitation.

"I apologize for my cousin's rudeness. He's never been graceful with the ladies. May you please bring us your finest champagne," he says.

The server came back with a bottle of Dom Perignon, and poured them each a glass.

"Thank you sir," replies Billy.

"Billy, please call me Francisco."

"Okay, Francisco."

"So Billy, I heard that you are a *nerd*, as they say here in

America," says Francisco.

"I don't know if I am that smart, but I do take great pride in doing my job."

"As did your parents."

"You knew my parents?"

"Not exactly, I read about your father years ago in my father's journal. He was a valuable asset to this company. My father called him a remarkable physicist and friend. He was at your parent's funeral."

Billy was proud of his parents, and the impression his father made on the Vega's.

"You have your father's drive and ambition. Though my father was a world renowned scientist, I was not raised to read books and solve equations. I was raised in a more combative, skilled art form."

Billy looked up in confusion at what Francisco said.

"What do you mean by combative art form," asks Billy?

"Never mind," says Francisco, "with you and I working together, we can lead this company into the future," he says as he pats Billy on the back.

"I still have a lot to learn, but I will do my best to help your company succeed."

Francisco paused and looked at Billy with a hazy glare in his eyes. He felt the effects of the scotch and champagne he drank.

"You are so humble Billy."

"Why thank you Mr. Francisco."

"That wasn't a compliment. Humbleness can be a weakness in the business world."

Vinares tapped Francisco on his shoulder. He leaned in as his cousin whispered something in his ear. Francisco stood up and adjusted his jacket.

"Well Billy, we must be going," he says.

Billy stood up and grabbed his jacket.

"Not you Billy. Vinares and I must be going, but you can stay and order anything you want. The server will put it on my tab."

"I guess when you are rich, you got it like that," mumbles Billy before he realize what he is saying.

"Excuse me?" says Francisco.

"I am sorry if I offended you Francisco."

"I see. I can't be casual with you Mr. Smalls, so from now on, call me Mr. Vega," says Francisco, "I will let that slide, but never forget that I am a busy and powerful man. I make profit from people like you."

Billy stared Francisco in the face to assure him, he was not weak, and that he was not intimidated.

"I will visit the plant later on tonight, to see your progress for myself," says Francisco.

They shook hands as their eyes locked into each other.

"Now that is a hand shake," says Francisco with a smile on his face.

They exited the restaurant as Billy sat back down. He thought to himself how, conceded Francisco and Vinares were. He also thought about what Hartwell warned him of earlier. Billy decided he didn't need Francisco's charity, so he grabbed his coat and left.

Chapter 9
The birth of legends

After lunch, Billy went home to get some sleep before work. He slept for several hours. During his slumber, he had an intense dream he was at the plant, and there was huge explosion killing dozens of his workers. In his dream, he ran into the blaze to rescue as many as he could, however, during his rescue the building collapsed on him. He woke up breathing heavily, and sweating as he looked around the dark room in panic. After he heard Mariah humming in the kitchen, he realized he was still at home, and needed to get to work. After a quick shower and dinner with his lovely wife, he left for work.

When Billy arrived on site, Alfred greeted him with a warning that Francisco was in the building. Billy assured him, he was aware and well prepared.

As Billy punched in for work, warning sirens started to glare. The voice on the intercom told people to evacuate. Billy ran towards the building to see what was happening as people evacuated. Suddenly, a huge explosion shook the building, stopping Billy in his tracks. Employees frantically ran from the building. In the distance, Billy and Alfred saw a bluish-green blaze of fire rapidly approaching them. They ran towards the exit just, as the blaze reached the door, and they barely made it to a safe distance. People continued to run out of the building, on fire, as Billy and Alfred struggled to help as many as they could.

"What happened," asks Billy, as he and Alfred tried to help people move away from the plant?

"I'm not sure. I have never seen fire that color. I think one of the reactors might have blown," shouts Alfred!

"That can't be, the structure looks like it is still intact! My God, people are still in there!"

Billy thought about the dream, just hours ago. He could not believe his nightmare was coming true. All he could think about was his workers, and who could be trapped inside. He took off running towards the plant as Alfred followed his lead.

"Billy what are we doing," shouts Alfred!

"People could be trapped in the basement. There isn't any time to lose. Quick, I need your resistant suit." says Billy.

"One or both reactors could blow up Billy!"

"Go back and do your job Alfred! You know what has to be done."

Alfred warned Billy of a potential radiation leak. Billy did not care. Reluctantly, Alfred took his suit off and gave it to Billy. He quickly suited up. Alfred mentioned that the Vegas were down in the basement earlier.

He told Alfred to make sure everyone was accounted for, and taken to the hospital once EMS and fire rescue arrived. He then told Alfred, he was going to search for survivors.

"As long as the reactors aren't compromised, the town will not be affected by the radiation from the explosion! I will be back, Alfred!"

Billy knew radiation leaks were probable. He also knew

that his resistance suit could only tolerate temperatures up to eight hundred degrees. However, without hesitation, Billy entered the fiery building, rushing through partially lit areas towards the basement.

The building was incredibly hot. The gauge on Billy's suit read six hundred degrees. There was smoke and debris everywhere, and with each step Billy took, he walked deeper into the point of no return.

When he entered the dimly lit basement, he called out to see if anyone was down there.

"Hello, Is anybody down here!" he says.

Billy carefully walked towards a light at the end of the hallway. Suddenly he heard a faint cry.

"Help, we are down the hall!"

Billy ran towards the end of the hall, where the light was located. Both Francisco and Vinares were in the room wearing a resistant suit. They were pinned under some lockers, struggling to break free. Billy ran into the room, and almost tripped over something. When he looked down, he gasped. It was Scott, his employee who lied lifeless and almost unrecognizable.

"Scott was showing us around, when the explosion occurred. He helped Vinares and I put on these suits," says Francisco.

Billy thought to himself how selfless Scott was, but he also knew Scott was a safety first type of person, and could not understand why he did not suit up first before he helped anyone else.

"Billy, I need help with Vinares. He passed out."

Billy glanced at their suits.

"My God, his suit is torn and so is yours!"

"It ripped while I was trying to lift Vinares. I twisted my ankle as well."

Billy moved the locker off of Francisco and Vinares. He helped Francisco to his feet, and heisted Vinares on to his back. Billy led the way, as they tried to escape the building.

"We have to get out of here! This area is unstable," shouts Billy!

They raced up the stairs as fast as they could. The alarm that was glaring suddenly stopped. Billy and Francisco stopped as well. An eerie silence filled the room

"The alarm stopped," says Billy.

"Great, "says Francisco, "that means we are safe now right?"

"Not exactly," says Billy.

"What do you mean?" demands Francisco.

"It means that the pumps are going again and the plant's reactor won't go into melt down, but we are far from being safe!"

"Meaning what," shouts Francisco!

"We can still die from heat and exposure We have to keep moving."

Billy and Francisco grabbed Vinares, and went to the top of the stairs. The door knob was red from the heat.

Billy used the fabric from his pockets to grab the partially melted door knob. The door was very hot and heavy, but Billy managed to slowly crack it open enough, for them to squeeze through. Francisco and Vinares went through. He took a few steps and looked back for Billy, but Billy was not behind them. Billy started to become woozy and disoriented, so he stopped at the door. He looked up at the ceiling, and heard a cracking sound above his head. Just as the ceiling was about to fall down, Francisco pulled Billy through the door. Billy lifted Vinares off of the floor, and the three of them hurried down the hallway.

As they moved quickly, there were small explosions behind the doors of laboratories on the main floor. Everything looked red to Billy, and for a moment he thought they were not going to make it out alive. Then he thought about Mariah, and all she lost in her life. He did not want her to suffer another loss, so he pushed forward leading Francisco and Vinares towards the exit.

When they finally made it outside, Alfred and an emergency team was waiting.

"Mr. Vega let me help you," says a rescuer.

Alfred ran towards Billy, but he told him to stay back. Though they were out of the building safely, their suits were still extremely hot, and they might have been exposed to radiation.

"I could not account for Scott. Did you see him in there," ask Alfred?

"He didn't make it Alfred. He is gone."

Alfred looked in disbelief, as Billy told him what happened to Scott.

"Make sure everything is sealed off for at least fifteen hundred feet from the perimeter of this plant."

"Okay," says Alfred as he ran off to carry out Billy's instructions.

Alfred came back with a suit on. He informed Billy that all of his employees on second shift made it out of the building safely. However the changeover shift was not so lucky. Three employees are missing, two were burned alive, and four were seriously injured. Billy demanded to know what triggered the explosion. However, at that point, no one had an answer.

"Where is my doctor?" demands Francisco hysterically.

"He has been notified and will be here shortly," says one of the rescuers.

"Billy, your suit is ripped," says Alfred.

Billy looked at his suit, and his eyes became wide in shock at how much his suit was torn. Billy sat down shaking and sweating profusely.

"Are you okay," asks Alfred?

Billy continued to shake and sweat, as if he did not hear Alfred. One of the paramedics called Billy's name, but he did not answer. His body temperature was climbing rapidly. Billy felt like he was on fire, and every organ inside of him felt like it was burning. All of a sudden, Billy bent over and begun to vomit. Emergency rescuers ran to Billy's aid and tried to get him out of his suit.

"I'm okay. I am just a little tired."

Billy's body was flushed. He had a few boils and gashes on his arm and thighs. He was lethargic and continued to repeat how tired he was, and how he needed to sleep. Alfred kept telling Billy to stay awake, but his eyes rolled into the back of his head, and he began to shake wildly with convulsions. Medics and rescuers tried to help Billy, as he had a seizure. The last thing Billy remembered seeing, was an extremely bright light in the center of darkness that resembled the sun.

When Billy woke up, he was in bed. He strained to focus on where he was. Mariah was sitting in the chair asleep, and unaware that her husband was awake. Billy fell back asleep for one more day, until he woke up in a state of panic.

"Help, Help!" he shouts as he frantically pulls at his sheets and IV.

"Billy, calm down," says Mariah.

Hearing Mariah's voice calmed him down.

"Mariah, where am I?"

"You are at Stone Mountain Medical. You were in a terrible accident at the plant."

Tears filled Mariah's eyes, as she watched her husband come back to her.

"The doctor said you were exposed to large amounts of smoke, fire, and radiation during the explosion. You have been unconscious for four days."

"You have to be kidding me," says Billy.

"Billy you were in a coma. We did not know if you were going to make it. We were all worried. Aunt Patty has been here every day praying for you, and asking God to bring you back to us. It's truly a miracle you are awake."

Billy looked at his wife and smiled. He reached out for her hand, and she gently touched it. He smiled and assured her, that he was fine. He even began to tell her about a dream he had.

"I had a dream," says Billy, "it was a beautiful and clear day. You and I were having a picnic, and I was lying down flat on my back throwing a little boy into the air. He was laughing every time I said, upsy daisy. We were so content and happy."

Mariah tried to tell Billy he needed to rest, but he insisted on continuing to tell her about his dream.

"Let me finish, please."

"Okay."

"So you called the little boy, Vernon and he called you mama. I smiled as you fed him some lunch. You had on a beautiful yellow sun dress, and your smile was as warm as a summer's day. As I stood up, I looked in the horizon and saw a firestorm headed our way. The fiery winds blew as screaming men, women, and children ran towards us. That was when I woke up in panic."

"Billy it is going to be okay. It was just a dream."

"No it wasn't," shouts Billy, "the last dream I had, became a reality, and I ended up in the hospital. Maybe this will come true, too!"

"Billy, I am going to get Dr. Sinto."

Mariah ran out of the room and came back with the doctor. He was a tall, slender, middle aged man with a medium sized beard. Dr. Sinto was the Small's family doctor, since Billy was a child. Not only was he the Small's family doctor, but he was also employed by Vega Incorporated.

"Billy I see that you are up. How are you feeling," he asks?

"I feel fine doctor."

"That's good. You gave everyone a scare."

"So I heard. Mariah was sitting here planning my eternal retirement party," jokes Billy.

"Billy that is not funny," says Mariah. "I was really worried about you."

"Relax babe. It was a joke. I am not going anywhere any time soon."

"Babe? Dr. Sinto can you please check Billy's head for a concussion? He is acting very strange."

"Actually, I do need to check you out Billy," says Dr. Sinto.

"Why? Haven't you checked me out for the past four days?"

"Yes, but now I need to check your heart, blood pressure, eyes, ears, and throat," replies Dr. Sinto.

"Ghee, will you need me to bend over a cough too," says Billy as he continues to joke.

Mariah looked at the doctor and shook her head. Dr. Sinto laughed at Billy humor.

"Humor is a great sign of recovery Billy." says Dr. Sinto," It appears that your heart rate is fine, and your blood pressure is normal. The results from the lab came back all negative."

"That is good news," replies Mariah.

"Though his temperature is a couple of degrees higher, it seems everything else checked out normal. You are completely radiation free," says Dr. Sinto.

"So doc when can I go home", ask Billy?

"Possibly in two days, but I still want to run more test on you."

"More tests," exclaims Billy!

"Billy you were exposed to high levels of radiation. It's a miracle you're alive and well. A couple more test, is not going to hurt you."

"I guess you're right doc."

"Billy, to the best of your knowledge, how long were you exposed to the radiation," ask Dr. Sinto?

"I would say about 15 to 20 minutes, though it felt like an eternity."

"Well, this is what puzzles me," says Dr. Sinto, "When you arrive in I.C.U. you had a two inch gash on your shoulder. It was greenish blue in color."

"Was it some type of infection, or did my body have an adverse reaction to the radiation?"

"We don't know Billy."

"What do you mean that you don't know?"

Billy reached for his shoulder and saw nothing. There were no bruises or gashes on his body.

"All we know is that your gash healed in two days," says Dr. Sinto.

"Well, I guess I can stay another night or two," says Billy.

"I am going to stay as well," says Mariah.

"That's fine Mariah," replies Dr. Sinto as he turns to leave the room.

"Dr. Sinto?"

"Yes Billy?"

"How are the Vega's doing?"

"I am afraid I cannot disclose that information," says Dr. Sinto.

"I just wanted to know if they were all ok," replies Billy.

"I know, but I can't disclose that information. I am sorry I can't tell you more," says Dr. Sinto.

Dr. Sinto left the room which, caused Billy to raise some suspicions about the Vegas. Billy asked Mariah for a newspaper. He told Mariah, how he felt about Dr. Sinto's reaction to his question.

"He is a nice doctor," says Mariah.

"I guess they are nice," replies Billy.

"What do you mean, they?"

"The Vegas. Did you hear what the doctor said?"

"What," ask Mariah?

"The doctor said he couldn't disclose the Vegas' information."

"I see your point, but the media has been around since this incident. Maybe they are trying to keep a low profile."

"It's all good, I am sure they are fine."

"Wow Billy! Since when did you start using slang? Are you trying to be hip or something?"

"Baby I am hip," replies Billy.

"Well, Mr. Cool, I am going home to get some more clothing for us. Don't get into mischief while I am gone."

"Hurry back, so we can both get into mischief. Bring me an ice cream from Spacely's," replies Billy shifting from side to side like a kid.

Mariah paused and looked at Billy weirdly.

"Baby, Spacely's closed ten years ago."

"Okay, then I will settle for your delicious pear pie."

Mariah smiled at her husband. She was so happy he was alive, but had concerns about his behavior. As she left Billy's room Alfred walked in. He sat beside Billy's bed, and looked at his friend with a sigh of relief.

Alfred and Billy talked about the accident. He told Billy the explosion occurred from an energy surge, caused by a bad generator. He assured Billy that Francisco took full responsibility for the accident, and paid for all of the repairs which included smoke, water, and radioactive damages. Parts of the plant were closed down, but they were still producing enough energy from the other reactor to power the nearby towns.

Billy asked Alfred about the employees who died and their families. Alfred explained that Francisco paid a generous amount of money to those families, as well as the injured employees.

Billy was impressed with Francisco's change of heart. He asked about their condition, and Alfred told him they only had a few burns and bruises, but nothing more.

"I almost died, and they barely have a scratch? Do you know if they are here in the hospital?"

"No. They are not even in the country," says Alfred.

"What," says Billy shockingly!

"The Vegas left two days ago," says Alfred.

"Really?"

"Yeah, and Francisco wanted to thank you for saving their lives. He says, he is forever in your debt. He even left you a parting gift," says Alfred handing Billy some keys.

"Keys?" ask Billy.

"Look out the window," says Alfred.

Billy got up out of his bed and walked towards the window. Alfred pointed towards the parking lot at a black British car.

"Whose car is that?" ask Billy.

"Yours," says Alfred, "Mr. Vega gave you a fully equipped, state of the art Aston Martin. He also wanted me to tell you to take the rest of the month off, with pay. He left his personal number for you to call him if you needed anything."

"I can't accept these gifts," replies Billy.

"And why not?"

"The blood of the dead is on my hands."

"I know we lost men during the explosion, and it haunts me also, but Billy you did the best you could."

Billy sat on the end of his bed rubbing his chin, and thinking back to the night of the accident.

"When we were trying to escape, Francisco was scared to death. I did not think a man that powerful could fear anything."

"Well Billy given the circumstances, the man thought he was going to die."

"Are you sure he is okay Alfred?"

"For the last time Billy they're fine. Why do you keep asking?"

"It just seems that his actions are intentionally humble, taking responsibility for the accident, giving money to our fallen employee's families, buying me a car, and then leaving. It was just a few days ago, he told me humbleness was a weakness. This is unlike him."

Alfred saw Billy's point and told him to rest. He knew Billy was on to something, but didn't want to get them more involved than necessary. When he left Billy's room, he got into his brand new Alfa Romeo that Francisco gave him. Beside him was a car phone that was plugged into the cigarette lighter. He looked out of the window at Billy's room in the distance, and made a call to Spain.

Chapter 10
The Era of Vega's Power

Somewhere, in an old and heavily guarded castle in Japan, an emotionally distraught Francisco tossed and turned in his bed. Remarkably, Francisco's rage became so intense, his body temperature increased, causing his bed to erupt into flames with him in it. He screamed out to Vinares, as his cousin and a group of soldiers stormed into his room, with semi-automatic weapons. When they entered Francisco's room, they saw his bed on fire, with him in it screaming for help.

"Hurry, get the fire extinguisher," yells Vinares as he pulls Francisco out of the bed!

"I have you Primo," says Vinares as he ordered the others to extinguish the bed before the room caught on fire.

Francisco seemed disoriented and delusional. He panted from being out of breath and continued to repeat himself saying, "His eyes. His eyes."

"Once the fire is out, get back to your post. I also want an informal investigation done to find out who started this fire," demands Vinares!

"Yes sir," replies the soldiers!

Francisco grabbed Vinares by the head, and looked him dead in his eyes.

"His eyes, his eyes," he continues to say.

"Primo, it was just a dream again," says Vinares.

"Billy, you and I were at the plant, and we were trying to escape the building when some man, or something with very long hair of flames dressed in red floated towards us. We couldn't see his face, but we could see his eyes, his red and vengeful eyes," says Francisco.

"Francisco, get a grip!"

"You and Billy tried to save me, but he vaporized the both of you with the snap of his fingers. He laughed insanely as the both of you burned. Then, he pointed at me and said, he was coming for me next."

"You have been talking about this dream of yours for days, but you never spoke of his face or voice, and you never woke up in a bed of fire."

"Well he did speak this time, and what frightened me the most, his voice sounded familiar and his eyes resembled mine."

"Don't worry Francisco. We are going to Master Soto in two days. He is going to help you with your internal struggles."

"You're right. If anyone can help me, he can. Master Soto is not only a master of martial arts, but also an expert in demonology," says Francisco.

"Agreed!" replies Vinares.

"Now where is my room?" asks Francisco.

"You are in your room," replies Vinares.

"Not anymore. This is your room now, and it smells like burnt flesh."

Vinares smiled and went with the flow. He agreed that Francisco's old room was now his new room.

"Primo, I think I have mastered the scrolls," replies Vinares!

"You think? It took me four years to master it, and you twelve years?"

"I know Francisco. I am almost there."

Vinares felt the cold sting of Francisco's words. He has always been looked down on by others, because he was not as smart as Francisco, or any of the other Vegas. What he lacked in knowledge, he gained in physical strength.

"Did I hit a nerve?" ask Francisco.

Vinares shook his head and walked towards the door with Francisco's bags.

"I will move your things into your new room, so you can go back to sleep," he replies.

"Don't you walk away from me when I am addressing you? I will dismiss you when I am good and ready," shouts Francisco!

"I am sorry Primo."

"Yes you are. Now you can go, and I will be in my new room in a few minutes," says Francisco?

Five minutes later, Francisco entered Vinares' room. He frowned when he smelled the musk of his stuffy, hot room.

169

He also noticed Vinares' white kimono was covered in green stains. He remembered that his doctors told them, green perspiration may be a side effect of the accident they encountered at the plant.

Francisco did not have that side effect, but he suffered terrible nightmares every time he closed his eyes. This side effect was emotional and filled him with guilt, paranoia and anger. He was always tired and sleepy, so he stopped caring about Vinares' housekeeping habits, and went to bed.

He slept and continued to toss and turn for two days, until Vinares woke him up and told him that Master Soto was ready to see him. Francisco asked for the demon mask Master Soto gave him when he mastered the strolls. Wearing it would be a sign of respect and honor.

Vinares was concerned about Francisco's health. He noticed a change in his behavior, because he surpassed the typical arrogance he genuinely displayed. This side of Francisco seemed darker and consumed with hate. Vinares thought about approaching Francisco about his new behavior, but he decided to keep his feelings to himself.

A few hours later, Francisco, Vinares and their body guards pulled up to a shrine located in a peaceful mountain village on the outskirts of Kyoto. At the walls of the shrine stood two guards. They drew their swords and carefully approached the limo. In silence Francisco quickly emerged from the limo with the mask of Soto in his hands. The two warriors bowed to him, and allowed them to enter.

The aroma of ginger incense filled the air. Francisco told his men to remain outside, but asked Vinares to come with him to see their Master. They walked towards the dojo at the end of the shrine. The walls were open, so they took their shoes off and entered.

Inside of the dojo, was a short old man with silver hair. He was sitting on a mat mediating. Master Soto, taught Francisco all he knew about Martial Arts, when he was sent to boarding school in Kyoto. He later met Vinares and taught him as well. When Master Soto sensed their presence, he opened his eyes and greeted them.

"I have been waiting for you boys," he says.

"Master it has been a long time," replies Vinares.

"Indeed it has."

Francisco looked around the room with suspicion, while Vinares and Master Soto talked.

"Primo, aren't you going to speak," ask Vinares?

"What is the meaning of this? Where is Master Soto," shouts Francisco!

"Are you insane, this is Master Soto," replies Vinares!

"Idiot, can't you see this is not our Master? Just because he is short, and has the white dragon kimono on, doesn't make him Master Soto you fool," yells Francisco!

"Master, please forgive him, he is sick from radiation poisoning," replies Vinares.

"You are correct Vega, very perceptive. How did you know I wasn't your Master?"

"Your confession explains it all. Only master's twin brother

Kenyatta called me by my last name. Since the accident in America, I am much more cautious," replies Francisco.

"I thought Master's brother Kenyatta died in a fight against him," replies Vinares?

"As you can see, I am alive and well," says Kenyatta.

"Where is Master Soto," says Francisco impatiently?

"I think you know the answer Vega," says Kenyatta.

"You killed him?"

"My brother brought great shame upon my family, because of you Vegas. You stole the sacred scrolls, and mask which has been in my family for generations."

"You are going to pay for this," replies Vinares.

"How dare you make threats to me? Both of you are in no condition to threaten me. If you think I am going to let you bathe in the sacred springs, you are both mistaken."

"Suit yourself, you old bastard. I guess I will have to take your life and the sacred springs in the process," says Francisco.

Vinares warned Francisco of his fragile state and told him that this may not be the best time to fight Kenyatta. Francisco told him not to worry and to go to the sacred springs. Francisco told Vinares to beware of the guards, and then he left the room in a hurry.

"I must admit, you fooled me. You deceived all of us, and now I will defend my Master's honor."

"What arrogance and disrespect you have boy. I know your skills Vega: Karate, Kung Fu, and Ninjitsu. Though you are good, you have no honor. After I am finished with you, I will take back the scrolls and the mask of my family. My men will cut Vinares down to size, if he is heading to the springs."

"Over my dead body!" shouts Francisco as he charges towards Kenyatta.

Kenyatta and Francisco engaged in an intense battle. They both moved nimbly and quickly. Francisco tried to end the fight by delivering a single strike to the heart, but Kenyatta was able to dodge his strike. Unable to deliver the death strike, Francisco used Kung Fu to throw Kenyatta off balance, but Kenyatta's defense was as equal to Francisco's speed and power.

Francisco realized he underestimated Kenyatta. With each powerful blow, Kenyatta struck Francisco with all he had. Francisco's youth and endurance gave him an advantage. His speed and power gradually increased to the point Kenyatta could not keep up the pace with him. In desperation, Kenyatta managed to grab hold his family's mystical Katana sword. He unshielded it, and pointed it toward Francisco. Francisco immediately changed his techniques to the defense, and prepared to stand his ground.

Meanwhile, Vinares and his guards were on their way to the springs. They ran into Kenyatta's guards and quickly defeated them. Worried about Francisco, Vinares told the guards to continue towards the springs while he checked on his cousin, but out of nowhere, there was an explosion that knocked Vinares to the ground. In the distance, Vinares saw a small cloud of smoke where the dojo once stood. He heard Francisco screaming, and immediately ran in his direction.

As Vinares sprinted through the burning forest, he realized he was not on fire though everything around him was. When he made it to where the dojo once stood, there was a huge hole in the ground. He called out to Francisco as he wondered what happened.

Suddenly, he heard a faint whisper.

"Vinares."

"Francisco, where are you," he replies looking around for his cousin.

From out of nowhere the ground began to violently rumble knocking Vinares to his knees. For a moment, he thought the explosion triggered an earthquake, but he soon realized that something was emerging from the crater where the dojo once stood.

Surrounded by dust, and light, Francisco emerged from the crater. He was engulfed in flames. His hair was long and black, and his eyes were red and glowing.

Vinares watched in terror as he witnessed something he never imagined possible. Francisco levitated towards him laughing and holding his hands out in amazement.

"Primo what happened to you," ask Vinares?

Francisco told Vinares about his battle with Kenyatta. He revealed his inner struggle and transformation. He also confirmed that Kenyatta was dead, and that he avenged their master's death.

Vinares looked at his cousin in disbelief. He was mesmerized by Francisco's story, but he also feared what he saw.

"How did you get these unearthly powers Francisco," ask Vinares?

"I don't know. Maybe it was the effects of the radiation poisoning. All of these dreams I've had about the man I might become was a mere premonition. Now, I can see clearly what my future has in store for me," says Francisco.

"So now that you've unlocked these extraordinary powers, do you still want to bathe in the sacred springs," asks Vinares?

"Absolutely not! This is a gift you fool," says Francisco as he looks at his own hands!

Vinares looked at his hands as well, and then looked at his cousin's power and strength.

"Primo, I have a confession. I have been having these similar crazy dreams of being on fire as well. I didn't want to tell you, because you have been dealing with your own nightmares. Do you think I may have this gift too," replies Vinares.

"It's a possibility. You were trapped down there, too."

"Wow! It would be amazing if you and I both had these special powers, after being saved by Billy," replies Vinares.

Francisco's face changed as a notion came to him. He

immediately demanded that Vinares search for the katana sword Kenyatta had. He said during the battle, the sword made him weak. He also told Vinares that he must get back to the castle and call his doctors immediately.

Vinares commented that he didn't think it was a good idea for Francisco to call his doctors. Francisco laughed at him and said, he was calling to check on a friend who was involved in an explosion. Vinares nodded and agreed.

"With my newly discovered powers, the world shall bow at my feet or feel my wrath. I have always dreamed of moving out of my father's shadow and now I truly can. I shall rule this world with iron fist, where only the strong will survive. Those who fear me shall follow me, and all who oppose me shall be crush unmercifully. I will usher in a new era. The Era of Vega," says Francisco!

He looked down at his hands as they continued to glow.

With Francisco's new powers, and Vinares potential to awaken his powers, the Vegas were on a crusade to rule the world.

Unbeknownst to them, back in Stone Mountain, Georgia, something truly remarkable transpired that will also have an impact on the world.

Chapter 11

A miracle in the womb

Mariah stared out of her bedroom window looking at the morning sun. She was smiling as the gentle breeze came in and blew through her hair. She was calm and radiated a remarkable glow, as she softly rubbed her lower abdomen. She turned around and looked at her husband sleeping in the bed peacefully. So, she walked over to him and kissed him on his forehead. Billy woke up and smiled at her.

"I must have died and gone to heaven, because an angel just kissed me. You are glowing sweetie, and the wind is flowing through your hair."

"You never cease to amaze me with your charm."

"Are you ok? You look like a kid in a candy store," says Billy.

"I'm late," replies Mariah with excitement!

"Late? Baby, Sunday school doesn't start for another three hours. Come back to bed."

"That's not what I meant Billy. My cycle is late, and that never happens."

"What," replies Billy as he sat up in bed?

"Billy, I think I'm pregnant."

"You're what!"

"I think I am pregnant. I took a pregnancy test last night

before I went to bed. I didn't want to get your hopes up, unless I was certain. The stick read positive."

"Praise God! We are going to have a baby!"

Billy jumped out of bed and swept Mariah off of her feet, and twirled her around. She told Billy to put her down, because she was getting dizzy, he apologized and gently placed her on the floor. Then, he started to jump up and down for joy.

"About how many days, months, hours are you," asks Billy?

"I am not sure. I am only a month and three weeks late. What made me suspect that I might be pregnant, was last night at dinner, when I felt sick after eating lima beans."

"Lima beans are your favorite. You must be pregnant if that made you sick."

Billy leaned down and touched Mariah's stomach.

"Hmm... it feels soft like a pillow."

Mariah slapped Billy on the head.

"More like you are soft in the head," she replies.

"Just joking. Your stomach is firm and flat," replies Billy.

"Thank you sweetheart," says Mariah blushing.

"But not for long. It will soon be round and fat," says Billy laughing as he runs from Mariah.

"Well at any rate, I am going to see Dr. Smith tomorrow and you are coming with me. Work can wait."

"Of course I am coming. Where else would I be?"

Billy pulled Mariah close and hugged her. He told, he loved her, and would be by her side throughout the entire pregnancy.

Billy decided to take the next two days off of work. He went to church with Mariah followed by a picnic in the park. They walked and talked for hours until the sun had set. When they arrived home, Billy tied his apron around his waist and grilled some food for dinner.

Mariah started to show her pregnancy within weeks after going to the doctor. They were told she was eight weeks pregnant. For several months, Billy and Mrs. Anderson watched over Mariah. They both cooked and cleaned up around the house. Billy was very protective of his wife, and she loved him for it.

Mariah gave birth during the beginning of her third trimester. Their baby was premature, but surprisingly, Mariah gave birth to a six pound, ten ounces healthy baby boy. Mariah and Billy named their son, Ev'ren.

They both shared tears of joy, for their little blessing. However, amongst their tears of happiness, a surveillance of darkness watched them closely.

Chapter 12
The Smalls' Legacy

It was a cool and rainy morning in Stone Mountain. Billy with an umbrella in his hand was walking to the doctor's office for his routine checkup. Suddenly, he heard struggling behind a deli shop. In the distance, he saw two men assaulting an old man dressed in an old sheriff's uniform. He rushed to the man's aide yelling for the two men to stop. When they saw Billy, they took off in a dash and ran away. Billy approached the old man who was curled up in the fetal position to protect himself.

"Hey, you all right," ask Billy?

"Get off of me," says the man hysterically!

"Hey I am just trying to help."

"I am fine," replies the man as he gets up slowly and out of breath.

Billy tried to help him, but he pushed Billy away. Billy looked at the man as if he knew him.

"Have I seen you from somewhere?"

"I don't think so," replies the man.

"Sir, aren't you Sheriff Lanksford," ask Billy?

"You mean ex-sheriff," replies the man, "but most people call me Lanksford."

The ex-sheriff scratched his head like he was trying to

remember who Billy was.

"I remember you now. You are Charles' son-in-law. We met a long time ago in front of Spacley's, and I saw you at his funeral beside his daughter."

"Yes it has been a long time."

"Billy is your name, correct?"

"Yes sir."

"So Billy, what have you been up to?"

"I have been busy working at the plant."

"Yeah, I heard about the accident and you saving everyone."

"Not everyone Lanksford. Good men and women died that day."

"Regardless Billy, what you did was remarkable. Your family must be proud of you. I've heard people call you a hero."

"Sir, I am no hero, but I am hungry. Would you like to join me for some breakfast?"

A minute later, Billy and Lanksford arrived at a deli. They could smell the food before they entered the building. As they entered the small deli, the pleasant atmosphere was replaced with bitter stares. Everyone eating stared at Lanksford. He brushed off his old uniform and took a seat with Billy.

The server came over to their table to take their orders. Billy ordered a hero sandwich. When she asked Lanksford what he wanted, he told her the same thing. The server frowned at Lanksford and made a comment underneath her breath. When she walked away, Billy asked Lanksford why she treated him that way. He shrugged his shoulders and changed the subject.

"You are like a town hero around here. You have protected this town as sheriff for many of years. I remember the day I went to the movies with the Clovers. You and my father in law were so close."

Lanksford's held his head down in dismay. His old and fragile face showed remorse and disappointment, as he confessed to Billy that he is not who he thought he was. He told Billy he has been homeless for a few months now. He also told Billy the town people hated him, and that he is not a hero.

When the server came back, she gave Billy his meal. She threw down Lanksford's hero sandwich and commented that he was never a hero in Stone Mountain. People in the background whispered and pointed at Lanksford.

Other people in the café made comments towards Lanksford. They called him a loser, and told him to leave. Billy tried to defend him, but the restaurant was in an uproar which forced them to leave. Billy asked to take their food to go, but changed his mind and decided he would never eat there again. When they left, he looked Lanksford in the eyes and asked him to explain, why they treated him that way.

"A few years ago, a tall white man tried to rob the National Bank of Stone Mountain. He took two hostages by gun point. One was a middle aged woman and the other was a

182

teenage girl. He made them get into a car. Meanwhile, I was in hot pursuit of the robber. The man shot his gun at me, but he ran over a pot hole and busted his tire. This caused the car to flip over with him and the two hostages inside. When the robber got out of the car, he forced the lady out of the car at gun point. I jumped out of my squad car and yelled for the man to stop. He looked at me and pointed the gun at her head demanding I put down my weapon. I was not about to give in to his demands, so I held fast to my gun. Meanwhile the teenager was still in the car as it caught fire. She screamed for someone to help her because she was trapped inside. The robber continued to move away from me as I asked him to drop his weapon. When the robber refused and threatened to kill the lady again, I placed my gun down. There was a cry from the smoking car. I can still see her face vividly in my mind. The robber shot the lady and open fired at me as he ran away. After I recovered to my feet and ran towards the car, it exploded. To make matters worse, when the paramedics arrived on site, they said the lady could have been saved if someone would have applied pressure to the wound. The café you took me to belongs to the husband and father of the two who died that day."

Billy looked at Lanksford with sadness in his eyes. He felt bad for him, and knew he was only doing what he thought was best at the time.

"To make matter's worst Billy, they did an alcohol test on me and determined that I was impaired by alcohol which clouded my judgment. I swear to you all I had was a beer. I was off duty when I heard the call, but I was close to the bank so I took the call. Now, I have no job, no house, no family or friends."

Billy gave Lanksford some money and his business card. He told him to stop by the plant for a janitor's job he was hiring for. Lanksford thanked him for his kindness and left.

About half an hour later, Billy arrived at Dr. Sinto's office for his annual checkup. Dr. Sinto checked Billy's reflexes, blood pressure and so forth. During the testing, Billy asked Dr. Sinto about his wife and two daughters. Dr. Sinto told him they were fine and asked about his family. He asked Billy questions about the accident again, which made him nervous, because he already answered those questions before.

"Do you still feel any side effects from the accident," asks Dr. Sinto?

"No," says Billy.

Dr. Sinto asked him again, and Billy replied that he hasn't.

"I noticed that your scars have completely healed."

"I guess I'm a fast healer," says Billy, "but there is one thing that concerns me."

"What is it," ask Dr. Sinto?

"Some nights I have dreams that I am on fire. It is like a nightmare that I have two or three times a week."

"Hum," says Dr. Sinto, "sounds interesting."

"What is it," ask Billy?

"I am going to prescribe some medicine to help you sleep. I do not want you operating heavy machinery, or driving when taking this medicine. Carefully follow the instructions on the bottle."

"Will this help me with my nightmares?"

"Yes, it will help you sleep. I will schedule a follow up in two weeks."

After Billy left, Dr. Sinto walked down to his office and closed the door. He picked up the phone and made a telephone call. He gave the person on the other end of the phone, a detailed report of Billy's medical progress. He also told the person about Billy's child. The mysterious person told Dr. Sinto he did not care about the child, but more so about Billy's dreams. Dr. Sinto told the caller, he didn't like breaking his doctor-patient confidentiality, and stated that he could lose his license to practice. When he asked if he would be rewarded for helping, the mysterious caller hung up.

A few hours later Dr. Sinto was rewarded with eternal silence for his information. He was found in his office face down with a hypodermic needle beside him. There was also a letter found next to him saying, *"Somethings aren't worth living for."*

Sheriff Lance Townsend, a mean middle age six- four, two hundred pound Texan with olive tan skin ruled Dr. Sinto's death a suicide. Townsend served in the US Marines for twenty years. He was in Vietnam as a Lieutenant, and was very successful in his missions. Townsend was also good friends with the Vega family, of which no one was aware of. He was known as the Texas Eraser. Whenever mistakes happened, Townsend made them go away, even if it involved a well-known doctor.

Meanwhile, after a long exhausting day of talking and screaming kids, Mariah prepared to depart Stone Creek Elementary with shopping on her mind. She jumped into her birthday gift, a red mustang convertible Billy gave her, and let hair down. She sped off from school with the music up and her shades on. A group of young boys drove up beside her and started to flirt. She showed them her wedding ring and drove off. A minute later she arrived at the mall to meet her friends Christina and Brenda.

Christina was a tall and beautiful model. She had beautiful blonde hair, and deep ocean blue eyes. Brenda was a tall, plus sized woman with curves. She had beautiful dark brown eyes, with the skin complexion to match it.

Christina and Brenda were old college friends of Mariah. They were in the area, and wanted to hang out with Mariah and do some shopping. The three of them embraced each other and talked about their current lives, and their college years.

After shopping, Mariah invited them over to her house for dinner and to see Ev'ren. Brenda said she had to get back to Atlanta, but Christina said she would stop by later that week to see Ev'ren since, she was there for a photo shoot.

After a cheerful reunion with Brenda and Christina, Mariah walked into the house and called out to Billy. She told him about her day at school, and her retail therapy with Brenda and Christina.

Billy joked with her about her friends as he played with Ev'ren and made silly faces. When she told him Christina would be stopping by later on that week, he teased and joked with her some more. Mariah blushed and softly kissed him on his cheek.

Billy picked Ev'ren up and went into the living room, to turn on the television and watch the news. He called out to Mariah when he heard some tragic news. She rushed into the living room to see what happened.

"Once again, it has been reported that Dr. Sinto was found dead in his office after he apparently injected himself with a syringe of oxycodone a powerful pain medication. It has been determined that he committed suicide. Stay tuned for more information as this story develops."

Billy shook his head in disbelief.

"Suicide? I was just in town this morning for a physical. He seemed fine to me."

"Yeah, when I saw him in the grocery store last week, I asked him about his family and he seemed happy," replies Mariah.

"Maybe he was depressed, but had nowhere to turn?"

"You have a point Billy. Now, I was wondering what time you will be at work tonight?"

"My shift starts at seven o'clock in the morning."

"I thought your shift started tonight at ten."

"Originally it did, but Dr. Sinto gave me some medicine to help me sleep. Maybe I shouldn't take it now," says Billy.

"I wouldn't. Who knows what was going through his head when he wrote you that prescription. Can we car pool tomorrow? I can call Aunt Patty to babysit Ev'ren."

"Okay. That is a good idea."

"Billy, I didn't know you were struggling to sleep? Please tell me what's wrong," ask Mariah?

"I have been having nightmares about the accident at the plant."

"What?"

"Yes, I have been dreaming about it since I was released from the hospital."

"You have been having these nightmares for a year Billy? Why didn't you tell me?"

"I am sorry Mariah. You were pregnant with Ev'ren and I did not want to add any unnecessary stress."

"Billy, I could have helped you, and I still can. I am calling Ralph."

"Ralph," says Billy?

"Yes, Cousin Ralph, the psychiatrist in Atlanta," replies Mariah.

"I am not talking to Ralph," exclaims Billy!

"And why not? He is a professional."

"He smells like fish Mariah, and I don't need a shrink."

"He is a psychiatrist Billy, not a shrink, and he is family. What other alternative do you have?"

"You're right. I will call him tomorrow."

"That is a great Billy."

"But I will go to his office instead of him coming here. I don't want him coming over stinking up our house. The only smell of fish I want in this house is your delicious fried flounder."

"Billy he has a medical condition, and it is not nice to tease him. I will let him know to expect you."

Billy and Mariah ate dinner, and prepared for bed.

Just as Billy locked the doors, the phone rang. Billy stumbled towards the kitchen to answer it.

"Hello?"

"Is this the Smalls residence," replies the caller?

"Yes it is, and whom am I speaking too," ask Billy.

The mysteries voice paused for a few seconds, and then warned Billy to prepare.

Billy looked confused, as he took the phone from his ear and looked at it, as if he was trying to see who was on the other end.

"Prepare for what," he asks?

"Prepare," says the mysterious voice again.

"Is this Hartwell," ask Billy?

Suddenly, the caller hung up, and the person on the other end was gone just as mysteriously as he called.

Mariah asked Billy if Christina called her. He told her about the strange call. She told Billy if the telephone rang again, she would answer it and gave the caller a piece of her mind.

Later on that night Billy secretly took the medicine Dr. Sinto gave him. As he slept, a dim white glow emerged from his body, and softly illuminated the room. For the first time in a year, Billy slept peacefully.

Chapter 13

The Supremacy of Life

Billy was awakened by the sights and sounds of thunder and lightning. He watched peacefully, as Mariah and Ev'ren slept in the rocking chair. He thought to himself how, beautiful they looked and how blessed he was to have them in his life.

He quietly crawled out of bed, onto his knees to pray. He closed his eyes and thanked God for his family. He prayed for his friends, his co-workers, and Mariah. He also asked God to watch over his beloved son.

After he prayed, he noticed that his sheets looked a little burnt. When he touched the area he slept in, he couldn't believe what happened.

Soon, Mariah woke up.

"Good morning Billy," she says.

Billy quickly wrapped up the sheets he slept in.

"Good morning sweetheart, how did you sleep," he asks?

"I slept well, even though Ev'ren and I rocked all night."

Mariah looked at Billy's trembling hands holding the sheets.

"Hey, what's wrong with those sheets," she asked?

"Nothing, I perspired a little, so they need to be washed."

Billy took the sheets and tucked them under his arms.

"You know what Mariah. I am just going to throw these away. We need some new sheets anyway."

Mariah looked at Billy puzzled.

"If you say so honey."

"I better go and take a shower."

"You can't shower in this weather Billy. It is storming."

"You're right. I will sponge off in the sink."

"Do you need some assistance with that," says Mariah coyishly?

"That sounds like a plan," says Billy as he starts to tip toe towards her.

Just as Mariah stood up to put Ev'ren in his crib, he woke up and looked at them both. They began to talk to him as he yawned, and then smiled.

"Look at my little man. Hey little guy," says Billy.

Ev'ren laughed and cooed at his dad, as he made silly faces. Mariah smiled as she watched Billy play with Ev'ren. A tear fell from her eyes as she thought about her husband's prayer she overheard this morning.

"I love you Billy," she whispers.

"I love you too, Mariah."

Billy walked towards Mariah and kissed her. Then, he walked into the bathroom. She smiled at Ev'ren and made funny faces like his daddy just did. Ev'ren giggled with joy.

There was a crackle of thunder and Ev'ren started to cry. Mariah picked him up and cradled him to calm him down. She looked into Ev'ren's eyes, and for a brief second, his eyes changed from blue to yellow. Mariah thought she was seeing things, but when Ev'ren stopped crying, his eyes were blue again.

A few minutes later, Billy and Mariah were dressed for work. Billy was wearing his yellow coveralls and Mariah had on a dress.

Mrs. Anderson arrived on time and ready to give Ev'ren his bottle.

"I know you are hungry," she says to Ev'ren.

Mariah and Billy kissed Ev'ren and told him goodbye.

"Have a good day you two," says Mrs. Anderson.

"Thank you auntie and take care little man," says Billy.

"Drive safe Billy. The weather out there is awful," she says.

As they drove off into the storm, Mrs. Anderson said a prayer for them. She had a bad feeling about them driving in this type of weather.

As Billy and Mariah cruised down the dark slick roads of Stone Mountain, they came upon a road block. Sheriff Townsend walked towards Billy and Mariah, and tapped on their window. Billy greeted the sheriff with a good morning and inquired about the road block.

"There is a highway emergency about a mile down the road, so you will have to turn around," he insists.

"Can't we take Lawrenceville highway or SR 8 near Decatur," asks Billy?

"Look, this highway is closed and no one is going to cross through. Got it," says the sheriff sternly!

"Wait a minute. You cannot talk to us like that," says Mariah!

"I already did. Now scram before I arrest the both of you."

"Billy, go around the barricade and forget this loser," says Mariah.

"No, we will turn around."

"I don't know how you were elected sheriff," says Mariah.

Sheriff Townsend came closer to their car and slammed his hands on the roof.

"You need to mind what you say to me," he says.

"You need to know that you don't intimidate us, and that I will press charges against you for harassing my wife and me."

"Get out of here," he says as he backed away.

As Billy drove off, Sheriff Townsend told his deputy to make sure they don't come back. He mentioned they will have to go through Hungry Neck.

As Billy and Mariah sped toward Decatur. They sat in silence, until Mariah exploded with anger.

"Lawrenceville highway was only a quarter mile away. He

might have set that road block up on purpose. What a jerk!"

"I know Mariah, but there's nothing we can do about it right now."

"I can't believe you sat there and let him talk to us like that."

"I spoke up and told him to stop, or we would take him court, and besides, you are a white woman and I am a black man. No matter how much times have changed, Stone Mountain is still behind the times."

"Take him to court? I would have taken him to the wood shed. He is a racist bigot," says Mariah!

"Look Mariah, I am taking a short cut through Hungry Neck, but I am trying to focus on this dangerous road, and this storm seems to be getting worst, so can we please drop this conversation?"

The weather intensified, as Billy strained to look out of the window at the lightning ahead.

"That's strange, I have never seen blue lighting before, and oddly enough there is no sound of thunder."

"It's unusual," says Mariah, "and what is that rumbling?"

"I don't know."

As they continued to descend down the dark mountain towards Hungry Neck, Mariah look up and saw a huge boulder rolling towards them. She told Billy to speed up so they would miss it. Billy quickly accelerated the car allowing them to barely miss the boulder. Shortly after, another huge boulder tumbled down the mountain towards them.

"Oh my God Billy! We made it," says Mariah with relief.

"Yeah, I have never seen Stone Mountain drop huge rocks like that."

"Now that you mention it, Stone Mountain's summit is round. Why would a bus size boulder tumble down it?"

"Lightning could have struck the mountain side," replies Billy as he turns his wipers up to the highest speed, and looks out of the window cautiously.

Mariah looked at the hood of the car, and started to panic. The paint on the car was melting as smoke and steam rose from the hood.

"Is that acid rain? What in the world," says Billy?

"How is this possible," ask Mariah?

"I don't know, but this is unheard of! We will be okay as long as we stay in the car," says Billy.

As they continued to drive in the acid rain, Billy and Mariah watched in terror as plants and animals died around them. A dense fog started to develop in the area. Then finally the acid rain subsided. Suddenly, they heard a loud boom and felt the car's rim bump against the road.

"Billy I think the front passenger tire is flat. We have to pull over."

"There is no place for us to pull over. Are you sure this is safe?"

"Once we make it downhill, I will pull over and change the tire. Until then, I will just drive slowly," says Billy as he tried to maneuver through the fog and rain.

All of a sudden, Billy drove over a pot hole in the road making the glove compartment swing open. Papers started to flow freely out onto Mariah's lap and the floor. Billy looked down to help Mariah with the papers. Mariah told him to keep his eyes on the road.

Standing in the middle of the road was a huge figure. Billy swerved and lost control of the car. As the wheels began to spin uncontrollably, Billy told Mariah to hold on. He slammed on the brakes as Mariah screamed. The car went off of the road and tumbled down into a deep gully about forty-five feet below.

A little dazed, Billy looked around the car which miraculously landed upright into the riverine. He tried to focus as freezing water rushed into the car. The windows were gone and glass was everywhere. He reached over for Mariah, but she was not there.

In a panic, Billy's senses heightened as he began to search for his wife. He called out to her, but she did not respond. He climbed out the window, and dove into the icy water to search for his wife, until finally, he saw her floating in the water faced down. He quickly grabbed her, and swam to the closest embankment. He cried out for her to answer him, but she didn't, so he immediately began to give her CPR.

"One, two, three... he says as he continues to give Mariah chest compressions.

Her chest moved up and down, as he attempted to breathe

life into his wife, but she was still unresponsive.

"Breathe sweetie, breathe," he says as tears roll down his face.

After a few more minutes of CPR, Billy checked Mariah's pulse, and there was none. Her lips were blue and her face was stone cold.

"Please Lord! Not her too!" says Billy hysterically.

Billy held his lifeless wife in his arms, begging her to wake up. She laid silent. He was in disbelief that his wife was gone.

He carried her lifeless body towards higher ground. Out of nowhere, he heard a voice.

"Stop crying. Grief weakens you," says the voice.

Billy looked around with caution.

"Who is there? Help me. My wife needs help."

Behind Billy emerged Vinares Vega out of the thick of the fog. Billy looked surprised to see him there. He looked down at Mariah in his hands, and pleaded for Vinares to help him get her to the hospital.

"Can't you see there is no life in her face," says Vinares.

He looked at Billy and called him pathetic as he laughed.

"Stop laughing! This is not funny you bastard! My wife is dying please help us," shouts Billy!

"She is dead because I killed her," boast Vinares.

"What do you mean," ask Billy?

"It was all part of the plan."

Billy looked at Vinares confused and out of sorts.

"You killed her?"

"Yes. As you and your little precious wife were driving, I appeared in the road, causing you to lose control of your car. When you two went over the cliff, I placed a needle into her heart, causing it to stop."

"Impossible! You couldn't have done that, because we were in the car."

Billy looked at Mariah as he cradled her. He placed her gently on the ground and touched her cold lifeless face. He looked at her dress, and noticed a tiny object protruding from the left side of her chest and became enraged.

"What did you do to her you monster!" demands Billy.

Vinares laughed at Billy's ignorance, as he kept his majestic stance about twenty feet away from them.

"Don't you see fool. I have super strength and speed. Not to mention I'm responsible for the acid rain and the boulders. With my newly found powers, I can do anything I want to do."

Billy looked at Vinares and noticed a dim glow illuminating from his body. He saw the difference in Vinares, and felt a heavy and dark energy around them. Anger took hold of Billy and without relent, he charged towards Vinares.

"Bastard," cries Billy!

199

Vinares casually stepped a few feet aside, which caused Billy to fall to the ground. He laughed as Billy quickly jumped to his feet and looked at him. His anger was intense, as he ran towards Vinares again. This time Vinares struck Billy across his face, knocking him several feet into the water.

Billy quickly jumped to his feet, and touched his face as he stared at Vinares. A normal human being would have been killed by Vinares' strike, but Billy barely felt Vinares' super human strength.

"You are going down! I have had enough of you," shouts Billy!

He charged towards Vinares again. This time, Vinares struck Billy across his back, causing him to fly into an oak tree. Billy fell to his knees and started to cough.

"Oh God, he almost took my head off. How did he get so strong, and why am I not dead yet," replies Billy to himself?

Vinares snuck up behind Billy, and placed him into a choke hold. Billy struggled to break free, but couldn't. The more he struggled, the tighter Vinares' grip became.

"Why are you doing this?"

"It is my method of persuasion," says Vinares, "a way to ask you to join our cause."

"A cause, what cause? You murdered my wife and you expect me to join your cause?"

"Yes. It was by design that you join us Mr. Smalls," replies Vinares.

"How did you find me," ask Billy?

"Since that accident at the plant and the nightmares, which I know you've had, we all have been connected. It is a numbing feeling to the cranium isn't it? Thanks to the sheriff, we were able to obtain you," replies Vinares.

"I knew the sheriff was up to no good. I should have listened to my wife, and ran through the barricade," says Billy.

"We are brothers, bonded by a single handed accident that changed all of our lives forever."

"What? Are you crazy?"

"I know about your abilities Mr. Smalls. I know that you can heal yourself."

"What are you talking about? I can't heal myself?"

"Okay. Let's take this slow, because obviously you are not the brightest bulb in the pack. How do you think you were able to survive the accident at the plant, and the car accident a few minutes ago? Let's not mention that you were able to conceive a child, after numerous failed attempts."

Billy had the look of disgust; at how much Vinares knew about his personal life. Then he thought about his wife lying on the ground lifeless, and started to struggle under Vinares' arms again.

"Mariah," he cries.

"Billy, get a grip! She would have eventually become an obstacle for you, and your true purpose."

"My true purpose?"

"Join us Billy. With your superpowers, we shall rule the world together."

"Rule the world? Who do you think we are? You sound ridiculous," laughs Billy sarcastically.

"I am serious Billy, so what do you say?"

"Hell no," yells Billy!

Billy managed to slip out of Vinares' hold, and stood at a distance from him panting in anger and fury.

"I will never forgive, or forget what you have done to my wife," he says.

Billy eyes began to glow yellow as an uncontrollable rage took hold of him. He had no formal training like Vinares did, all he knew at that moment was anger and hurt.

A twister of flames, formed around Billy as he prepared to attack. Vinares was in shock at the heat and energy Billy exerted. Then all of a sudden Billy vanished. Vinares laughed at Billy and taunted him like they were playing hide-and-go seek. He called out to Billy looking, for signs of him, but he did not see him anywhere.

"You stupid fool! Did you just vaporize yourself?"

As Vinares continued to laugh and walk away, Billy reappeared. He charged towards Vinares and struck him in the face. Billy continued to strike Vinares across his face until he knocked out a tooth. Vinares screamed out in anger and started swinging wildly, while Billy watched him unaware that Vinares could not see him. When he realized he was invisible to Vinares, he began to smirk.

Vinares held out his hands and launched needle like objects from his nails. Billy dodged them with ease.

Both of them were surprised at Billy's unknown abilities. Vinares was no match for Billy's super speed. Billy reappeared and punched Vinares in his torso sending him into an oak tree. Just as Vinares stood up, Billy struck him again. In fury Vinares stood up, and started to swing wildly destroying surrounding trees. As he continued to swing, he began to get tired. Billy seized the opportunity to repay Vinares the favor, by slipping behind him to apply a rear choke hold. Vinares attempted to break Billy's hold, but despite his incredible strength, Billy's speed and vibration to shake Vinares' grip was unmatched.

"Can you feel it, the life leaving your body like it did my wife?"

"Let me go," replies Vinares as he struggles to break Billy's hold!

"I am never letting you go! Your time is up and the only thing I want right now is your absolute silence!"

"Billy is this what your wife would have wanted? For you to be a cold blooded killer," ask Vinares?

"How dare you bring my wife into this? She didn't deserve to die. If you wanted me, you should have come for me, not her, and to answer your question, yes she would have wanted me to kill you."

"Billy if you let me go, I will never bother you again. I am sorry about your wife. I should have left her out of this. I will do anything to make this up to you. Just let me go!"

Vinares began to gag and pant for air. He slowly felt everything going dark.

Inside, Billy knew that Mariah would not want this, so he bargained with Vinares.

"Promise to go away and never bother me, nor my family again?"

"I promise. You have my word as a gentleman," says Vinares.

When Billy released Vinares, he fell to the ground coughing and gasping for air.

"Go and never come back again," says Billy.

Vinares continued to cough as Billy turned to walk towards Mariah's corpse. Suddenly, a smile came across Vinares' face as he crept up behind Billy, and stunned him from behind. Billy fell forward, a few inches from Mariah.

"You stupid fool. You are so weak. You should have finished me off."

Billy looked up at Vinares and quickly recovered to his feet. Billy appeared behind Vinares again to place him in a choke hold.

"I will show you weak! I will show you just how weak you are, when I finish you this time," says Billy!

From high above, Billy and Vinares heard the word *"Toro"*. A blast of light came out of nowhere like a heat wave, and knocked Billy to the ground. Vinares seized the opportunity to attack Billy with a punch to the face.

Billy was caught off guard from the blast that struck him. He began to spit blood out of his mouth, as Vinares kicked him over and over again in the stomach. One last kick sent Billy flying into the side of the mountain. When he landed, part of the mountain collapsed onto him.

Vinares looked above the mountain and smiled.

"At last primo. You came," he says.

From high above the mountain, Francisco began his descend to the ground. He was wearing a demonic mask and a black elastic body suit. He majestically floated to earth and landed beside his cousin.

Francisco wasn't happy at all. He saw the mess Vinares left and it infuriated him. With a quick move of his wrist, Francisco struck Vinares down to the ground.

"Don't say a word to me. I watched it all," he says.

Vinares lowered his head in shame.

"You killed that man's wife! You were not supposed to do that! How would you expect him react after that you fool?"

"I thought you wanted me to end her life," replies Vinares.

"I told you to use her as bait. Not to kill her. You are so incompetent. Now we have a mess on our hands. The anger in him you've created has caused him to unlock his powers, and now he will never join us."

"I am sorry cousin. I messed up!"

"We have to dispose of him now, before something else happens," says Francisco bitterly.

"He's probably dead after the side of the mountain collapsed on him."

"He is not dead, because I can feel his energy rising again. Get ready to fight."

There was rumbling beneath the rocks where Billy laid. The earth began to shake as an explosion came from the mountain side. Rocks and boulders the size of cars flew in every direction. Billy stood directly in front of them as he wiped pebbles from his face.

"So you are the master mind behind this Francisco? After I saved your life in the plant explosion, you repay me back by killing my wife? You are going to pay!"

"I didn't think the bank was open this early in the morning, so don't write a check you can't cash Billy. Your wife would have been a distraction," says Francisco.

Enraged, Billy attacked Vinares and Francisco at the same time. He charged into Vinares and knocked him to the ground. Then, he turned his attention to Francisco. Despite Francisco's superior fighting capabilities, he was not prepared for Billy's speed or invisibility. He was always a step ahead of Francisco which aggravated him. Each punch or kick Francisco gave, Billy was able to avoid it. Francisco took to the sky and fired volleyball sized energy waves toward Billy. Billy easily dodged each of his attacks, as Vinares uprooted a tree and tossed it at him like a dart.

Billy saw the two of them ganging up on him, so he

vanished like he did before. Unable to find him, Billy watched them carefully. Francisco pointed at Vinares and kneeled. Vinares did the same. They looked as if they paused to pray.

Francisco and Vinares developed the powers of telepathy during their training. They were able to communicate with each other without Billy hearing them. That way they could formulate a plan.

"We have to work together to defeat Billy, he is invisible plus his speed makes him impossible to locate. If it starts to rain again, use your Blades of Acids Rain attack," says Francisco.

"It doesn't have any effect on him," replies Vinares.

"Just do it," demands Francisco.

Francisco flew above the surface and began to gather energy from high above. Vinares recovered to his feet and fired needles from his hands in every direction. Billy easily dodged them and hid amongst the trees and bushes.

As Francisco ascended to into the clouds, his heat energy triggered a light drizzle. Pleasantly surprised, Vinares used that opportunity to shoot his projectiles. Then he did as Francisco asked and retreated.

The rain water turned to acid rain and slowly destroyed plants and trees around Billy. Once the rain coated Billy, Francisco was able to see him.

Billy heard a cry from high above.

"GAMMA CANNON!"

Francisco unleashed his energy attack. Everything within a quarter of a mile was leveled. A few minutes later, he and Vinares returned to the ground below and found Billy semi-conscience on a bed of rocks.

"Look at him. He is truly pathetic," says Vinares.

Francisco stood over Billy watching him as he remarkably began to heal.

"He will keep coming. This will never end if we do not finish him," says Vinares.

Francisco reached behind him and pulled out his newly forged Katana sword.

"This sword was said to be unbreakable. This sword has unbelievable power. The power to discharge heat energy. Another incredible thing about this sword is that it can also absorb light," says Francisco.

He unshielded the sword and drove it into Billy's glowing body. Billy cried out in pain, and called out to Mariah, as light energy expelled from the sword and into his body.

"Don't worry. You will be joining her soon, Billy," replies Francisco.

Billy eyes rolled back into his head, as a tear ran down his face, which soon turned dark and wrinkly. The sword drained all of his energy, as he continued to call out for his wife.

"Die," shouts Vinares!

"Why," says Billy as he takes his last breath and falls silent?

Billy's lifeless body disintegrated and turned into dust.

The Vegas started to laugh and celebrated their victory.

Francisco told Vinares to clean up any signs of foul play, while he took care of a project in Kuwait.

Vinares told him not to worry and called some people they paid off to clean up the mountain. By time they were done, it was as if Billy and Mariah never existed.

Vinares called Francisco to let him know the job was complete. He was delighted.

"What about the boy. Don't they have a child," ask Vinares?

"Leave him to me," says Francisco with a sinister voice, "I have always wanted a son."

Chapter 14
Ev'ren's education

"Alright Gentleman, welcome to football tryouts 2014. I am Coach Cheesebro, and these are my assistant coaches, Watermaker, Tang, and Williams."

Cheesebro coached the football team at Stone Mountain High School. He was a tall dark skinned man in his middle ages. He use to play professional football, but after an injury, he retired and starting coaching at Stone Mountain High School.

"Today we are going to do some basic fundamental drills without contact. Do you understand," says Coach Cheesebro.

The team replied like a military squadron and said, "Yes coach!"

"If you do not follow these simple instructions, you will not be on my team," says Coach Cheesebro.

"Yes Coach!"

Each of the young men was dressed for battle, wearing t-shirts and shorts. Coach Cheesebro's job was to weed out the weak, and create a winning football team. There were at least fifty teenagers on the field ranging in different shapes, sizes, and heights.

For try outs they had to do various stretches, sprints, weight training, and testing their knowledge of the game. He also looked to see who was serious about the game. Coach

Cheesebro came upon two of the trainees laughing about something.

"You two," shouts Coach Cheesebro!

'Yeah," says the boys.

"First of all, it is Coach Cheesebro," he says.

"Sorry Coach Cheeseburger…I mean Coach Cheesebro," snickers the young men.

Coach Cheesebro's eyes pierced into theirs, with anger as they fell silent.

"You guys think you're funny, huh. I see we have a couple of comedians."

He walked so close to them, he could see the sweat forming on their foreheads.

"Well I have jokes, too."

Coach Cheesebro told everyone, they would be running five additional miles thanks to their two comedians. The guys moaned in agony as they, all looked at the two, who made it possible for them to stay later.

"You will also be practicing on Saturday mornings for the next three weeks. So that's Monday through Saturday. Four hours in the evening starting at four. And you better be on time!"

The guys were furious with the two jokers who opened their mouths. They sighed and whined as Coach Cheesebro continued to talk.

"If one messes up, we all mess up, but if one succeed, we all succeed. That is what makes a team," says Coach Cheesebro.

He then turned to the other coaches and nodded.

"If they want to bring the wood, we will set the fire, because no one will make a fool of us," he says.

For the next few hours, the coaches put the young men through rigorous workouts. A few couldn't handle the pressure and decided to quit, including the two who made fun of the coach. Others excelled and achieved their goal, which gave Coach Cheesebro a sense of potential in the candidates.

After try outs, Coach Cheesebro met with his two other coaches for a full report.

"How did our other candidates do in the weight room," asked Cheesebro.

"Everyone can bench over one forty-five and squat over two hundred pounds. Marco Tines, our senior blocker benched three hundred fifty pounds, and squatted seven hundred pounds of weights," says one of the coaches.

Coach Cheesebro asked about the offensive and defensive line.

"Orlando Stone, weighs three hundred ten pounds. He is benching three hundred pounds, and squatting seven hundred and fifty pounds," replies the other coach.

"Excellent," says Cheesebro.

The coaches continued to give Coach Cheesebro their assessment, as he stroked his thick beard.

"It looks like we are going to have a strong team," he says.

"Oh, and this new kid Smalls, is five feet eleven, weighs one hundred sixty-five pounds, but he can bench two hundred eighty-five pounds and can squat five hundred pounds without breaking a sweat," says one of the coaches.

Coach Cheesebro stopped stroking his beard and looked up.

"You're joking right," says Coach Cheesebro.

"No Coach. No Joke."

"Where is this Smalls kid right now," ask Coach Cheesebro.

"He is with Coach Williams doing some laps."

They both hurried over to the track to see this trainee in action.

As they watched him on the track, one of the coaches proceeded to give Coach Cheesebro information about him.

"He is supposed to be a freshman, but he skipped one grade and is a sophomore. From what I was told, he is some kind of child prodigy. Extremely smart," says the coach.

The coaches walked out onto the track to see this kid up close. He raced Marco, their fastest player and left him in the wind.

After the race, Coach Cheesebro wanted to talk to him. When he came over, Coach Cheesebro looked at him from head to toe. He was smaller than the average football player. He looked like he belonged on the science team, not the football team. His skin was light brown in color, with rusty brown curly hair. It was easy to see his ethnicity had a mixture of rich cultures, but what really gave it away were his ocean blue eyes. Coach Cheesebro shook his hands.

"What's your name kid," he asks?

"My name is Nitro Smalls," he says.

Coach Cheesebro looked at him as if he was joking. He thought to himself, maybe this kid had an ego problem. Some of the other kids laughed at his response, but he was sincere.

"Son is that your real name?"

"Yes Coach. As a child I was always energetic. My aunt would let me run outside at an old family farm to burn off energy. She said I was an explosive runner, so she started calling me Nitro."

"Awe how sweet," says one of the players sarcastically.

Some of the players laughed at him, until Coach Cheesebro made them stop. He wanted to test Nitro Smalls' speed.

"I have a little test for you. I would like for you to race one lap around the track. Run as fast as you can, and when you come back to your starting point, stop. Is that clear?"

"Yes Coach," says Nitro.

Coach Cheesebro watched as Nitro prepped himself to run. Once he gave the signal, Nitro quickly took off. When he made it back to his starting point, everyone looked at him and was speechless. His teammates were all in awe.

"Unbelievable. You ran half a mile in eight seconds."

Marco walked up to coach Williams and looked at Nitro's time.

"That can't be right Coach. I'm the fastest runner on this team. This must be beginner's luck," he says.

"A half mile in eight seconds... in other words, you were the fastest person on this team," says one of the coaches.

Marco demanded a rematch on running against Nitro. Coach Williams told him to give it a rest, but Marco refused.

"Let them go for it," says Cheesebro loving a friendly competition, "I would like to see some real sportsmanship."

Marco and Nitro went to the starting point and prepared for a re-match. On the count of three they took off in a dash. Within eleven seconds Nitro was back, and Marco was not half way around the track.

Most of the candidates gazed with their mouths open. Others gave Nitro a pat on the back. Coach Cheesebro was extremely impressed.

"All right guys knock it off. I am going to let you all run your last lap thanks to Nitro, and call it a day," says Coach Cheesebro.

The guys were happy and took off running. Coach Cheesebro asked Nitro Smalls to stay behind and talk. He told Nitro he was impressed with his performance that day.

He also warned him that he did not tolerate druggies. When Nitro assured him he has never even smoked a cigarette, Coach Cheesebro smiled.

"Is your name really Nitro Smalls?"

The boy smiled and told him his real name was Ev'ren Smalls.

The coach smiled at his humbleness.

"Ev'ren, if you make it through try-outs, I would like for you to play the position of wide receiver. You did great today, and I look forward to seeing what you can do tomorrow."

After an intense day of screaming coaches and sweating, Ev'ren finally arrived home. He was greeted by his German Sheppard, and the smell of Barbeque as he entered.

"Yo Auntie I'm home," say Ev'ren as he walks through the front door and into the kitchen.

"Do I look like a yo-yo to you? Have some respect boy."

"Yes ma'am. I'm sorry," answers Ev'ren.

"You know I raised you better than that. Now how was practice and school? "

"I did good Auntie! I was the fastest runner out there," replies Ev'ren.

"I knew you would do well my little Nitro. You must be hungry?"

Ev'ren blushed and rubbed his stomach.

"Yes ma'am. I am starving," replies Ev'ren as he sits at the table ready for a plate of food.

Mrs. Anderson looked at Ev'ren with her hands on her waist. She told him to go clean his room first, if he wanted dinner.

Ev'ren walked upstairs with a hunched shoulder as his stomach growled.

"Oh, I all most forgot to tell you Megan Zands called."

Ev'ren took out his cell phone to call Megan.

"No sir Ev'ren Nitro Smalls. If you know what's good for you, you best put that cell phone down and clean up first," says Mrs. Anderson.

"Yes ma'am, "answers Ev'ren.

Ev'ren sighed as he felt his cell phone vibrate in his pockets. He looked at the screen and saw Megan's number appear. Quietly he decided to answer the phone once he arrived in his room. When Mrs. Anderson yelled for him to hang up the phone, he jumped and told her okay.

Like most teenage boys, Ev'ren's room was a complete mess. He found a two day old greasy pizza box, which still had a slice left in it. He took a few bites of it while he cleaned up. He picked up his socks, underwear, and pants from off of the floor, and then looked at his messy dresser and sighed. He walked over to his dresser and picked up a dusty frame. He used his shirt sleeve to dust it off. Ev'ren stared at the picture of Billy and Mariah. He talked to their picture from time to time to get through the day. He heard they died in a car accident when he was baby, but no one found their bodies. All they found was the car in a riverine. It was a mystery to him. He hoped someday, they would be found. Sometimes Ev'ren wondered if they were still alive, trying to find their way back home to him.

"I promise to make you proud of me one day," he says.

After doing his chores and eating dinner, Mrs. Anderson allowed him to meet his friends at Little Africa, the neighborhood basketball court. There, he was greeted by his best friends Megan and Tye.

Tye was six feet four inches. Some said he may be the second coming of Jordan, because he was a great basketball player. People at Little Africa called him Shooter, and girls flocked to him all of the time.

Megan and Ev'ren were friends for a very long time. She was spunky with big brown eyes to match the color of her silky honey brown skin. People thought she was very pretty, but also opinionated because she always spoke her mind. Ev'ren and Megan talked every day, which was usually the highlight her afternoons.

"Yo Ev'ren, how was practice," asks Tye?

"I ran like a gazelle in the savannah, and I think they were impressed," says Ev'ren.

"For real, for real," ask Tye with his hip slang?

"Oh yeah," replies Ev'ren.

As Ev'ren and Tye continued to talk, Megan entered and immediately walked over to them.

"Well guys. How was the first day of school?"

"Well you know me. All the upperclassmen girls were checking me out," says Tye.

Megan rolled her eyes at him and directed her attention to Ev'ren.

"Well Ev'ren, how was football practice?"

"It was great. I think I made the team."

"Think? Ev'ren you are the fastest runner I know. You'd better make that team, or they will have to answer to me."

Tye looked at Megan and winked. She sucked her teeth at him and proceeded to tell them about her day.

While she was talking, these two basketball players, new to the neighborhood walked in. They were both sporting a Chicago Bulls number twenty-three Jersey. One of them made a comment to Megan about her booty, which set her off. Furiously, she yelled at them both and told them not to address her like that, and to have some manners.

"Manners? You need to show us some respect. We are ballers and this is our court now."

Both of them were over six feet tall. They were darker in skin complexion, and had a haircut with the design of a basketball etched on the sides.

"Excuse me," says Tye, "but this is my court, and anyone who think otherwise need to think again."

"And why is that?"

"Because we have yet to taste defeat in any game," answers Tye.

"Do you want to put it to the test and play one game with us?"

Tye looked over at Ev'ren and nodded in agreement.

"You're on," he says.

"One game, one basket will count as two points. Hope I didn't lose anyone. Whoever gets to twenty points first wins, this court becomes theirs, and they have to do what the winner says," says the baller.

They all agreed and started to play basketball. As the game became more intense, people began to gather around and watch them. One of the ballers attempted to back Ev'ren in the low post. The more he attempted to back Ev'ren into the post area, the more open he left himself. Ev'ren saw his opportunity and stole the ball. He crossed over and smiled at him. Then, Ev'ren scored.

Both teams scored eighteen points, Tye asked the crowd to start the countdown. They started to count from ten as Ev'ren crossed the half court line. He looked to his left and right to see if there was an opening for him to take, but the baller was too tall and lanky. Ev'ren attempted a desperation shot, before the crowd counted to one. He jumped up and shot the basketball from where he stood. The crowd held their breath, as the ball went through the basket. He scored the winning shot.

Tye was elated as he ran towards Ev'ren, and lifted him up onto his back. The two ballers shook their heads in disbelief of Ev'ren's shot. They asked Tye what he wanted them to do because they lost. Tye told them to apologize to Megan for being rude, and to kiss his shoes. Ev'ren told him that was enough, but Tye pointed to his shoes. They reluctantly bent down and kissed his shoes, as the crowd laughed.

Tye and Ev'ren pounded each other's fist, and patted Megan on her head.

"Well guys, it's late and I have an early day tomorrow," says Ev'ren.

"You don't want to hang out and celebrate our victory," ask Tye?

"I'm tired, and my aunt will skin me alive if I arrived home late," says Ev'ren.

Ev'ren left Little Africa delighted with him and Tye's victory, but he was extremely tired. When he arrived home, he took another shower and headed straight to bed.

The next day, after finishing up a long school day and football practice, Ev'ren arrived at One-Mile Lake. Megan, Tye, and Tye's new girlfriend was there to celebrate their first week of school. Ev'ren told everyone, he made the football team. They all cheered and congratulated him, especially Megan. She wrapped her arms around him and gave him a big hug. Tye and his girlfriend were shocked at Megan's reaction to Ev'ren.

"We're going to get some more fire wood," says Tye.

"Besides, I think Megan has something to discuss with Ev'ren."

221

Tye and his girlfriend left to get more firewood. Ev'ren and Megan sat around the warm camp fire roasting marshmallows.

"Discuss what Megan?" asks Ev'ren.

Megan held her head down, and paused to get her thoughts together.

"Tye said you have something to say, so tell me what's on your mind."

"It's nothing really."

"Megan I have known you for thirteen years. I know when something is bothering you or not, so don't beat around the bush."

Megan started to fidget and bite her lower lip.

"I have a friend who sort of has a crush on another friend. My friend told me she likes him, but she doesn't know if it is reciprocated. What should she do," asks Megan?

"Who is this friend?"

"You don't know her, because she moved into my neighborhood this summer, and became close friends with a boy in our subdivision. They are both students at our school."

"I think your friend should tell that person how she feels. It is not good to keep secrets with your friends. Look at us, we tell each other everything," says Ev'ren.

"Yeah that's easy for you to say," she mumbles.

"Your friend should follow her heart, unless this guy is in a relationship with someone else."

"No they are not dating other people to my knowledge."

"Cool. Then I think your friend should go for it," says Ev'ren smiling.

"Perhaps I will," she utters.

Ev'ren heard Megan's response and started to ask her a question, when his cell phone rang. He flipped it open to see who is calling, and saw that it was his aunt.

She called to ask him if he needed an umbrella for the showers tonight. He laughed at her, and explained they were camping out to see the meteor showers, not rain showers. After he hung the phone up, Tye and his girlfriend returned with wood.

When he asked Megan to continue with the conversation and see what Tye thought, she hesitated and said never mind.

She came so close to telling Ev'ren how she really felt about him. She looked into the clear night sky and thought about Ev'ren advice. She felt like, she may truly have a chance with him.

As they continued to look into the sky, they saw lights appear in the distance and fell towards the earth.

"Look everyone," she shouts, "the meteor shower has started!"

"Wow! I have never seen so many," replies Ev'ren.

"Yeah, these are a lot of shooting stars," says Tye.

"Tye, these are meteors, not shooting stars. They were once part of a larger space mass that broke apart," says Ev'ren.

"What do you mean professor," jokes Tye.

"I heard meteors can be the size of a golf ball or even as large as a building. I also read that large meteors are called asteroids," says Megan.

"Didn't they kill the dinosaurs?" asks Tye joking.

"Seriously Tye? Comets, meteors, and asteroids travel from galaxy to galaxy for lifetimes. For example, imagine if a huge asteroid or comet were to hit earth. All life on this planet would cease to exist," replies Ev'ren.

"So a meteor did kill the dinosaurs," says Tye?

"Give up Ev'ren. Talking to Tye is like talking to a dinosaur," replies Megan.

They all laughed at Megan's response as Tye threw a wood chip at her.

"I understood what Professor Smalls was saying. He just gets so serious at times. Can we just enjoy the light show without a science class, or talk of the end of the world," says Tye.

Ev'ren looked up at the meteor shower with serenity. All of a sudden, he felt a slight change in his heart beat, along with a pain in his chest. Though he became uneasy, he did not tell Tye or Megan.

The following week, Ev'ren took off jogging down the

dusty dirt road, when out of the corner of his eyes, he saw a stray dog running behind him. He wondered where the dog came from, but allowed him to catch up with him at the bus stop. The stray licked Ev'ren on his hand and then started to bark. In the distance, a black cloud of smoke came towards them. As it came closer, a rusty old school bus back fired as it stopped in front of him. The dog tucked his tale between his legs and ran away. Ev'ren looked at the bus and started to laugh.

"So this is my new ride to school?"

The bus door slowly creaked open as Ev'ren heard kids on the bus coughing.

"Get in," says the grumpy old bus driver.

Ev'ren shook his head, took a deep breath and walked on the bus. He saw Tye and sat next to him. They talked about their weekend, and the second week of school.

"All I want to do is get by this year," replies Tye.

"Seriously Tye," says Ev'ren.

"You are one of the few people I know, who gets excited about school."

Suddenly there was commotion on the back of the bus. Ev'ren and Tye looked back to see what was going on. A small white kid, with square glasses was being bullied by, some kids sitting in the back of the bus.

"I'm not going to let some thugs dump me into the dumpster as some ritual," he says.

"Hey, I know that kid," says Ev'ren, "his name is Shrimp."

When Ev'ren told them to leave his friend alone, they immediately stopped and moved away.

"Hey Shrimp. What are you doing on my bus? I thought you lived in the city," says Ev'ren.

"I did, however since my parents travel a lot, I am staying with my aunt now."

Ev'ren introduced Shrimp to Tye, and explained they met at science camp over the summer.

"What's up Shrimp?" replies Tye.

"So you are Tye," says Shrimp rubbing his barren chin.

"In the flesh baby, I'm the one who scored fifty points in middle school. My reputation speaks for itself," replies Tye.

"Yeah, and I heard that two brothers from Little Africa have plans for you today. They are going to throw you into the dumpster," says Shrimp.

"Where did you hear that from," says Tye.

"Well you did say your reputation speaks for itself," says Shrimp.

"Hey, slow your roll short fry," says Tye as he moves closer to Shrimp.

"Look, don't shoot the messenger. They never forgot about what happened at Little Africa last week, and they are out to embarrass you," says Shrimp.

"So they are planning on throwing me into the dumpster. I thought that ritual was a thing of the past?"

"You shouldn't have gloated and made them kiss your shoes," replies Ev'ren.

"What," says Shrimp with a delirious expression?

"They shouldn't have claimed my court," says Tye.

Ev'ren told Tye not to worry because he had his back. Tye told Ev'ren he could handle it himself.

Within a few minutes they arrived at school. All of the students were hanging out at the bus, waiting for Tye's arrival. Kids were laughing, talking, and staring as they walked off of the smoky bus. Megan rushed over to tell them about the guys from Little Afrika.

"I cannot believe all of this uproar. They are saying those two guys from last week are planning on throwing Tye into the dumpster."

Tye looked a little nervous, but smiled at Megan in his usual cool manner.

"No one is making me a dumpster diver," he says calmly.

Megan looked at him and shook her head at his reaction. Then she glanced in Ev'ren's direction and saw Shrimp standing with him. He looked like he was in a daze, as he starred at Megan. She saw what he was doing, and immediately frowned at him.

"Ev'ren, who is this crazy white boy," she asks?

"Megan, this is Shrimp."

"Shrimp," says Megan with a puzzled face.

"The honor is all mine Megan," says Shrimp holding his hand out shake hers.

"Yeah, yeah whatever," replies Megan pulling away from him.

"Wow, feisty and spicy. I love a girl with an attitude," says Shrimp!

"Ok enough with the love connection. So Megan, any word on those ballers," asks Tye?

"I saw them earlier. They bragged about dumping Tye into dumpster. When I told them to leave you alone, they said they wouldn't bother you if I agreed to go out with the two of them. What perverts."

"So what time is your date," asks Tye.

"Date, I told them to fly a kite, take a hike and kick rocks," exclaims Megan!

"Thanks a lot Megan, some friend you are."

As Megan tossed her head back and walked off, she slapped her butt, and signed for Tye to kiss it.

"That's why I am in trouble right now. You're always telling someone to kiss something Megan," says Tye.

"She makes me nervously happy! What a babe," says Shrimp.

"Shut up Shrimp, why are you hanging around us anyway," asks Tye?

"It's my first day of school, and I need friends," he says.

Ev'ren told them to cool it, so they could all go to breakfast.

"I am not hungry. My stomach hurts," replies Tye.

"Are you scared Tye? You wanna lie down or poop," asks Shrimp sarcastically?

"Are you guys going to argue all day? Let's eat," says Ev'ren impatiently.

As they walked towards the cafeteria, a student passed them running towards the bathroom drenched with garbage on his head. Students were looking at him laughing and pointing. When Tye asked what happened, he was told someone was dumped in the garbage by two tall guys. Tye took a deep breath.

"What a break for me," he says.

Just as Tye thought he was in the clear. Someone grabbed him and Ev'ren from behind. It was the two ballers from Little Africa, along with a couple of friends. Shrimp quickly ran away.

Tye and Ev'ren begged for them to let them go, but they refused. Tye struggled, as he was carried towards the dumpster. Ev'ren had broken free from the other baller, and ran towards his friend. Two friends of the ballers blocked Ev'ren from getting close to Tye. They were on the weight lifting team, so when Ev'ren pushed them, they didn't budge. One of the bullies swung at Ev'ren, but he easily dodged him. Ev'ren threw a jab to both of their mid-sections causing them to double over in pain. As he walked towards the two ballers who had Tye held down, the students watched in awe.

"Let him go now or else," he says!

"Or else what," says one of the ballers.

"Or else you will end up in that trash can," says Ev'ren.

"You and what army, loser."

Just as Ev'ren walked closer to the ballers, ready for battle, Marco and Orlando walked up beside him wearing their letterman jackets.

"You heard the man. Let him go," says Marco.

The two ballers moved back and told Marco to back off and stay out of their business.

"If you dump him into the dumpster, it will be our business and you will be dealing with the entire football team," says Marco!

The two ballers looked at each other and released Tye. Ev'ren asked him if he was okay, as Tye brushed himself off in embarrassment.

The ballers and their group of guys walked away. Megan came over to see if they were okay. Ev'ren held his hand out to give Marco and Orlando a high five.

"Thanks guys. How did you know what was going on," ask Ev'ren.

"Your friend Megan found us and said you were in trouble," says Orlando.

Megan looked at Ev'ren and smiled.

"Shrimp found me and told me what was happening," replies Megan.

Tye thanked Shrimp, Megan, Orlando, and Marco. He then turned to Ev'ren and thanked him for having his back.

"I have never seen you fight like that before Ev'ren," says Tye.

"I have been watching a lot of kung-Fu and Karate movies. I just used some of the moves I saw on television," jokes Ev'ren.

As the class bell ranged, they all walked towards the school building. Tye invited everyone out for burgers after school, but Ev'ren, Marco, and Orlando declined because of practice. Megan and Shrimp agreed to go and celebrate another victory against the ballers.

A few minutes later, Ev'ren arrived in his physics class. Shortly after he took a seat in the front row of the class, a short medium build Japanese man dressed in an old black suit walked into the classroom. The students were talking and laughing. He asked them to be silent as he opened his brief case.

"Good morning class, my name is Dr. Henzu and I will be replacing your teacher from last week," he says.

Dr. Henzu pointed to Ev'ren, and asked him to introduce himself. Ev'ren was a little nervous, but he did as he was asked. Then, one by one, all sixteen students stood up and introduced themselves.

"Do you like surprises," asks Dr. Henzu?

Unanimously the class all agreed and smiled with delight. Dr. Henzu told the class to take out their paper and pencil, for a surprise pop quiz. Everyone moaned and groaned with anger, for the exception of Ev'ren. He loved pop quizzes, so he embraced the challenge and took the quiz. When they went over the questions afterwards, Ev'ren passed with flying colors. After class was dismissed, Dr. Henzu pulled Ev'ren aside.

"I have never seen anyone make a hundred on my test before. I must say, I am impressed. Keep up the good work," replies Dr. Henzu humbly to Ev'ren.

Ev'ren thanked Dr. Henzu and left for his next class. As Ev'ren departed from his last class of the day, he heard over the intercom that his old bus was being replaced with a new bus, which made him happy. He ran to the gym and changed for football practice. Everyone on the team was talking about, how he was able to fend off four students earlier. Ev'ren told his teammates, he couldn't have done it without the help Marco and Orlando, but was happy they were there.

The team had a scrimmage that day. Ev'ren scored two touchdowns. After practice, Marco took Ev'ren home. When Ev'ren walked through the door he was greeted with the smell of fried chicken, macaroni and cheese, and green beans. He followed the smell to the kitchen, where his aunt was, and gave her a kiss on the cheek. He and Mrs. Anderson talked about his day. She fussed with Ev'ren about fighting at school, but was happy he wasn't hurt. Then she grounded him, because he should have avoided the fight and told a teacher.

After dinner, Ev'ren sat in his bed holding the picture of his parents. Tears filled his eyes, as he wished his father and mother were there to give him advice. He wondered if his dad was ever in a fight at school, and wondered how he would have handled bullies like those ballers. Later on there was a knock on his door, as Mrs. Anderson asked for permission to come in. She had a glass of milk, and fresh baked chocolate chip cookies.

"Ev'ren I brought you something," she says sweetly.

"No thanks Auntie."

"Are you sure? Your grandfather used to bring your mom chocolate chip cookies, and milk when she was upset."

Ev'ren looked at his aunt and attempted to smile. Mrs. Anderson placed the cookies and milk on Ev'ren's night stand, and sat beside him on the bed.

"Your father used to be bullied by this boy called Leroy. Every Friday, he would come home with a black eye, or clothes that smelled like garbage. When he finally tried to stand up for himself, he was beaten really badly."

Ev'ren's eyes widen, as he listened to his aunt talk to him about his parents.

"Your father was smart and patient, so one day, he and some friends decided to teach Leroy a lesson, which they did. Needless to say, Leroy never bullied your dad again...well at least not physically."

"What do you mean," asks Ev'ren?

233

"Well, Leroy and your mom started to date. Your father was furious, and it tortured him every day. For him, that was worse than being physically bullied."

Ev'ren looked at his parent's picture as Mrs. Anderson shared more about their childhood. Somewhere deep down inside, he knew Mrs. Anderson was right about fighting.

"In the end, no one ever wins," she says as she gets up and kisses him goodnight.

Ev'ren was happy his aunt spoke to him about his parents. It made him feel closer to them. It also answered his question about what his father would have done, if he was bullied. He loved Mrs. Anderson and knew she helped raise his dad. So that night he fell to his knees and prayed for his aunt. He thanked God for allowing her to live for as long as she has.

Chapter 15
Secrets

Somewhere in the hot and unforgiving desert of the Sahara, a small group of nomads watched a pair of fiery twisters from a far. The frequent sounds of thunder and lightning filled the arid air as the fiery twisters collided with each other.

One of the nomads says, "It seems as if the twisters are fighting each other."

The leader of the nomads replies, "I can feel the intense heat from here and yet, they are miles from here. We must leave this cursed place."

As the nomads mounted their camels, both of the fiery twisters accelerated toward them. Like the leaves in an autumn breeze, the nomads were quickly overtaken by the fiery giants. Their agonizing screams were muffled by the crackling of the flames. Then all of a sudden, the mighty twisters had dissipate, and the nomads were no more.

Emerging from the dust and flames of the twisters were two men. One was slender built, and dressed in a black. He had long dark hair that was slicked back with a speckle of grey in the middle. His dark eyes were as sharp as his suit. The other was a gigantic man with a scar across his right eye, and a steel breast plate embedded into his chest. He wore black military fatigues as if he was prepared for war. Both of them stood facing each other.

As the ashes of the nomads fell like snowflakes to the

scorched ground, the slender gentleman unshielded his sword, and pointed it at the giant's throat.

"You've gotten faster, Fran...I mean Vaul," says Vinares.

"No one must know who I am you idiot," says Vaul.

"Please forgive me," begs Vinares.

"Despite a lapse in judgment, you have improved. However, your technique is still sloppy. Use more Ki and less needle attacks to be more affective. It's a shame that after all these years, you still haven't mastered the scrolls," replies Vaul.

"But if it wasn't for those miserable humans," says Vinares with rage.

"Save your petty excuses for someone who cares. Now get on your knees loser."

"Ok Vaul."

"My goodness, you even waste energy even when you kneel. If Francisco saw you now, he would be ashamed of you. Did you use your reflection technique to reflect the sun's rays," ask Vaul?

"Yes," says Vinares with hesitation in his voice.

"You sound unsure, yet you managed to deflect my fire ball. Now rise, and use those massive arms of yours to create your fiery funnel attack. And don't depend on your strength. Use your Ki," replies Vaul.

"It's hard using my Ki. I can't control it very well," says Vinares.

"Instead of whining like a two year old, use the powers which have been bestowed upon you."

Vinares hesitated for a moment to think about what Vaul was really saying. His eyes widen as he came to a realization.

Just as Vinares prepared himself for Vaul's attacks, a transmission came in from one of Vaul's spies stationed in America. Vaul touched his temple to receive the S.I.C. message. Then, he started giving orders.

"This is Vaul...I see...really...interesting. Keep an eye on him. I will send someone to relieve you in two days. Communicate with Agent 4, and notify Agent Nightfly. I'm in the middle of an important mission right now. Give agent Nightfly the before information about Operation Spin. Brief them, and they will know what to do, end transmission S.I.C."

S.I.C. was a satellite that Vaul helped create for military use. Satellite Intelligent Computer was the abbreviations for S.I.C. It was also a mini space station. The satellite could send or jam signals, and messages from space without being detected. It also had unbelievable fire power at its disposal. If ever attacked it carried weaponry such as plasma cannons, lasers, and missiles. S.I.C. was staffed by highly trained soldiers and some of the world's top scientists. It was a formidable satellite, unlike any other.

Vaul and Vinares continued to spar. With each attack, Vaul advised Vinares on his flaws. When they were finished, Vaul appointed Vinares as his General. With a sinister laugh he shared his plans to conquer the world. He planned to attack within a few months, after his troops were ready.

237

Back in Stone Mountain, Georgia things seemed normal. Ev'ren was engaged in days of intense practice and weight training. He proudly sported his black and gold football jersey, with the number eighty-one on the back of it. He and his team prepared for their first football game of the season.

That morning he spoke with some of his friends and teammates, until it was time for his first class. Ev'ren sat in his usual seat next to Megan, who decided to take physics as well. He pulled out his physics book and began to read. Megan glanced at Ev'ren as Dr. Henzu walked into the class with a new student.

"Good morning class, we have a new student at our school," he says.

He turned to the beautiful young girl and motioned for her to stand beside him.

"Good morning class, my name is Willamina Goldberg. I am from the country of Georgia, and it is a pleasure to meet you all."

The class looked at Willamina curiously as she motioned towards Ev'ren. She took a seat next to him, while his eyes followed her with fascination.

He was captivated by her mysterious beauty. Willamina's skin was milky white, and her hair was dark and cut into a jagged bob, with thin streaks of blond framing both sides of her round face. Her eyes were the color of a light brownish gold coin. She was dressed in a fitted black leather jacket with a black T-shirt underneath that read "Prodigy". She also had on a pair of fitted jeans and boots that made her look like a model. She noticed Ev'ren looking at her.

"May I help you," she asks?

Embarrassed, Ev'ren told her no as he stuttered his words. Dr. Henzu saw Ev'ren's lips moved, so he asked him to read aloud from their text books. The class erupted into laughter as Ev'ren blushed and pickup up his book to read.

Dr. Henzu asked Ev'ren to share his book with Willamina. Ev'ren smiled and started reading. While he was reading, Megan looked at Willamina and stared with envy.

After class was over, Megan attempted to stop Ev'ren as he ran out of class behind Willamina. She was infuriated with Ev'ren's sudden attraction to Willamina. After she gave up trying to catch Ev'ren, she sucked her teeth and walked to her next class.

Ev'ren found Willamina at her locker. He cleared his throat and approached her.

"Hey Willamina, we haven't been properly introduced, my name is Ev'ren, and you're Willamina. I wanted to apologize for embarrassing you in class today," he says.

Willamina looked at Ev'ren with a puzzled expression. Her light brown eyes did not blank as Ev'ren spoke to her.

"I know my own name stupid. And you didn't embarrass me; you embarrassed yourself," replies Willamina.

Ev'ren turned a shade of red as his embarrassment took root again. To calm his shame, he talked about football and asked her to come to his game. When Willamina declined, he became persistent. She told him, she had to study so she could catch up in all of her classes.

"Who studies on a Friday night," he says.

"I can't Ev'ren. I really do not know anyone here, and I don't know you like that. Besides, you might be an axe murderer or a pervert," replies Willamina.

Ev'ren looked at her and smiled charmingly.

"I understand, Willamina, but I am really a nice guy, once you get to know me. I was just hoping you could come out tonight and support our first game of the season. There will also be an after party, which would be a great way for you to meet people."

"I see that you don't know when to quit," replies Willamina.

"I don't give up so easily. I am very persistent," says Ev'ren.

Willamina agreed to show up, if she finished studying. Elated with her response, Ev'ren smiled and shook her hands. When he grabbed her hands, papers fell out of her back pack. Ev'ren quickly bent down to get them for her. She bent down as well scrambling up her papers, until she looked up at Ev'ren. His eyes met hers, and he smiled. His dimples showed a lighter side of him, and Willamina smiled back.

"Can I get directions to the party tonight," she asks.

"Sure," says Ev'ren.

"I will email it to you, if you give me your email address."

Willamina wrote down her email address on a piece of paper. Ev'ren placed it in his pocket, and ran off towards his next class, telling her that he couldn't wait to see her at the party.

Later that afternoon, the kick off pep rally began. Cheerleaders and announcers energized the students making them jump, stump, and scream as the players were introduced. When Ev'ren's name was called, he came out in his jersey. He looked up and saw Megan, Tye, and Shrimp holding a banner that said "Nitro." He looked around for Willamina, and saw her standing in a corner with her arms crossed. She looked uninterested in the pep rally and out of place. Ev'ren smiled and waved at her. She slightly nodded back at him.

The energy of the pep rally carried over into the football game that night. As each member of Stone Mountain High's football team was announced, a sea of black and gold stormed the field as they took on their cross town rival and state champions, Spring Mill High. On the opening kickoff, Ev'ren ran a ninety-five yard touchdown. That energized the crowd even more and sent the team into a frenzy. As the game progressed, it became more intense. Every tackle, catch and mistake was magnified.

Back and forth the game went. Stone Mountain's quarterback threw an interception on the one yard line. The cornerback for Spring Mill caught the ball and ran like a pack of wild dogs were after him. Ev'ren from the back of his own end zone gave chase. Despite the cornerback being forty yards a head, Ev'ren locked on like a missile and gained speed passing the other players. He closed in on the cornerback, but the cornerback crossed his goal for a touchdown which gave Spring Mill the lead. Two minutes were left in the fourth quarter, so Stone Mountain called a time out.

Marco ran over to Ev'ren.

"Good grief Ev'ren you ran down Ellington. He is one of the top five fastest guys in the nation," he says.

"I didn't catch him. He scored and they are up by eleven points," replies Ev'ren.

Ev'ren walked over to the side-line clapping, trying to keep his teammates positive.

"Let's get a score guys this isn't over," he shouts!

The coaches gathered the entire team together. They huddled as Coach Cheesebro gave them marching orders. The special teams unit ran on to the field. Ev'ren told one of the blockers to toss him the ball if it came there way.

The blocker agreed, but the kicker kicked the ball deep into the end zone towards Ev'ren. He caught the ball and took off with speed until he reached the ten yard line. Then he sped towards the sideline as his teammates cheered him on. When Ev'ren made it to the end zone, the crowd screamed and yelled his name. The team congratulated Ev'ren after he made the touchdown. Ev'ren ran to the sideline to speak with Marco.

"Marco we need a turnover, and if you can give us the ball, I promise you we will win the game," he says.

"You got it amigo," replies Marco.

Coach Cheesebro called the defense to the sideline, and told them they had three timeouts left and needed a turnover in the worst way.

The defense stormed the field ready for battle. On the first play, the opposing offense ran the ball and gained four yards. Marco quickly called a timeout with one minute, fifty seconds left in the game. Spring Mill's offense lined up and snapped the ball, they gained three more yards. With one minutes, thirty seconds on the clock, Stone Mountain called timeout again. On the third down, the coach of Spring Mill called a screen pass as the running back picked up the first down. Then suddenly, out of nowhere, Marco ran down the running back and stripped the ball out of his hands.

The ball went in and out of the hands of several players until, Marco recovered the fumble. The crowd along with his fellow teammates went wild.

The coaches called the offense to the field. Coach Cheesebro told the offense to spike the ball when they are awarded a first down, or run out bounds. He told them to save as much time possible.

The team shouted, "Yes coach," in agreement.

Coach Cheesebro called back to back screen plays, which gained twenty yards a piece and a first down. In each pass, the receiver ran out of bounds to save the last time out. On the very next play they gained twenty-five more yards, but Orlando ended up hurt. Coach called their last and final time out. After Orlando's injury, the team fell silent. Macro and the other players, called the team into a huddle. As Orlando, is helped off the field, he told them to win for Orlando.

The tension was unbearable, and the crowd was on the edge of their seats. The quarterback went under the center, and snapped the ball. When Ev'ren caught the ball, he almost fell to the ground. After he regained his balance, he sprinted towards the end zone, where opposing players awaited him. Ev'ren dived for the end zone as all three Spring Mill tacklers dived on top of him.

The referee ran over to the four man pile up and peeled each person back to see where, and who had the ball. Ev'ren looked up as he clutched the ball. The line judge raised both of his hands in the air indicating that Ev'ren scored the winning touchdown. The crowd erupted in victory.

While on the field, Ev'ren's teammates and coaches mobbed him and lifted him up into the air. Coach Cheesebro applauded him from a safe distance, until he, too was whiffed away by the crowd.

One of the nearby news stations were there, and asked a lot of questions about the team and Ev'ren. They knew nothing of him and wanted a complete exclusive. Coach Cheesebro, Marco and Orlando spoke on the team's behalf and announced, they were planning on going all the way to the top that year.

After celebrating a big victory on the field, an even bigger celebration occurred at Orlando's parent's huge luxurious log cabin home. It was like being at Time Square on New Year's Eve. Kids were dancing in the huge living room area and by the swimming pool. Once the football players arrived, people began to cheer. Soon after, Tye and Megan arrived and were greeted by Orlando. People asked if Ev'ren was with them, but he wasn't. Ev'ren tried to sneak into the party through the back door, but he was caught and bombarded by everyone. He laughed as his teammates pulled him into the crowd.

"Ev'ren, we have a surprise for you," says Orlando.

"Ok," says Ev'ren?

The team carried Ev'ren into the living room, where he was congratulated by some of the hottest girls in school. As Ev'ren danced his way through the crowd, Tye and Megan greeted him. He stopped to have a conversation with his best friends, but they were constantly interrupted by people who were partying, and trying to take pictures with Ev'ren like he was a superstar.

Megan attempted to give Ev'ren his spotlight, but she lost her composure and began to cause a scene. With all of the commotion going on, Ev'ren didn't notice someone coming up behind him. Willamina tapped him on his shoulder and smiled. Tye was speechless and spellbound when he saw her. Ev'ren smiled showing his dimple and introduced Willamina to Tye and Megan.

"We've met already," says Megan with an attitude.

"Pay her no attention," replies Tye.

"Thank you for coming out to the party Willamina. It is nice to see you," says Ev'ren.

Willamina looked around in amazement.

"What a wild party," she says.

"It's about to get wilder, because Ev'ren and I are about to turn it out on the dance floor," says Tye!

Ev'ren and Tye walked out to the dance floor and began

dancing. A crowd of people surrounded them. The crowd cheered them on as they danced. Ev'ren grabbed Willamina by the hand, and started to dance with her. Megan became so angry, she stood behind Ev'ren and started dancing with him as well. The crowd watched and shouted for them to continue, as Ev'ren was sandwiched between Megan and Willamina.

Once others started to dance again, Ev'ren and Willamina made their way through the crowd and left Megan standing on the dance floor. Tye looked at Megan and shrugged his shoulders as Megan pouted.

Ev'ren and Willamina walked out to the balcony away from the party. The moon was full and bright.

Ev'ren and Willamina sat on the balcony, and talked about the game and party. They laughed as crickets chirped in the distance.

Willamina's curiosity took over as she began to question Ev'ren.

"How do you feel about Megan," she inquires?

"I care about her a lot. We practical grew up together. She can be a bit of a drama queen, but we are buds."

"Just buds, huh? It seems to me you two are a little more than that."

Ev'ren looked puzzled at Willamina's comment.

"What do you mean when you say *more than that*?"

"Have you not noticed the way she acts around you?"

"She always acts like that. Seriously, there is nothing going on between Megan and me."

Willamina grimaced at Ev'ren's naivety.

"So, is there something going on between Megan and Tye?"

Ev'ren laughs and responds in sarcasm, "Let me know if it snows in July!"

"I will take that as a no."

Ev'ren looked towards Willamina inquisitively, and felt the need to return the game of twenty questions.

"So mystery lady… tell me a little about yourself?"

"What exactly do you want to know?"

"Tell me about your family."

"Well, I am the oldest. I have a younger brother, who I love to death, and my parents died when I ten years old."

"I am sorry to hear that about your folks."

"It's okay. My brother is my only family now, and as I long as I have him in my life, I will never be alone."

"So where is your brother?"

"He is home with a personal friend of the family."

Ev'ren nodded as he thought about what it would have been like to have a brother.

"What were your parents like?"

247

"My mother was a model, she worked for Finest Inc. Her name was Christina Goldberg."

Ev'ren looked astonished by her response.

"Seriously? *The* Christina Goldberg! She was a native of Stone Mountain. She is like a legend in these parts."

"I see you're a fan," says Willamina smiling.

Ev'ren blushes, "I did a report on your mother for a school paper. She was beautiful, and from what I can see the apple doesn't fall far from the tree."

"Yeah, I bet you say that to all of the girls?"

"Not really. I don't really communicate with girls I like," says Ev'ren.

Willamina ignored his response and continued to talk about her parents.

"My father, Vincent Goldberg was a well-respected business tycoon and my hero."

"I have heard of your dad, too. He was in Fortune magazine's top fifty businessmen in the world. Your dad was in the shipping industry, real estate, and nuclear energy. He was one of several businessmen who helped fund *Operation Clean Slate.*"

Willamina was shocked at how much Ev'ren knew about her parents.

"Did you do a report on my father also?"

"No. But I know of his philosophy that clean energy is the

wave of the future. He talked about climate change and how limited resources and carbon dioxide are causing global warming. He is a huge reverent of how the greenhouse effect changes our environment."

Ev'ren continued to talk, while Willamina listened to how much he knew about nuclear energy.

"Vega Inc. was where my father worked. It was because of people like your dad, and other private corporations that Operation Clean Slate received funding. It really helped save this town."

Willamina nodded her head in agreement, but hearing about her parents made her uncomfortable. So she shifted the conversation to find out more about Ev'ren's parents.

"Tell me about your parents Ev'ren?"

"I don't know much about my parents. They died in a car accident when I was an infant."

"I apologize for asking. I didn't know."

Ev'ren shook his head saying, "It's okay. My mother was a beautiful school teacher. She was really feisty from what my aunt says. My dad worked for Vega Powers. According to the history books of this town, and my aunt, he saved the town from a nuclear meltdown. He also saved the life of Francisco Vega."

"That's truly remarkable. Mr. Vega is the richest man in the world."

"I know. He seems like a cool person, and he does so much for the environment and our town. The plant is still as

249

prosperous as ever. My father lived for his family, friends, and this town. That's why I want to be a nuclear physicist."

Willamina admired Ev'ren's humble response.

"Ev'ren, I think it is noble you want to follow in your father's footsteps."

"If it's to better Stone Mountain, I will do all I can. It's what my father would have wanted."

Willamina gazed at the stars in the sky as Ev'ren talked.

"Why are you interested in me," she asks?

Ev'ren looked at her with his eyes widened. He was impressed by her straight forwardness, but nervous as well. She and Ev'ren looked into each other's eyes, as they drifted closer and closer. However, before Ev'ren could answer the question, his phone rang. It was Mrs. Anderson. When Ev'ren answered the phone, she fussed at him for being out past his curfew. Ev'ren smiled in embarrassment and told Willamina he had to go, and he would see her at school. Willamina told Ev'ren to wait, and gave him her cell phone number. In shock Ev'ren asked her if it was a hoax. She assured him it wasn't.

"Goodnight Willamina," says Ev'ren hurrying down the fire escape instead of through the crowd.

Willamina replied in her native tongue.

"Ghame Mshvidobisa."

"What," asks Ev'ren in confusion?

"It means goodnight," she says waving at him laughing.

Ev'ren blushed and walked away.

As the week progressed, Ev'ren and Willamina began to trust each other more. He would call her during the day, and Willamina would text him well into the night. They spent most of their time together talking about school and their futures. Their feelings for one another started to grow as each passing day went by.

When fall approached, Ev'ren asked Willamina to go with him to the county fair. She accepted his offer and told him she would pick him up in her limo.

After getting off of the phone with Ev'ren, she arrived at his home. Mrs. Anderson greeted her at the door, and invited her to come in and have a seat while Ev'ren finished cleaning his room.

"How are you young lady?"

"I am well. Your house is very nice. It reminds me of a little antique store," says Willamina.

"Thank you," says Mrs. Anderson as she sat down, "so Ev'ren told me you're a foreign exchange student, but your mom is from Stone Mountain."

"Yes ma'am," says Willamina comfortably.

Mrs. Anderson observed Willamina while they sat and talked. She squint her eyes at Willamina's wardrobe. She had on black jeans, a black jean jacket, and a red camisole. Her makeup was dark as well, which made her look a little older than her age.

"So how old are you dear," she asks?

Willamina was shocked at how straight forward Mrs. Anderson was. Just as she was about to comment, Ev'ren came running down the stairs.

"Hi auntie, my room is clean and I will see you later," he says in a hurry.

"Ev'ren. Be home by ten o'clock tonight," replies Mrs. Anderson.

"Come on Auntie how about eleven? It is Saturday night," says Ev'ren pleading.

Mrs. Anderson smiles and says, "How about nine o'clock then?"

Ev'ren covered his face with embarrassment.

"Okay auntie ten o'clock," he says and kisses her on the cheek.

"It was nice to meet you Willamina," says Mrs. Anderson.

"The pleasure was mine ma'am," smiles Willamina.

Ev'ren and Willamina got into the limo. A few minutes later, they arrived at the fairgrounds. Ev'ren called Megan and Tye earlier, and asked them to join them. They were not at the fair yet, so Ev'ren and Willamina took their time and walked around to survey the rides and games. One of the games they stopped at was called "strong arm." It was a game that involved a sledgehammer and a bell.

"How strong are you," asks Willamina?

"I'm strong enough," replies Ev'ren.

252

She grabbed Ev'ren by the hand and led him to the sledgehammer.

"Prove it, and win me that big panda bear," says Willamina with a smile on her face.

The gentlemen hosting the sledgehammer event told Ev'ren it would be two dollars to play. Ev'ren smiled, and paid the gentleman. He rubbed his hands together, and took the sledgehammer into his hand. He lifted the sledgehammer above his head, and brought it down with great velocity. The lever moved quickly to the top of the meter, but didn't reach the bell. Ev'ren kicked the ground in disgust and said he was cheated. Willamina folded her arms and nodded in agreement. The gentleman smirked at them both, and told Ev'ren maybe he should let Willamina win the panda bear for him instead. Then he called Ev'ren string bean as they walked away. When Ev'ren heard his comment, he became furious and walked back over to the gentlemen.

"Here is two more dollars. I want another try," he says.

"Ok kid, here's the hammer and you're lost," says the gentleman.

Ev'ren brought the hammer down again sending the meter to the top, but the bell did not ring. The jolly gentleman laughed at Ev'ren again.

"Is that the best you can do string bean," he says.

"Come on Ev'ren, don't worry about it," replies Willamina grabbing his hand to lead him away.

"Wait! I want another crack at it!"

Ev'ren paid the gentleman again. In anger and determination he grabbed the hammer, and without thinking, he brought the hammer down swiftly and fiercely. He hit the lever so hard, the bell went flying off into the night air. Willamina and the gentleman were stunned by Ev'ren's strength.

"Wow," she said.

Ev'ren looked at the gentleman with the look of accomplishment and demanded that he give Willamina the panda bear.

"That was amazing. Here kid, take three pandas. I've never seen anything like that before in my life!"

Ev'ren took three and gave them all to Willamina. Her hands were so full, she didn't have room for anything else.

"Thank you Ev'ren, I knew you could do it," replies Willamina.

They both walked off chatting and laughing at Ev'ren's victory.

"Ev'ren, I am going to buy you a popcorn ball to congratulate you."

"Thanks," says Ev'ren.

A few minutes later, Tye and Megan arrived at the fair. Megan saw Ev'ren and Willamina from afar and immediately became defensive.

"Why is Willamina here?"

Tye rolled his eyes at her comment and avoided her

question. When she asked him again, he told her that it was a free country and Willamina could go anywhere she wanted.

Megan told Tye to stop being smart at the mouth.

"Here they come now," says Tye.

Ev'ren and Willamina walked up to them laughing and eating popcorn.

"What's up guys?" says Ev'ren.

"Wow Willamina, look at all of those stuffed animals. Did you win all of those," asks Tye?

Willamina laughed and pointed at Ev'ren.

"You're the man Ev'ren," replies Tye!

"Ev'ren won the strong arm game. He hit the meter so hard, the bell flew off!"

"Really," says Tye.

"Yep, the bell flew like a bat in the night," says Willamina.

They all started to laugh as Willamina and Ev'ren relived his small victory. They were all having fun for the exception of Megan.

Tye replies, "Sounds just like Ev'ren. He doesn't know his own strength."

Willamina had a puzzled look on her face.

"What do you mean by that?"

Tye looks at Ev'ren, "Man I have to tell Willamina what happened."

Ev'ren rolls his eyes and says, "Oh boy, here we go again!"

Tye began to explain a bizarre story that happened to him two years ago.

"Ev'ren, Perverus and I were in the woods cutting down some oak trees for Mrs. Worth. It had rained for two straight days, not to mention it was windy. You should have seen the trees falling left and right as we cleared a path in the forest. We were cutting trees down at a good pace, and then out of nowhere, a huge oak tree fell on me pinning my legs down. I cried out for help, because I was in a lot of pain. Perverus heard me, and came a few minutes later. He tried to move the tree, but he couldn't. I was shocked Perverus couldn't move the tree, because he was a big and strong dude who could squat 350 pounds easily. He ran off to get help, because my cell phone was under the tree. I was left there for about two minutes, though it felt like two days. When Ev'ren found me, I was screaming and yelling in pain. We both started to panic, because I started to sink deeper into the wet and soggy ground. Ev'ren started to lift, but he couldn't move the tree. I thought all was lost, but Ev'ren was determined to get the tree off of me. Out of nowhere, he suddenly found the strength and lifted it off of me. He told me to pull myself from underneath the tree, and saved my life!"

Willamina was amazed.

"Then what happened," she asks?

Tye replies, "Ev'ren saved my life. I heard of people doing

amazing things when adrenaline kicked in, and it was remarkable what Ev'ren did."

Megan started to get annoyed. She was not happy to see Willamina there.

"Come on Tye, give it a rest," she says.

"How would you feel if an elephant sat on your legs," he says.

"Whatever," says Megan.

Willamina interrupted them again and commented to Ev'ren.

"That is remarkable. You're a hero!"

She kissed Ev'ren on his cheeks as Megan angrily bit her lower lip.

"Why don't you two get a room," she replies bitterly.

Ev'ren was stunned by Megan's comments.

Willamina stroked Ev'ren's head while looking at Megan and replies, "Perhaps we will."

Then Willamina kissed Ev'ren on the lips. Ev'ren did not know how to react, so he held Willamina and kissed her back as well. He was light headed and intoxicated by her touch.

Enraged, Megan stormed off. Ev'ren asked Megan to wait, but she kept walking. Tye told Ev'ren he would talk to her.

"What is wrong with her," asks Ev'ren?

Willamina replies, "Didn't we discuss this earlier?"

"She has been acting a little weird lately."

"Weird, I thought she was always moody?"

"Since this past summer, she has become extremely sensitive and moody."

"Ev'ren, I really think she likes you."

"Who? Megan? That's absurd! What would someone like her see in me?"

"You know, that's a good question," she replies.

"Hey, that hurts."

Willamina looked at Ev'ren with a sinister smile.

"You know Ev'ren. I think we should burn some of this fair food off."

Ev'ren blushed.

"How do you suppose we do that?"

"I will explain on the way to my house."

Ev'ren became nervous as provocative thoughts filled his head.

"Your house, huh," he replies.

Willamina grabbed Ev'ren's hands and led the way towards the exit.

After a thirty minute ride into the foothills of the Blue Ridge

Mountains, they arrived at a steel reinforced gate with a gargoyle sitting on the top of it. They drove through the entrance after the gates automatically opened.

Ev'ren playfully asks, "Are we there yet?"

"We have a little more time before we arrive to the house. Do you want a drink of water?"

"Sure," he says.

As they drove through the estate, Willamina explained the landscape of her home. She has one hundred fifty acres, with a few gardens and an estate home. There was also another house on her estate with two bedrooms. Ev'ren was in awe.

As they continued through Willamina's estate, Ev'ren saw trees and shrubs trimmed into whimsical animal shapes like elephants, bears, and giraffes. When they finally arrived at Willamina's house, Ev'ren was stunned by the size. Butlers and maids greeted them at the walkway.

"This isn't a house, this is a palace," says Ev'ren.

Willamina smiled at Ev'ren and whisked him inside. She told Ev'ren she would give him a tour later. She was more focused on the two of them burning off some energy.

Ev'ren became very nervous and stopped Willamina in her tracks.

"I'm not ready yet. This is moving all too fast."

"But I want to spar with you," says Willamina with an innocent look on her face.

"Spar? That is what you meant?"

"Um, yeah," says Willamina sarcastically.

"Ok, then lead the way," says Ev'ren.

"Stay close, because we have six rooms and an aquarium to pass by. This house has forty rooms."

Ev'ren laughed and mocked Willamina.

"Forty rooms she says. Like it's no big deal, six rooms and aquarium she says. Who needs to spar when can just walk through the house," says Ev'ren with sarcasm.

"Quit crying and run," says Willamina as she takes off in a light dash.

Ev'ren followed Willamina and ran beside her, as they passed paintings, pictures, statues, and a state of the art aquarium.

"Where are you taking me Willamina, Shangri la?"

"Not exactly."

When they stopped, Willamina opened a sliding wooden door to a huge open space. As they walked in, it felt peaceful there. There were windows throughout the entire room. The floors were made of bamboo, and covered with white mats. Japanese scrolls hung on each side of the golden Buddha that sat at the front of the room. Two swords hung above their heads.

"A Dojo," shouts Ev'ren!

"What do you think Ev'ren?"

"It's nice. It kind of resembles the one I use to train in, but without the swords and Buddha statue."

Willamina raised her eyebrows at Ev'ren's comment.

"I thought you never train in martial arts?"

"You didn't ask. I took youth martial arts for five years in Atlanta during the summer. There was a studio called Kempo. They had an excellent summer camp, and I enjoyed it. It's been years since I practiced martial arts."

"Well in that case, I will take it easy on you," says Willamina.

Willamina took her shoes, top, and skirt off. She had on a pair of black leggings and a tank top. She picked up a black box and tossed it to Ev'ren. Then, she walked to the middle of the floor.

"What is it," asks Ev'ren.

"A gift," she says.

He opened the box and saw a lime green karate gi.

He looked at Willamina and laughed.

"Do you seriously want me to spar in this?"

"Yes," she says without a blank or stutter.

"If I have to wear this, can you wear a blue bikini," replies Ev'ren?

"Enough with the jokes, the time for talk is over. Let's get it on," says Willamina.

She clasped her fist and assumed the mantis stance.

"Mantis wow, I didn't know you knew martial arts like that. Can we at least stretch," says Ev'ren.

"You're right," says Willamina.

After a quick series of stretches, Ev'ren and Willamina assume their fighting stances. Ev'ren once again interrupted Willamina before they began their match.

"Willamina, why do you want to spar with me?"

Willamina did not answer. Her stance was strong and the look on her face was intense like she was a different person. She attacked Ev'ren and threw him on the floor. Ev'ren was surprised by her speed and power. He recovered to his feet and tried to catch his breath, but Willamina struck him several times. Ev'ren kept telling Willamina to take it easy, because it was just a sparring match, but she was in a zone. She attacked Ev'ren again and again by slamming him to the ground, but he quickly recovered to his feet each time.

As he planned his attack he thought to himself, "Who is this girl?"

Willamina attacked Ev'ren again as he desperately attempted to block her fierce attacks. She was quick and relentless as she struck him on his stomach and back.

"Ouch," he screams, "that's enough. I think I have a bruised rib."

As he grabbed his side in pain, Willamina picked up a cane and started to attack him. He pleaded with her to stop, but she continued. The more Ev'ren pleaded with her, the more intense her attacks became. Ev'ren became annoyed and angry with her!

"Stop," he shouts as Willamina struck him in the arm!

"That's it, I am going home," he says.

"Ev'ren stop acting like a wimp," says Willamina.

"Wimp, I invited you out to the fair to hang out and have fun, not get my ass kick?"

"Man up," she says.

Willamina's comments angered Ev'ren, as he thought back to what the guy said about him at the fair. He turned towards her and assumed a defensive position. As Willamina continued her attacks, Ev'ren started to match her speed and tenacity. Though Ev'ren continued to take a beating, he studied her moves and began to learn them. Willamina continued to attack Ev'ren without remorse. Though she injured him, she noticed he continued his pace. What she didn't notice was that Ev'ren's patience had just run out.

"I warned you to stop, now you are really making me angry," he shouts!

Ev'ren counter attacked with a series of kicks and punches making Willamina collapse to her knees. She was stunned by his speed, accuracy, and power.

"I don't like hitting girls. It is not the gentlemanly thing to do," he tells Willamina.

Willamina stood up and touched her face. She looked at

Ev'ren and smiled as she wiped the speck of blood from her lips. Ev'ren was shocked at what he did to her.

"I'm so sorry," he says.

"No. Don't apologize for striking me Ev'ren, "she says.

"I don't hit women. Don't ask me to spar again."

"Fine, but what kind of attack was that?"

"I call it my survival. I thought you were going to kill me!"

She told Ev'ren she hadn't seen speed and power like that since her master.

"Your master," he asks?

"Don't worry about that," she says avoiding his question.

"Those last few punches and kicks you threw Ev'ren, illuminated a light from you. I also felt the heat from your fist."

"Yeah right Willamina. Must be the lights in your eyes," he says smiling at her.

"Your speed was incredible. I could barely defend myself against you. It looked like you threw a hundred punches and kicks all at once," says Willamina.

"Come on Willamina, you're over exaggerating," says Ev'ren.

"So Ev'ren, have you ever heard of Ki?"

"Yes. It's the drawing of energy from everything around

you. I see that kind of stuff on martial art movies and video games. It is a bunch of mumbo jumbo," replies Ev'ren.

"You think so? Well stay right there and I will be right back, nonbeliever," says Willamina.

"Where are you going?"

Willamina came back with a candle.

"What is this...witch craft, voodoo, root or something," replies Ev'ren.

"I don't practice witch craft or voodoo, and what is root?"

"Never mind," says Ev'ren, "what are you doing?"

"I am going to make you a believer in Ki. Please place this candle ten feet from us on the table," says Willamina.

Ev'ren did as he was told. Willamina assumed an open stance and took a deep breath.

"Willamina, what are you doing," whispers Ev'ren?

"I need your silence please. All will be revealed," whispers Willamina back to him.

The room was quiet while Willamina gazed at the flame. She began to move her arms in a circular motion. Her hands were stiff, but her shoulders and wrists were relaxed. About a minute later, the flame of the candle grew bigger and started to flicker. Ev'ren was amazed by what he saw. Then, Willamina violently thrust her hands forward causing the flame to go out.

"That's impossible! How did you do that," shouts Ev'ren!

"Years and years of practice, I'm still working on my technique, because I'm still fairly new at it," she replies.

"I couldn't see it, but I could feel the force you released. It made the hairs on the back of my neck stand up. Do you have superpowers," asks Ev'ren?

"No silly. Every living or non-living thing gives off energy or Ki. We walk, talk, eat, sleep and die! Even the dead gives off energy, or Ki, because of decomposition. Only a special selection of people have mastered this technique. With training, you can channel your life force also. You have to be perfect. Your stance has to be perfect. Your mind and body has to be as one. However, using this technique also has its' draw backs," says Willamina.

"Such as," ask Ev'ren?

"Remember, it is your life force you are wheeling. It can drain you. Also, if used improperly, you can injure or kill someone," says Willamina.

"Don't worry. I won't ever try that technique. All I need is my fist," says Ev'ren.

"There may be a time, when you will need more than a mere fist to beat your opponent. You should try to tap into your Ki. That's if you can focus your energy," replies Willamina.

"I can't do that. I am not an expert like you," says Ev'ren.

"Go on Ev'ren. What's the worst that can happen," replies Willamina.

Willamina assumed her stance again. Ev'ren closely looked

at her and copied it. She glanced over at Ev'ren to make sure he was paying attention.

"Good. Your life force comes from the earth and the sun. Focus on it," says Willamina.

Ev'ren focused and tried to use his Ki, but nothing happened. Willamina patted Ev'ren on his back. She told him it was ok, and when the time came, he would be able to master it. She also told him, he was rusty at martial arts and needed to practice every day. When she offered to practice with him, Ev'ren nodded in approval.

"Are you hungry?"

"Does a hog like slop," replies Ev'ren.

"You truly are a pig Ev'ren. Let's go porky."

"That's Mr. Swine to you miss. So where are we going," ask Ev'ren?

"We are going to my dining hall. I will give you a tour of my mother's home."

"Your mom," ask Ev'ren?

"Yes. Though she moved away, she always had a soft spot in her heart for Stone Mountain, Georgia. My father built this house for her as a retreat to get away from city life. When my mom died, she left this house to me," says Willamina.

"The only place I ever saw with this much land was my great uncle Joe's farm, and to be honest, your front yard is bigger than his farm." says Ev'ren.

Willamina grabbed Ev'ren's hand and led him through her house. As they walked, she apologized for tricking him into sparring with her. She mentioned that when she heard he took on four guys at school, she wanted to put him to the test.

"I am lucky and honored to have an accomplished martial artist, such as you to challenge me, not to mention beautiful," replies Ev'ren.

"Ev'ren for someone who doesn't have much training in martial arts, you are truly a natural. You have the potential to be a great warrior," replies Willamina.

"Warrior," replies Ev'ren with a puzzled look, "thank you, but I don't want to be in the military, or go to war."

Ev'ren shifted the conversation to Willamina and asked her about the types of martial arts she knew. She told him she knew Uechi-ryu, Tai-Chi, Judo and Ninjitsu. She told him she has been practicing martial arts for thirteen years.

Within a few minutes, they arrived at the dining hall. Ev'ren was once again in awe.

"Wow! This place is huge. It looks like the dining hall of Buckingham Palace," says Ev'ren, "though I have never been there."

"Not bad Ev'ren. It is a smaller replica of Buckingham Palace's dining hall," says Willamina.

"These are some beautiful oil paintings," replies Ev'ren.

"Thank you," says Willamina, "this is my family painting."

"It's priceless," replies Ev'ren.

Willamina's family painting was in a twenty-four karat gold painted frame. She explained to Ev'ren it weighed about three hundred pounds.

"And here is a painting of Stone Mountain Park in the bloom of spring," says Willamina.

"Stone Mountain Park was once a beautiful place, but now it is a wasteland," replies Ev'ren.

"What actually happened there," ask Willamina?

"According to reports, there was an explosion. Nothing lives out there anymore. The city and governmental officials says, it's forbidden to go out there now."

Willamina and Ev'ren continued to walk the hall and look at pictures, while dinner was prepared. As they continued to walk, Ev'ren came to a dead stop at a painting called "the friendship of love." Ev'ren paused with his mouth open in amazement.

"What's the matter?" asks Willamina.

Ev'ren couldn't say anything. He pointed towards the picture that had three young ladies in it. It was a picture of Willamina's mom. She was gorgeous with blonde hair. Beside her was a black lady with an afro, and a beautiful red hair lady with blue eyes.

Willamina became very uncomfortable and tried to continue with the tour, but Ev'ren wouldn't budge. She became frustrated and tried to change the subject.

"I hope you like surf and turf for dinner," she says.

Ev'ren continued to stare at the painting and point. Finally she decided to address the painting.

"My mother said these were her best friends, when she was in college."

Ev'ren continued to stare as he walked up to the portrait and touched it.

"I can't believe it," he says.

"Believe what," says Willamina, "that my mom had friends in college?"

"No. I can't believe that *my* mother is in this portrait," says Ev'ren as he points to the young lady with red hair and a gorgeous smile.

Willamina looked at Ev'ren and then the portrait.

"That's impossible. I thought you were young when your parents died. How would you know if this lady is your mom," replies Willamina.

"I know what my mother looks like, ok! I have seen pictures of her. This is my mother. Your mother and my mother were best friends. And now, many years later, we are boy and girl friend?"

Willamina told Ev'ren not to get ahead of himself. She told him they were not a couple, and were just friends.

Ev'ren scratched his head in disappointment and disbelief. He asked her about the kiss she gave him at the fair, but she told him she did that to make Megan upset.

"I see what this was really about. You wanted to make me and my friends look like a fool, but you know what, I lost my appetite and I am ready to go home."

Willamina called her driver and told him to take Ev'ren home. Rejected, Ev'ren folded his arms and went home.

Willamina clenched her fist in frustration after he left.

"This was not supposed to happen. The picture, dinner, sparring, and kissing, I can't believe he saw the portrait," says Willamina to herself.

A few minutes, later Willamina asked one of her servants to meet her in the dining room. When the older Hispanic man arrived, Willamina questioned why he did not follow the orders she gave him about the picture. When he told her he forgot, she struck him against his face and called him an insolent fool. She told him to remove the painting immediately and fired him.

As Willamina thought to herself about Ev'ren and her feelings towards him, she decided she needed to change her strategy. She felt the energy from him, and knew he was the one.

A few minutes later, she went into her meditation room. The room was dark and filled with hundreds of black candles. She entered and closed the door. As she took a deep breath and kneeled to meditate, she sensed, she was not alone.

"Are you going to sit there in the shadows all night, or come out," she says.

Suddenly, out of the shadows of the room the tall image of a ninja emerged. The figure was dark, and moved swiftly.

"Forgive me Lady, I didn't want to disturb your mediation."

"That is very honorable of you, but that doesn't give you the right to break into my house. Who are you," asks Willamina?

"My clan calls me Xi of the Ike Clan. I have been receiving S.I.C. signals about your progress with the boy. I have learned about the football game, his transparency, what happened at the fair. Not to mention the story about the tree and your sparring match. This is no ordinary boy," says Xi.

"Ev'ren is mine to deal with," replies Willamina.

"He belongs to the organization, and don't you forget it Lady Nightfly," says Xi.

"I should kill you where you stand ninja!"

"I didn't come to fight with you Lady Nightfly. I came here to do my job and warn you. You have a week to accomplish your mission, or you will have to suffer the consequences."

"Leave this place before I show you the consequences of threatening me."

Just as quickly as he appeared, the ninja, Xi disappeared. Willamina was angry someone sent him.

"I am Lady Nightfly. People make threats, I make promises and I will see this through," says Willamina.

Willamina left her meditation room and went to her office. She looked over to her desk, and saw a red light blanking on it. She walked over to it and took a deep breath. She rubbed her index finger on the screw of the brief case to identify her DNA. Once the brief case unlocked, she opened it. Inside of it appeared something shaped like a giant clam shell. She placed her hand on the shell, and it slowly opened into a computer.

The computer started booting and then a S.I.C. emblem appeared on her desktop. After her password was accepted, she was greeted by the head of S.I.C., Vaul.

"Greetings master, how are you doing," asks Willamina as she bows respectfully?

"Depends on the information you have for me. Did you follow my instructions," ask Vaul?

"Yes. I sparred with Ev'ren."

"And what were the results," ask Vaul?

She knew Vaul had received information from Xi, and she reluctantly told Vaul about Ev'ren's hidden powers, and other events. Vaul was pleased and asked of his where-a-bouts. When she told him Ev'ren went home, Vaul was furious. He called her incompetent, and told her to do whatever it took to get Ev'ren to join them. She surrendered to his wishes. And told him about Xi breaking into her home.

Vaul laughed at her, and nonchalantly told her that he owed her no explanation. Then, he proceeded to tell her this project was too much for her to handle, and she may need some assistance. Willamina was furious, and told Vaul she was a big girl and could handle Ev'ren. He told her she had one week to get him to join them, before the arrival of Hope.

273

"What about Hope," asks Willamina?

"Did you read the report?"

"No, I didn't."

"I suggest you read the report. You have seven days, and failure is not an option," says Vaul.

After the transmission ended, Willamina took a deep breath and rubbed her temple. She asked S.I.C. to bring up today's report on Hope. As she read the report, fear entered her eyes.

"S.I.C can no longer jam other satellites. N.E.O (Near Earth Object) will impact the planet in nine days from today. It will be a global event causing earthquakes, tsunamis, and possible volcanic eruptions. According to scientific measurements, the only safe place will be the "alpha passage" located in Africa."

Willamina feared the worst as she looked out towards the midnight sky, and saw an abnormally bright star beside the moon.

She says to herself, "So it has finally come down to this… the beginning of the end."

Chapter 16
World Crisis: A change in the winds

The next morning Ev'ren arrived at school with his normal look of excitement, however he was tortured inside with thoughts of Willamina and the argument they had. He felt dumb and naïve for thinking she was interested in more than a friendship with him.

When Ev'ren walked into his physics class, he took a deep breath and managed to put a big smile on his face. He sat beside Megan and greeted her with a smile and an apology about the night before. Megan accepted his apology and told him it was water under the bridge.

Ev'ren told Megan, he and Willamina were over before they started. Megan saw the hurt in his eyes, and told him that she was sorry about what happen. He smiled at her with reassurance, but it quickly vanished when Willamina entered the classroom.

She wore a red leather mini skirt with black fish net footless tights underneath. She also had on a matching red leather vest. Her t-shirt was black and fitted. It had a single red rose on it with blood dripping from its thorns. She sat between Ev'ren and Megan and signed like nothing happened. Though he tried to look the other way, Ev'ren couldn't help but notice how attractive Willamina looked. She turned towards him and apologized, but Ev'ren looked at her and said nothing. Willamina knew she had hurt his feelings, but she also knew she could never get involved with him.

When Dr. Henzu entered the classroom he greeted everyone and told them to pair up with their lab partner. Ev'ren gritted his teeth, because he and Willamina were lab partners. Megan looked at Willamina with a murderer's intent as she pulled her desk away from Ev'ren.

"I am sorry again," says Willamina to Ev'ren.

"We have some work to do so, let's get this done," says Ev'ren.

The two of them worked as a cohesive team, despite their differences. When class was over, Willamina attempted to talk to Ev'ren, but he walked out of the classroom and ignored her.

A few hours later, Willamina caught up with Ev'ren. He was sitting underneath a pine tree eating an apple. She approached him, but Megan intercepted with her arms folded.

"Willamina, where do you think you're going," ask Megan?

"I am going to see Ev'ren," replies Willamina with attitude.

Megan walked a little closer towards Willamina and stood in front of her.

"Ev'ren doesn't want to be bothered by you anymore. You got that," says Megan waving her finger in front of Willamina.

"Megan, you better move your finger from my face," replies Willamina impatiently, "I don't have time for your childish antics, and I *am* going to see Ev'ren."

Megan defiantly stumped her foot into the ground like an enraged bull.

"Over my dead body," shouts Megan!

Willamina smiled at her with delight, as she told her that could be arranged.

Ev'ren heard the commotion between Willamina and Megan and ran over to them. Tye saw them as well and ran over.

"Stop you two!" shouts Ev'ren as he and Tye stand between them.

"What's all the commotion about," asks Tye?

"She was coming over to mess with Ev'ren, so I intervene," replies Megan abruptly!

"Ev'ren we need to talk in private," says Willamina.

"Why should he talk to you after what you told him," replies Megan!

"Well if I didn't know any better Megan, it seems like you have feelings for Ev'ren," taunts Willamina!

"Why you dirty tramp," shouts Megan as she motions toward Willamina!

"Tye please take Megan for a walk while Willamina and I talk," says Ev'ren.

"Ev'ren, don't do it," pleads Megan.

"Megan I will be okay," says Ev'ren.

As Megan and Tye walked away, Megan glanced back at Ev'ren. He nodded to her in reassurance.

Ev'ren and Willamina both took deep breaths and signed.

"Before you speak, I have something to say. I am sorry for walking out last night, and acting like a jerk this morning. I have never met anyone like you before. You are incredible and I like being around you, so I would rather have you as a friend than not have you at all," says Ev'ren.

Willamina was shocked at Ev'ren's actions. She thought he was going to be rude like most guys she knew, but he was the opposite. For a moment she was speechless, but she knew that Ev'ren was a kind hearted person. That only made her feelings for him stronger.

"I can't do this to you anymore. There is something you should know," says Willamina.

"What is it," ask Ev'ren?

Before she could confess, the school's fire alarm sounded. In a panic, students trampled over one another as they fled the school like wild horses. A student yelled out that there was an asteroid called *Hope* coming to destroy the Earth, and school was being dismissed. Megan and Tye ran over to Ev'ren and Willamina with fear and disbelief in their eyes. Then, amongst the panic, Ev'ren received a phone call that Mrs. Anderson was involved in a bad car accident.

He told his friends about his aunt and that he needed to go to the hospital. Willamina, Tye and Megan all said they were coming with him.

As they sped towards the hospital, the whole town was in

278

panic. People were frantically preparing for the end of the world as they packed bags, filled their cars with gas, and raided grocery stores.

When they arrived at the hospital, Ev'ren, Willamina, Tye, and Megan ran to the receptionist desk.

"I am here to see Mrs. Sarah Anderson," says Ev'ren.

"She is in intensive care," says the receptionist.

Out of the corner of his eyes, Ev'ren spotted his family doctor. He called his name, and walked briskly towards him.

"What happened to my aunt," ask Ev'ren.

"She was in a car accident. She is unconscious, but in stable condition," says the doctor.

"Can we see her," ask Ev'ren?

"You can, but your friends are going to have to stay here. I will be over there in a few minutes," replies the doctor.

Ev'ren left his friends in the waiting room and made his way to the intensive care unit. Along the way, he smelled bleach and felt the cold all around him. Ev'ren hated hospitals after growing up without his parents. When he arrived at his aunt's room, he gasped in shock at the wires and machines attached to her. Ev'ren kneeled beside Mrs. Anderson's bed. He softly stroked her hair and began to cry. The doctor walked in and explained that she suffered a broken rib, a punctured lung, and a concussion. He also told him she briefly woke up and asked for him.

"That's a good sign, right," asks Ev'ren?

"Possibly, but I would not get my hopes too high," says the doctor.

"How did this accident happen," ask Ev'ren?

"She was involved in a head on collision. According to the police report, the person driving the car had on a mask and was seen fleeing the scene on feet. A witness said the driver looked like a ninja. The police also said they found a star like weapon in your aunt's rear tire," says the doctor.

"Oh God! What are the cops doing to apprehend this person?"

"They are working on it."

"That's not good enough. Someone hurt my aunt and got away with it, and all the cops can say is that they are working on it?"

"Calm down Ev'ren, there is more," replies the doctor.

"What is it?"

"A few years ago, I ran some test on her lungs and spotted a growth. However, I just did an MRI and discovered it has grown into a tumor. The biopsy shows that it is cancerous. I am so sorry Ev'ren."

Ev'ren listened in disbelief and anguish as the doctor told him about the biggest secret his aunt ever kept from him.

"Are you saying my aunt had cancer all this time and did not tell me?"

"She promised me to secrecy, and never came back for a follow-up visit. The test indicates the cancer cells have metastasized. I need to operate, but I need your consent."

"I can't believe this. This is too much."

"I realize you are still a minor and this is a big decision, but the longer we wait, the more fatal this tumor can become."

Ev'ren looked at his doctor and then at his aunt. He thought about life without her, and how alone he would be.

"Save her doctor," he says.

After Ev'ren signed the papers, he held his aunt's hand and kissed her on the forehead. He left the room and promised he would return.

When he arrived back into the waiting room, his friends all gathered around him in support. Ev'ren told them what happened to Mrs. Anderson.

When Willamina heard about the driver looking like a ninja, she clutched her fist in anger. They were relieved she was stable, but was in shock about her having cancer and not telling him.

Tye and Megan told Ev'ren their parents wanted them home because of the asteroid. Just as they were leaving, the sheriff walked in. Ev'ren signaled for the sheriff to come over, so he could get more information about his aunt's accident.

"We don't have any leads right now kid."

"What do you mean," shouts Ev'ren, "my aunt is in a bed fighting for her life, and you should be out there looking for the perpetrator!"

"Why don't you worry about school, books and girls, and let me worry about catching criminals," says the sheriff.

Every one of them for the exception of Willamina, spoke out in anger towards the sheriff and his response to Ev'ren.

The sheriff tried to ignore them, but he finally grew impatient and demanded them to leave and go home. He threatened to lock them up if he caught them out after the town's curfew. They all fell silent and walked away.

Ev'ren was furious with the sheriff, and his aloofness towards him and his friends. His rage took over as he stormed out of the hospital ahead of his friends. He was so determined to get away from the sheriff, he didn't realize he left them behind. He panted and raged about his aunt, and the driver who got away with attempted murder, until a sudden glow began to illuminate from him. As the sun shined overhead, his eyes changed from blue to yellow. He clinched his hands into fists as the rage inside of him grew.

Suddenly, his concentration was broken by Willamina, who caught up to him in enough time to tell him to calm down before something happened.

Ev'ren looked at her confused, but soon he heard Tye and Megan calling his name in the distance as they approached them.

"Is everything okay," asks Megan.

"Of course," says Ev'ren.

"Are you sure?"

"For the last time... yes," says Ev'ren angrily!

They all stood around Ev'ren shocked at his anger.

"What are you guys staring at?"

"Bro, you have two burnt holes in your t-shirt," says Tye.

Ev'ren looked down and saw holes burnt into the chest part of his t-shirt. Ev'ren didn't know what to say to his friends as they stared at him.

"I burned him with a lighter to calm him down. It is customary in my country to use heat to extinguish a fire. Isn't that right Ev'ren," she says.

"Yeah, I guess so," says Ev'ren.

"Okay guys, we have to go before the curfew takes effect," says Tye.

A few minutes later they arrived at Megan's house. Tye told Ev'ren he was going to leave town with Megan's parents, because his parents were out of town. They offered for Ev'ren to come with them, but he refused to leave his aunt.

Tye, Megan, and Ev'ren hugged each other and said their goodbyes.

A few minutes later, Willamina and Ev'ren arrived at his great uncle and aunt's old farm on the outskirts of Stone Mountain. It was Ev'ren's hope, his aunt would get better within the next day, so she could leave Stone Mountain with them.

As the sun started to set, Willamina looked out of the window and wondered if she should tell him about his unknown fate. If she does, her fate would be sealed. She knew time was running out for the both of them, and she also knew they were being followed.

Ev'ren walked over to her with a glass of water. He sat beside her and looked out of the window. He thought about her and Megan, and how confused he was about everything that was happening.

"Ev'ren do you know me," ask Willamina?

"What's that supposed to mean," he replies.

"Do you know me, Ev'ren?"

"Well yeah. You're Willamina," he says as he slightly chuckles.

"That is not who I am," she says sternly, "and now it is time for me to be honest."

Ev'ren was confused about Willamina's comment. He was even more confused when she stood in front of him, and showed him a tattoo of a black butterfly on her stomach.

"My name is Willamina Von Penakova. My father changed our last names to protect us from a malicious crime organization in Russia. My code name is Lady Nightfly."

"Really? Lady Nightfly," jokes Ev'ren as he touches her tattoo.

"I am not joking Ev'ren. There is something I must tell you, but you need to prepare yourself. Once I tell you this information, there is no turning back."

Ev'ren stared at her without blanking and motioned for her

to proceed.

"Our moms were best friends. The painting you saw the other night at my house was a painting with your mother in it. My mom was a world famous fashion model who fell in love with a crime lord from the Ukraine. My dad had ties with the Vegas, and did a lot of business with Francisco. He met my mother in Stone Mountain when he travelled there with Mr. Vega. With my mother's fame and my father's business connections they were extremely wealthy, but they were also extremely indebted to Mr. Vega. After my brother and I were born, they tried to get from under Francisco's control. Unfortunately they didn't make it out alive."

"What are you saying Willamina," asks Ev'ren?

"I am saying that my parents, as well as yours died at the hands of Francisco Vega."

"Impossible! My parents were in a car accident, and according to police records, their bodies were never found. For all I know, they could still be alive."

"Ev'ren, your dad was involved in a major accident that happened at the nuclear plant decades ago. Francisco, his cousin Vinares, and your father developed some extraordinary powers no one else on this planet has. Mr. Vega believes that these powers exist within you as well, and wants you to join his team."

"Join his team for what?"

"He wants to be the most powerful being on Earth. That is why he sent me here for you."

Silence filled the room as Ev'ren stared at Willamina. He found it hard to believe what she was telling him. He thought about all of the stories his aunt talked about, and the research he did on his parents as well. Everything started to make sense as an effortless ball of rage grew inside of him.

"You and the Vega's can fly straight to hell! I will never work with the man who murdered my parents."

Willamina reached into her bag and pulled out an old Japanese farm blade that was used during the feudal era, called a Kama. She grabbed Ev'ren and held the blade to his throat. Ev'ren paused in shock.

"I am out of patience Ev'ren! They have my brother, and I can't leave without you. Therefore you must join us or else!"

"If you are going to kill me Willamina, then do it. You never cared about me anyway," replies Ev'ren.

The tip of the Kama glowed, as Ev'ren's heart became consumed with hate and betrayal. Willamina paused and withdrew it from his throat.

"They are holding my brother as ransom for me completing this mission. I was told that if I didn't convince you to join us, they would kill him, and you as well. Being in your world these last few months, have meant a lot to me, but it has also shown me how much of my childhood was lost."

"What do you mean Willamina, you are a child."

"I'm an assassin Ev'ren. I kill for a living. It is what I was raised to do after my parents died. Though I am a few years older than you, I have never lived the life of a child."

As Willamina stared into Ev'ren's eyes, she gently grabbed his hands and pulled him towards her. She closed her eyes and kiss him. Ev'ren didn't stop her. He could smell the scent of her perfume, and she could taste the fear in his mouth.

After the kiss was over, there was a brief moment of silence between them.

"What was that for," he asks?

"I can't kill you Ev'ren. I care about you too much to hurt you."

Willamina sighed and shook her head as she dropped the Kama. Then suddenly, dozens of razor sharp shurikens came through the window and penetrated the wall. Willamina grabbed Ev'ren, and told him they had to leave the house immediately.

They left the house from the back, and ran towards an abandoned barn a few miles away.

"Who is attacking us?" ask Ev'ren.

"They are ninjas. I saw two of them hiding in a tree as we left your home. They are following us from above."

"Are you sure it's two of them? It seems like ten of them."

"Ev'ren they are masters of disguise. They can hide amongst the shadows without being noticed. We have to hide and stay out of the shadows."

As Ev'ren and Willamina entered the barn, Willamina told him to hide. She quickly closed the doors and hid as well. A moment a later, the doors flew open with Xi and his younger brother Len standing in the door way. Both ninjas looked around for Willamina and Ev'ren, but there was no sign of them. They began to shower the barn with more shurikens, but there was no movement. Xi told Len to find Ev'ren and finish him with the sword. He told Len, he would deal with Willamina personally.

Len disappeared into the darkness in pursuit of Ev'ren. Xi walked around in the light calling for Willamina to come out and fight him. He called her a traitor and a fraud.

As Xi continued to taunt Willamina, Ev'ren remained silent amongst a stack of hay. He could feel his heart beating rapidly, and tried to calm down. Then he suddenly heard the unsheathing of a sword, as the blade reflected from behind him. He turned around expecting to see Len, but Xi was behind him with his blade drawn and ready to strike. Ev'ren eyes widened as he surrendered. Then from nowhere, Willamina dropped from above and landed on Xi, knocking him to the ground.

They both recovered to their feet and prepared to battle. Blood dripped from Xi's masks as he warned Willamina that her brother was going to pay for her betrayal. He slowly drew his sword as Willamina searched for a weapon.

"Don't you have a weapon to fight with Lady Nightfly," he says taunting her.

"A weapon doesn't make the warrior. The warrior is the weapon," says Willamina.

Willamina jumped into the air extending her legs and kicked Xi in the chest, as he fell to the floor. Xi recovered to his feet and relentlessly attacked Willamina with an array of moves and sword play. She effortlessly dodged his attacks, and then went on the offense, striking Xi several times. Enraged with Willamina's attacks, Xi swung his sword and cut Willamina on her leg. She felt the warmth of her blood mixing with the cold sting of Xi's blade, as she fell to one knee. Xi looked at her and smiled with delight.

"You are a great fighter Lady Nightfly, but it will be only a matter of time before I find Ev'ren."

He held his sword up and brought it down, but Willamina rolled over to dodge the blade. She landed underneath a thick chain.

"You can run but you can't hide. I will cut through that chain Lady Nightfly, and you will be finished," says Xi.

He swung his blade at her again and sliced through the chain. Just as Xi thought he had the advantage, Willamina mounted a counter attack, striking him numerous times with the chain. She wrapped the chain around his neck, and proceeded to strangle him.

"It is time for you to die," she says.

Willamina wrapped her legs around Xi's waist and forced him to collapse to his knees. He dropped backward and landed on her. He struggled to break the hold, but with every move he made, Willamina tightened her grip. Xi's eyes starts to roll back into his head as he gasped for air. When he took another breath, Willamina squeezed one last time and broke his neck.

"The last things you will ever hear on this earth, is my voice saying goodnight," she says.

His head dropped backward as she pushed his lifeless body off of her. She looked around the barn and sighed in pain, as she grabbed her leg where Xi's sword wounded her. She noticed a discoloration in her cut and began to panic. When she staggered over to Xi's sword, the blade had a light blue film on it.

"Poison," she thought to herself as she looked around for Ev'ren.

She started to become light headed as she wondered if Len, found Ev'ren. She looked around, but she saw no one.

"Come out you coward," she says.

Then, out of nowhere, three shurikens emerged from the darkness and flew towards her. Willamina deflected them as Len laughed and threw three more from beyond the shadows.

"I thought you wanted to get to the point?" says Lens.

"Ninja, I know your powers, but I don't think you know why they call me Lady Nightfly."

Willamina stabbed the sword into the ground and assumed a defensive stance. Len laughed at her calling her crazy, but she focused her energy and created a force around her. Three more shurikens were launched, but they deflected off of her.

Suddenly, Willamina was engulfed in flames. The barn illuminated a green hue as she forced her energy into a ball. When she saw Len's shadow, she launched the fireball, but

Len's shadow disappeared. He threw three more shurikens in her direction, but this time she spotted him and sent a fire ball in his direction. She sent him crashing to the ground.

Willamina collapsed and fell to one knee. She didn't know where Ev'ren was, but told him to stay hidden. She tried to get up, but her injuries from the blade and poison nearly paralyzed her.

Willamina looked over at Len who was motionless, but she wasn't sure if he was dead. When she saw his chest rise and fall, she tried to get up. Len slowly crept to his feet, and moved towards Willamina. He had burns, and his right arm was broken. He used his left arm to grab his sword and aimed it at Willamina.

She had no feeling in her leg, so she anchored her body with her arms and hands to move away from him.

One look into Len's blood shot eyes, made her aware of his rage and fury. She knew she was at his mercy.

"I am going to kill you slowly Lady Nightfly, while your sorry excuse of a boyfriend watch me cut you into fish bait."

Willamina looked around for Ev'ren to make sure he was not in sight.

"Don't listen to him Ev'ren. Your survival means everything. I am expendable, but you are the key to the fate of this world."

"Shut up traitor. It's time to die!"

Len drew back his sword to deliver the final blow. Willamina closed her eyes in preparation for her imminent death. Just as he motioned his sword forward, Ev'ren emerged from hiding and demanded Len to leave Willamina alone. Len turned toward Ev'ren and smiled at him.

As he stared at Ev'ren, he moved his sword towards Willamina and cut her on the arm. She screamed out in pain.

"Oops," he says smiling.

Ev'ren was infuriated with Len's actions. He told him to leave her alone, as his eye color suddenly changed to yellow.

"I will not stand here and let you hurt her or anyone else," says Ev'ren.

Len continued to laugh, as he taunted Ev'ren about running his aunt off of the road. Len gloated about how he and Xi were sent to kill Mrs. Anderson.

"You're the one responsible for hurting my aunt?"

Ev'ren became enraged with fury. His breathing became heavy as his body began to glow. He cried out in anger as a red glow surround him.

Len looked around as the barn started to shake. He gave Ev'ren a devious smile and drew his sword towards him.

"Let's do this boy," shouts Len!

The barn continued to shake as the temperature grew hotter by the second. Soon the entire area around Ev'ren ignited into flames. Ev'ren's energy pushed Len back, and caused him to drop his sword. Len quickly reached down to regain possession of his sword and charged towards Ev'ren.

"Don't let him touch you with the sword Ev'ren," cries Willamina!

As Len came closer to Ev'ren, he screamed out in pain from the intense heat. The closer he got, the more he burned. Soon, Len's body was completely on fire as he screamed in agony. The barn and everything around Ev'ren was on fire. Willamina crawled towards the door of the barn, and attempted to flee the area. When Ev'ren saw her struggling to survive the effects if his rage, he quickly shifted his focus and ran towards her. He took her into his arms and carried her out of the barn just before it collapsed.

Ev'ren looked down at her weakened body and gently moved her hair away from her face. As he attended to Willamina's wounds, she looked down at her watch and pressed a button that started to flash.

"Help is on the way Ev'ren," she says.

"Willamina are you comfortable?"

She smiled, and told him she would be fine.

"I should have come out sooner, then you would be okay right now," says Ev'ren throwing his fist into his hand.

"No, Ev'ren. I am happy you did not get hurt."

Willamina touched Ev'ren's face, and thanked him for saving her life.

Ev'ren looked back at the barn and then at his hands in disbelief.

293

"Willamina, what just happened to me?" he asks.

"You were beginning to transform."

"Transform into what? I don't understand how all of this happened."

"I don't either Ev'ren, but I need you to listen to me very carefully."

Willamina sighed and grabbed her wounded leg.

"Something is about to happen and you need to prepare yourself. Francisco is about to shut down the plant in Stone Mountain."

"He can't do that! The plant is the heart and soul of this town!"

Willamina asked Ev'ren to calm down and listen, as she continued to explain Francisco's next plan of action.

"Francisco will be coming for you. He and his team have begun to mobilize, which is why the ninjas Xi and Len appeared tonight. They were sent to kill you, if you did not choose to join Francisco's team. Now that he is certain you have no plans of joining, he will be releasing a new terrifying weapon called Sunstrokers."

"What are Sunstrokers?" asks Ev'ren.

"Sunstrokers are humanoids, with incredible strength. They feed on energy by biting or touching humans to increase their strength. They have an insatiable appetite for energy. Before I came to Stone Mountain, I saw the child prototype. Though it resembled a little girl, it broke one of the guard's arms in three places. They are very strong Ev'ren, but they are also slow," says Willamina.

"Are they like zombie bio-weapons?"

"Not quite. You can try to out run them, but there will be thousands of them all over the world."

"What will happen if they bite or touch someone," asks Ev'ren?

"They will continue to drain you until your dead."

Ev'ren began to worry as Willamina told him about the fate of the world. His heart raced as he felt overwhelmed about Francisco, Hope, and the Sunstrokers.

Willamina knew it was a lot for him to absorb, but her hands softly touched his to reassure him everything would work out.

"Ev'ren, you have to remain calm. That is the only way you will be able to understand what these creatures can do."

Ev'ren took a deep breath and nodded as Willamina continued to talk.

"During the day time, they look just like you and me. They talk and show emotion, but in the dark, you can see a green skeletal interior beneath their skin."

"These creatures sound impossible to defeat," says Ev'ren?

"They have the power to regenerate limbs and even the head. In the prototype I saw, their fail safe was in the belly button. Hitting them there, should shut them down as long as they are not at maximum power. If they are at maximum power, the only way to stop them is striking them three times in the stomach, or waiting until they run out of energy."

"Who in their right mind is going to sit and wait for them run out of energy? Why would Francisco release something like this into the world?"

"It's simple Ev'ren. He wants to create fear in the heart of every human on this planet. He craves power and wants to keep world governments in disarray so he can take over. I am hoping this asteroid scare might slow down his plans to release his humanoids, but Francisco thrives under chaos."

"I can't believe this. We are talking about ninjas, asteroids, and humanoids," says Ev'ren.

"Francisco and Vinares are going to be your biggest adversaries. Vinares possesses the strength of one hundred men. His right hand can fire needle like projectiles that can puncture through anything, and his left hand can morph into a whip. If he grabs you, I don't have to tell what will happen. He hasn't mastered the Sacred Scrolls of the Honzo Clan, but he depends on his strength mostly. He is a very aggressive fighter, but doesn't always display the best control in his techniques."

"What about Francisco," asks Ev'ren?

"Francisco is an expert martial artist. He has mastered kung-Fu, Ninjitsu, and a plethora of other techniques. His power is incredible. He has mastered the Sacred Scrolls of the Honzo Clan. Francisco has an energy wave that is much stronger than Vinares. He has no weakness that is known to anyone, and he is a master swordsman."

Willamina's voice became intense as she continued to explain Francisco's powers.

"His most powerful weapon is his sword. It is an unbreakable weapon that can drain you of your powers. This sword was made to kill people, even beings with special powers. He used it to kill your father, because like you Ev'ren, your father possessed great powers. The one thing you have over all of them Ev'ren is your incredible speed. You have yet to discover your true powers, so there is a lot to be done if you are to save the world."

"Save the world Willamina? If they are as powerful as you say they are, I don't stand a chance against them. It just me! What can I do," he asks?

"Ev'ren, you must try, or all you know and care about will cease to exist."

Ev'ren looked at Willamina and knew she was still in pain. Her words haunted him, because he knew he couldn't let anyone else get hurt.

"How will I do this? Who will help me find these powers you are talking about?"

Ev'ren heard the sound of thunder. He started to look around for another attack.

"What's wrong Ev'ren," asks Willamina?

"I hear thunder," he says.

"I don't hear anything."

Ev'ren looked towards the sky, as his ears heard the sound

of a helicopter.

"I see a helicopter in the distance. It is coming in fast from the west."

"It belongs to me. I called for help. My God Ev'ren, you can hear and see my helicopter before I can. You must have some type of heightened senses," says Willamina in surprise.

"What's going to happen to my family and friends," he asks?

"I will try to protect them as much as I can. I have secret agents looking over them as we speak, but with the scare of Hope, no one can out run the asteroid."

A few minutes later, Willamina's helicopter arrived as she grabbed Ev'ren by the arm, so he could pick her up. The helicopter landed as Willamina's butler, and a group of soldiers came running out to grab her from Ev'ren's arms.

They told her the sun was giving off strange solar flares. She was also informed that her brother and Ev'ren's family were safe, but they needed to leave immediately. Willamina told them to wait, as she looked over at Ev'ren.

"Things are going to happen very fast Ev'ren, but you will be ready. Your trainer is on his way and will arrive soon. Hide until he gets here. You will only have a few days to train, but you must stay focus. Every moment counts."

Ev'ren told them to leave and take care of Willamina. She looked at him one last time, and told him to promise her he will survive.

Though filled with doubt, he told her what she needed to hear.

As the chopper took off into the sky, a feeling of uncertainty fell upon him. Once it was out of sight, Ev'ren quickly dove into the bushes to hide as Willamina instructed him to do. Minutes later, a grey car pulled up to where the old barn once stood. The car door slowly opened and out of it stepped a familiar face, the person called out for Ev'ren.

He emerged from the bushes with his fist drawn and ready to attack.

"Put down your fists son. I did not come here to fight with you. We have no time to waste if I am going to train you."

Ev'ren looked at his physics teacher and says, "Dr. Henzu, you are the trainer Willamina told me about?"

"Yes," he says.

"Now, please get in the car."

Ev'ren got into the car and they drove off.

They rode for an hour as the night progressed. Ev'ren and Dr. Henzu rode upon a blockage in the middle of nowhere. They parked the car near a river and quickly jumped out to cover it with bushes. Once the car was covered, they squeezed through the blockage and began to run. They ran through eight miles of dead forest, as Ev'ren looked around to see if he was running into a trap. They came to a cave that was covered with dead overgrown vegetation. Dr. Henzu told Ev'ren to come in and keep his head low. As Ev'ren walked into the cave, he stumbled over something and fell.

"How can you see?" asks Ev'ren.

"I don't see," replies Dr. Henzu, "I feel each step. Now please be quiet so I can listen," he says aggressively.

About a quarter mile into the damp cave, there was a glimmer of light. They entered a room filled with lit candles, and a small cooking pot over a fire. Ev'ren looked around and then stepped towards the pot. He took a quick peek inside and saw some beef and potatoes.

"Mmm," he says rubbing his stomach.

Dr. Henzu laughed at Ev'ren's reaction to the dinner he prepared.

"I was expecting to be eating alone, but when Willamina signaled for help, I stepped in to help. So here we are," replies Dr. Henzu.

Ev'ren looked around at the coldness of the room. He couldn't understand why Dr. Henzu was there and how he knew Willamina so well.

"Why couldn't we stay at your place," he says scratching his head.

"Francisco and his team know my true identity now, and they would have killed us on the spot, if we were at my apartment. This is our safe house for now, as well as our practice facilities for the next several days."

"Okay…who are you really, and where exactly are we," asks Ev'ren.

"I am the teacher you know, but I am also the last of my

bloodline, the Honzo Clan. My ancestors possessed ancient scrolls with secret martial arts techniques. Now to answer your other question, we are on the outskirts of town. The locals call this the forbidden place. This place was blocked off from Stone Mountain, after a terrible accident years ago."

"What type of accident," asks Ev'ren?

"The death of your parents," says Dr. Henzu.

Ev'ren became frozen and stared at Dr. Henzu in disbelief.

"The day your father and the Vegas fought, so much damage was done due to their nuclear powers. It was too much damage to clean up, so the town deemed it inhabitable. The area has begun to revive itself. The radiation is gone, but no one knows."

"So how do you and Willamina know each other?"

"Are you hungry Ev'ren?"

"Like a run-a-way child! I am also extremely tired," says Ev'ren.

Dr. Henzu walked over to the cooking pot and prepared their meals.

"I see you don't want to answer my question Dr. Henzu."

Dr. Henzu sat down on the mat, as he placed a small bowl in front of Ev'ren with stew in it.

"About eight years ago, when I was in my final years of teaching in Japan, Willamina was a student in my class. She was small with pale skin and dark eyes. She was a quiet

girl who kept to herself, and made friends with no one. One stormy night I saw her being chased by a group of ninjas on my way from the grocery store. They ran into a back alley to fight. To my surprise, Willamina fought with skill, knocking both ninjas to the ground. I yelled for them to leave her alone, which distracted her. Within the next few seconds, Willamina was knocked out. When I ran into the alley, the two ninjas ran off. I picked Willamina up off of the ground and took her to my apartment that was close by. When I placed her on my couch to get first aid supplies and blankets, she woke up. When she saw me, she felt threaten and tried to attack me. I assured her I was no threat, and only wanted to help her, but she remained silent and stood her ground. I slowly back away and asked her why she was being chased by ninjas. She did not answer, so I asked her if she was in trouble, and once again she said nothing. Then, there was a knock on my door a few minutes later. When I answered, Vinares Vega was standing at my door. He told me he came to pick up Willamina. I didn't know how he found us, or why he wanted her. She quietly went with him without hesitation. I asked her if she was going to be okay, but she just gave me a blank stare and walked away. Vinares laughed and thanked me for watching over her. They both left, as quickly as they came and went into the chilly rainy night. The next day at school, I didn't see Willamina. I was a little worried, but she came back the following day. We made eye contact and I waved at her, but she just stared and continued to walk by. As the year progressed, I slowly gained her trust. She began to open up to me and I became her confidant. She told me she was a student by day and an assassin by night. I was floored by what this young girl told me. In my mind, she was just a child and couldn't kill a fly. Then one day, one of my colleagues was killed who taught at my school. My colleague was said to have been caught up in a mob scandal, so the word on the street was that a hit was put out on him. Shortly after my colleague's death, Willamina disappeared and relocated. I didn't see her again until years later."

Dr. Henzu explained to Ev'ren that Willamina was abused as a child. He also explained how Francisco was holding her brother hostage, and threatened to kill him.

Ev'ren felt a new level of remorse for Willamina. Dr. Henzu yawned and told Ev'ren it was time for bed. He told him to get some rest, because the next few days were going to be the toughest in his entire young life. Building endurance, strength, and technique is paramount. Ev'ren agreed, and thanked Dr. Henzu for the meal. As Ev'ren slept, Dr. Henzu scratched his beard, thinking about the road ahead, and wondered if Ev'ren could really defeat Francisco like Willamina said. He knew she had strong feelings for him, and hoped he really was the miracle the world needed.

Chapter 17
Training day

The next day, Ev'ren was awakened just before dawn. It was a cool, crisp and dark morning as Dr. Henzu prepared Ev'ren for training. He tossed a cereal bar and bottle of water towards him, and told him to eat and drink it.

Ev'ren ate quickly, and began to do some stretches as Dr. Henzu explained his first day of training.

"Today I am going to have you jog five miles to test your speed, strength, endurance, and agility," says Dr. Henzu.

Ev'ren yawned and bowed to his trainer, assuring him how easily he could perform that task.

"No problem," he says as he takes off.

Ev'ren yawned again and commenced running, but within his first few steps he stumbled down a rocky path. He recovered to his feet, but with each step, it felt like he was carrying a ton of bricks.

Dr. Henzu was shocked at how hard it was for Ev'ren to run. Ev'ren struggled for a while and could not understand why he felt so tired. He thought it might have been due to his battle the night before, so he continued to struggle as he attempted to put one foot in front of the other. Dr. Henzu watched him with concern, and questioned if he could even defeat Vinares let alone Francisco.

Just as Dr. Henzu was about to call it a morning and re-group his training strategy, the sun began to rise. A ray of sun broke through the trees. Ev'ren's skin glowed from the rays of light, as he slowly began to move with more ease. With each step he took, he ran faster and with more precision. Then suddenly, he took off in a dash and quickly finished his five mile run.

"I'm back," says Ev'ren as Dr. Henzu looked at him in amazement.

"Great. Now we are going to really see what you are made of," he says.

Dr. Henzu tested Ev'ren strength. He told Ev'ren to lift up a heavy boulder rock. Ev'ren told him it was impossible for him to lift a rock that heavy. Dr. Henzu explained to Ev'ren how he has unlocked many of his powers, and that he would not know unless he tried. As he stooped down and braced himself to pick up the basketball size rock, weighing about one hundred pounds, he lifted it with ease and threw it farther than the eyes could see. Ev'ren was surprised at his strength, and began to jump up and down with excitement. Then, Dr. Henzu told Ev'ren to pick up the heaviest rock he could find and throw it. Ev'ren did not know which rock to pick up, because there were so many big ones.

Dr. Henzu saw a large rock lying beside a tree. The rock was the size of a small car tire and weighed about 400 pounds. He told Ev'ren to pick it up. Ev'ren walked up to the huge boulder and picked it up with one hand. Then, he tossed it effortlessly in the air. Dr. Henzu was surprised, but he hid his enthusiasm. He walked Ev'ren to the side of the cave, and pointed at a larger rock that was the size of a small car. Ev'ren walked over to the rock and scratched his head. He doubted whether he could lift it or not, so he prepared himself for failure. He stooped low enough to put both of his hands underneath the rock. Then, he took a deep breath, before he started to lift it. He was amazed at how light it was. After he lifted the rock up and threw it twenty feet, he questioned Dr. Henzu asking if he created fake rocks.

Dr. Henzu laughed as he told Ev'ren he did nothing to the rocks. When he told Ev'ren the last rock weighed about one ton, he almost tripped over himself in shock.

"Ev'ren, when you lifted the last rock, I noticed a change in your muscle mass. It grew," says Dr. Henzu.

"Wow, are you serious," exclaims Ev'ren!

"Yes, and now I want to test your ability to leap, by jumping as high as you can," he says.

Ev'ren braced himself as he leaped high into the air. Dr. Henzu was stunned by Ev'ren's leap. His eyes followed Ev'ren into the air, as he estimated sixty feet between the ground and Ev'ren. As they continued with the assessment, he was asked to do a series of front and backward flips to show his flexibility. With each move, Ev'ren was light and nimble on his feet.

Also, he told Dr. Henzu that his sight and hearing had enhanced, since the barn fire the night before. He explained how he could see objects from far away, and could clearly hear faint sounds.

"Ev'ren you are unlocking a lot of amazing powers. Do you have x-ray vision, too," asks Dr. Henzu?

"Of course not, I'm not Clark Kent," says Ev'ren jokingly, "but after last night, I think I may have infrared vision."

Dr. Henzu nodded as he continued to ask Ev'ren a series of questions about things he can see and hear. He explained to Ev'ren that he developed his super powers from his dad who was exposed to massive amounts of radiation. He also told Ev'ren about the dangers of Francisco's plan, and explained to him that Willamina felt he was the only one who could defeat him.

Ev'ren was aware of some of his father's abilities after meeting Willamina, but he had no idea his strength was superhuman. Dr. Henzu reminded Ev'ren that Francisco had superhuman strength also, and how he would need more than his abilities to defeat him.

"Spar with me Ev'ren," says Dr. Henzu as he assumed the stance of a crane.

Ev'ren smiled at Dr. Henzu, because he didn't know what to expect from him. When Dr. Henzu attacked Ev'ren, he was not merciful. His aggressive multiple kicks made Ev'ren wobble left to right and caught him off guard. Dr. Henzu was extremely light on his feet, which surprised Ev'ren as he continued to dodge his attacks.

"Hey Dr. Henzu, do you know Kempo," asks Ev'ren?

"Yes. Do you," he asks surprisingly?

Ev'ren smiled again and took his stance.

"Let's do this boy," he says.

Dr. Henzu told Ev'ren to show him what Willamina taught him. Ev'ren mounted his attacks against Dr. Henzu as he launched a series of quick jabs and kicks. Dr. Henzu dodged them until, Ev'ren caught him in the chest with one of his kicks. Ev'ren stopped for a second to make sure Dr. Henzu was okay.

"I am so sorry," he says, "are you alright?"

Within a matter of seconds, Dr. Henzu grabbed Ev'ren by the wrist and slammed him to the ground. When he did, the ground beneath Ev'ren cracked.

"As you can see, I'm fine. Never underestimate your opponent," says Dr. Henzu.

They continued to spar back and forth with each other.

Dr. Henzu was impressed by Ev'ren's speed, strength and agility, and Ev'ren was impressed with Dr. Henzu's guile and abilities.

"Okay Ev'ren," says Dr. Henzu, "enough sparring."

"Why, old man? Am I wearing you out?" says Ev'ren jokingly.

"Not even. I have something very special to show you."

Dr. Henzu lifted his hands toward the sky. All of a sudden, a light expelled from it. He slowly brought his hands down to his stomach, holding the energy between his hands. Ev'ren watched in awe as the energy swelled in Dr. Henzu's hands.

"Dragon's Moth," yells Dr. Henzu as he released the energy ball towards Ev'ren!

Ev'ren barely dodged the special attack aimed at him. He looked at Dr. Henzu with disbelief, as multiple energy balls came towards him. Dr. Henzu laughed as he watched Ev'ren play hop scotch with his technique. Before long, he struck Ev'ren to the ground.

"How did you do that?" asks Ev'ren.

"Years upon years of practice my boy," replies Dr. Henzu as he walked towards Ev'ren, and grabbed his hand to pull him up from the ground.

"Can you teach me that," asks Ev'ren?

"I will do my best to teach you, but it takes time, patience and a lot of practice to master this technique."

"I saw Willamina attempt an energy attack last night. She also tried to teach me how to create one when we sparred. Last night something happened to me in that barn to cause the fire, but it was nothing like your energy attack," says Ev'ren.

"Then I am sure she has told you the dangers of using this technique. You could hurt others, or potentially blow yourself up," replies Dr. Henzu.

"I didn't know about the blowing up part, but I will do whatever it takes to perfect this technique. Francisco will not get away with this," says Ev'ren.

Dr. Henzu looked at Ev'ren with concern.

"Ev'ren you are a determined and spirited fighter, but I am going to be honest with you. That fire was caused by rage…a rage that is hidden deep within you."

"Rage, you can't be serious," replies Ev'ren.

"You have a lot of manners and respect, but the rage I see is buried deep within your heart Ev'ren, and I fear someday it will surface."

"You make it sound like I am some demonic person."

"You are not," says Dr. Henzu, "but anger is within you, and you must not let it consume you. There is no telling what you may do in the heat of battle or immense frustration."

Ev'ren sat on a boulder and looked away.

"I know this isn't the easiest of circumstances son," says Dr. Henzu.

"The past forty-eight hours have been one twisted turn of fate for me. I found out that one of my closest friends is a spy, and an assassin. My physics teacher is a master martial artist. I have superhuman powers I never knew I had, and the world's richest man wants me dead. He also murdered my parents. Let's not forget that my aunt was almost killed, and the world is supposedly about to be destroyed by an asteroid. Things like this come out of comic books, but not Stone Mountain, Georgia."

"It must be hard coping with all that is happening," says Dr. Henzu?

"I saw what happened to Willamina and feel like it's my fault," says Ev'ren, "she could have been killed, because of me."

"Ev'ren, you are not responsible for what happened to Willamina. She was sent here to trick you into joining Francisco's team. Instead, she protected you, because she started to care about you. She knew the risk."

Dr. Henzu pointed at the sun shining in the distance as it began to set.

"Ev'ren, I think you may have the ability to harness the sun's power. If I am right, then you truly have a remarkable gift."

"Like nuclear energy," asks Ev'ren?

"The jury is still out on that one my boy. I am going to change your training. Your superhuman abilities far exceed simple sparring and strength training. We will re-direct our focus, and practice energy waves and mediation. If you have the ability to burn down a barn, just think of what you could do with focused and controlled energy," says Dr. Henzu.

"Yes Master," says Ev'ren as he bows.

"Ev'ren, I am no master. I am merely a physics teacher with a family legacy to preserve."

"Fine, I will not call you master, but at least allow me to treat you like one."

Dr. Henzu knew this was a lot for Ev'ren to process; after all he was just a teenager. His heart went out to Ev'ren and the burdens he has to bear. He knew Ev'ren was in for the fight of his young life.

"Ev'ren, sometimes the answer you seek comes when you least expect it," says Dr. Henzu giving him more consolation and encouragement.

Ev'ren looked at him and nodded in agreement.

Dr. Henzu told Ev'ren to meditate. As he meditated the sun

continued to descend. Beads of sweat rolled off his face, while visions clouded his serenity. His solitude was overwhelmed by visions of an asteroid that landed off the coast of Florida. It created a massive tsunami that devastated North America, South America, the Caribbean, parts of Europe and Africa. In his vision, he saw earthquakes that ravaged most of the Earth, throwing the planet into disarray. Millions of people died, and those who survived, struggled due to the rising of Francisco's oppression. He watched in horror as he saw his love ones burned alive by Francisco's hand. He saw the delight in Francisco's eyes as they screamed in agony.

During meditation, Ev'ren body began to glow. His eyes opened. He was filled with so much emotional torment. His breathing became sporadic and heavy, as sweat poured from his face. Unaware of what was happening around him. The ground started to tremble as the glow around his body became red. Dr. Henzu felt the ground tremble and ran out of the cave to see what was happening. He saw Ev'ren engulfed in flames as he mediated. Dr. Henzu feared he might reach a point of disaster, so he ran towards Ev'ren, shouted out his name, in hopes to break his meditation.

He continued to call Ev'ren's name, but he was in a deep trance. Finally, Dr. Henzu ran to get a bucket of water.

With each step he took, the ground continued to shake from Ev'ren's emotional breakdown. The ground around him began to crumble and cave, but Dr. Henzu knew he had to get back to Ev'ren before the entire area collapsed. He quickly ran towards Ev'ren who sat twenty feet below him in a crater. Dr. Henzu took the bucket of water, and threw it on Ev'ren.

The shaking stopped as Ev'ren opened his teary eyes. He was drenched in sweat, and trembled as he looked up at Dr. Henzu. He gazed around at his meditation spot, and saw crumbled rocks and stones all around them. Dr. Henzu was speechless as Ev'ren looked at him for answers.

"This can't be," he says, "I couldn't have done this?"

"Yes Ev'ren, you did, but you were supposed to be meditating. What happened?"

Ev'ren told Dr. Henzu about his vision. He thought that maybe he fell asleep, but Dr. Henzu told him his eyes were open. When he saw the fear on Ev'ren's face, he assured him it was only a vision, and it has not been written in stone. He and Ev'ren both helped each other out of the crater as the sun finally sat. They stood at the edge of it looking down in astonishment.

"I'm so sorry," says Ev'ren.

"It is okay. I've always wanted a fire pit," says Dr. Henzu laughing.

With a horrid look, Ev'ren saw what he was capable of and knew he had to find a way to control his newly found powers, or he could potentially hurt innocent people.

Dr. Henzu patted Ev'ren on his back and motioned for him to move away from the crater.

"You shouldn't worry about your powers Ev'ren. You have the raw energy of the sun inside of you. It took Francisco years to reach his full powers, but you are still learning and have yet to reach yours. There is always a risk when you attempt something. I promise to help you master your

313

powers. You have no other choice if you want to defeat Francisco."

"Wait, has Francisco reached his full potential?" asks Ev'ren.

"Willamina said Francisco likes to boast about his power. She watched him spar against his guards and even Vinares. Some of his attacks were lethal for the guards. Vinares was more like Francisco's whipping boy, she recalled. His most favorite and deadliest attack "*Lightning Blast*" not only leveled a city in Iraq sixteen years ago, but he used his attack against Vinares. According to Willamina, there was a flash of light that went through Vinares and exited through his chest. The attack was so fast Vinares could not avoid it. Needless to say, it caused him serious injuries which is why he sports a metal breast plate today. No one knows if Vinares has fully recovered from Francisco's attack, but I think he has."

"What a messed up family. Francisco is so evil, he would attack his own cousin with his deadliest attack. I have to find a way to stop him. I just have to," says Ev'ren as he pounds his fist into the palm of his hand.

Dr. Henzu told Ev'ren he has a way to see how much power a person has through the use of physics. It's called the transference of energy. He asked Ev'ren to put both of his hands into his and kneel. Ev'ren gave Dr. Henzu a weird look, but did as he was instructed to do.

"Dr. Henzu, your hands are cold and clammy," says Ev'ren.

"That's from fishing in icy rivers," says Dr. Henzu, "please concentrate."

Dr. Henzu began to concentrate along with Ev'ren. As he held Ev'ren's hands in his palm, he began to sweat. Ev'ren's grip became hotter and stronger as Dr. Henzu felt his power. His hands started to sizzle, as he uttered and yelped. Finally, he pulled away when the heat was too much.

Dr. Henzu stared at Ev'ren, but smiled as he confirmed Ev'ren's amazing power.

"You are really like the sun, explosive and unpredictable." he says with amazement.

Ev'ren saw a burn wound in the palm of Dr. Henzu's hands and became worried.

"Your hands, I am so sorry," says Ev'ren.

"I'm fine Ev'ren. I am a fast healer, but if I held your hands a few more seconds longer, they would have combusted."

Dr. Henzu told Ev'ren to continue to meditate, because it would help him better control his powers. Ev'ren agreed, but began to yarn from exhaustion. He became extremely tired like he was that morning. Dr. Henzu saw the fatigue on Ev'ren's face, and decided to end his training for the day. As they began to walk towards the cave, Ev'ren called out just before he passed out.

Dr. Henzu tried to shake Ev'ren and wake him up, but he was unresponsive. When he heard Ev'ren snoring, he smiled and slapped him in the face calling him a slacker.

He picked Ev'ren up and carried him inside. As he watched over Ev'ren, he began to wonder why Ev'ren's energy faded so quickly. Physically he was very fit, but he struggled earlier that morning with a simple run, and then passed out asleep while he was walking to the cave. Dr. Henzu rubbed his stubby chin as he tried to put the pieces of this mystery together.

"That's it," he says to himself, "why didn't it come to me sooner."

The next day around four in the morning Dr. Henzu threw a pail of cold water in Ev'ren face. Ev'ren woke up infuriated. Dr. Henzu told him how he made several attempts to wake him, but he did not respond.

"Ev'ren, go fill these buckets with water and bring them to me," says Dr. Henzu.

"Yes Sir," says Ev'ren as he rubs his eyes in exhaustion.

When Ev'ren stood up, he took a few steps forward and fell towards the ground. Dr. Henzu told him to get up and walk. Ev'ren moved slowly towards the entrance of the cave, and then fell to his knees again.

"I am so tired, and I can barely stay awake right now. I feel like a ton of rocks are on top of me. What's happening to me," he asks?

"It is funny you should ask that question Ev'ren. Last night I had to carry you into the cave after the sun went down. I began to think about solar energy and the key components of it. Consider yourself a conductor of energy. Without your source of energy, it is hard for you to function."

Ev'ren looked at Dr. Henzu with confusion.

"When the sun sets, you become incoherent and tired. It is

my theory, the sun is your source of power, and you are a conductor of its energy."

"So you are telling me that darkness makes me weak?"

"Yes," says Dr. Henzu nodding his head, "but I also think cold temperatures do the same thing."

"This doesn't make sense. I have never experienced this issue before."

"Ev'ren, when you were playing football, did you ever feel weak at night?"

"No, which is more reason why this doesn't make any sense."

"Since you've unlocked some of your powers, your body has started to change. It needs more energy, because you are using more energy. Your body depends on its source, and that is the sun."

"I get it," replies Ev'ren like he aced a quiz.

"You will have to overcome this weakness, which means, you must learn to function when the sun goes down, or when there is extreme coldness."

"That is impossible," says Ev'ren, "I feel so tired when it gets dark, like I have no control. This is hopeless."

Dr. Henzu looked at Ev'ren, and snatched him by his shirt.

"Do you think feeling sorry for yourself is the answer? It's not hopeless! If I am wasting my time with you, say it, and we will leave this place now!"

Ev'ren could barely look at Dr. Henzu as he continued to talk. He felt stupid and immature for saying what he said.

"The entire world is depending on you, and you are acting like a little kid who wants to run home with his thumb in his mouth. You have to pull it together and stop freaking out. Suck it up! Conquer your fears and do it now, before it is too late. We don't have a lot of time."

"Yes, Sir!" exclaims Ev'ren.

"Good, now go out there and get me some water."

After Ev'ren came back with the buckets of water, he went outside and began to run. As he ran, he thought about the people who depended on him. The sun slowly came over the horizon, as Ev'ren began to run faster and faster.

After he completed his run, he went to the riverside to mediate. About an hour into his mediation, Dr. Henzu walked over. Ev'ren arose from his mediation.

Dr. Henzu raised his hands to the sky, and cried out, "*Koga's Howl*." Suddenly, a bright light emerged from Dr. Henzu's hands, and struck a pine tree in the distance. On impact, the tree split in half.

"How did you do that? Your hands were at a different angle," ask Ev'ren.

"You can discharge your wave attack from any angle. It takes years of patience, practice and perseverance. Hand and foot techniques are very important to launch an energy attack. Just copy my stance Ev'ren, and we will see if you can do this or not."

Ev'ren concentrated and copied every single move Dr. Henzu did.

"Good Ev'ren, inhale through your nose and exhale through your mouth. Focus your energy from your gut, and give your attack a name."

Ev'ren breathed through his nose, and out through his mouth. He called out to it hoping something would happen, but nothing materialized. He hung his head low in disappointment.

"Darn it."

Dr. Henzu folded his arms as he looked at Ev'ren's reaction.

"Don't be disappointed. Your stance is great, and that is a huge accomplishment."

"That is not good enough. I want to try again," says Ev'ren.

"Ev'ren it's starting to get dark. We need to head back to the cave, because I don't feel like carrying you again."

Ev'ren refused to stop. He wanted to try again one more time. He closed his eyes and copied Dr. Henzu's stance. As he brought his hands from the sky, a dim white light emerge with it. The light began to surround Ev'ren as he focused it into the size of a basketball. The light became blood red, as Dr. Henzu looked with astonishment. Ev'ren opened his eyes and cried out *"Red Giant."* He released the energy ball smashing it into a giant boulder.

Dr. Henzu was impressed with Ev'ren's determination.

"I knew you could do it. Great job! Now, don't forget that

feeling Ev'ren," he says.

"I won't," says Ev'ren

"Energy balls are your life-force. They come from inside of you, so you can tire yourself out quickly if you are not conditioned. You will need to practice, but only in the day time, so attention is not drawn to us."

As the sun begun to set, Ev'ren started to become tired and weak again. Dr. Henzu saw his fatigue, so he told him to call it a day.

"I have another surprise for you Ev'ren."

"Really, what is it?"

"You will see."

As they entered the cave, Ev'ren noticed it was warmer and much brighter. Immediately, his energy began to increase. He saw a nice size fire, so he gravitated towards it and sat down.

"I noticed that when you were sleeping, the flames from the fire pulled towards you. So I made it bigger and created solar conductors to give the cave a little more light," says Dr. Henzu.

"Wow! Thank you so much," says Ev'ren jumping up and down like a kid.

"Absorb as much heat as you possibly can during the day to remain strong," says Dr. Henzu.

"I was outside all day, but I'm still weak," says Ev'ren.

"That is because, you didn't absorb any sunlight, not to mention you are hungry son."

Ev'ren grabbed his growling stomach because he didn't eat since breakfast.

"You are right."

"I am making fish stew and rice. It will be done soon."

Ev'ren and Dr. Henzu discussed energy waves over dinner. That night he went to bed early, so he would be refreshed for his next day of training.

The next morning, Ev'ren woke up groggy, but he was excited about his training. As he walked towards the exit of the cave, he began to get weak again. As he exited the cave, to his surprise, there was snow on the ground. Ev'ren cringed. However, despite the cold and grey day ahead, he pressed on and did his morning run. During his run, he felt like passing out from exhaustion, but he convinced himself "mind over matter" and continued on.

After he finished his morning run, he went to a spot by the river to meditate. After an hour of meditation, he practiced shadow boxing and Kempo. As the day progressed, Ev'ren gained more energy as the sun peaked in and out of the grey sky.

Ev'ren stopped at the river side, and stared into the water at his reflection. He thought about his past. He saw the reflection of his parents he didn't know, the aunt who raised him, and the friends who needed him.

"Mind over matter," he says to himself as he takes his jacket, shoes and socks off.

He took a deep breath, and plunged into the slow moving river. He immediately began to shake from the intense cold, and as quickly as he entered the river, he got out just as fast.

"Oh God, hypothermia," he says to himself shivering, "what the hell was I thinking?"

He searched for his jacket, ready to call it a day, but he began to feel guilty for giving up.

"I have to get back in there, no matter how cold or tired I am," he admits.

Ev'ren walked into the icy water again and immediately started to shake. He assumed his fighting stance, and raised his hands to the sky.

"This isn't so bad. If a bunch of old men and women in the Polar Bear Club can dive into icy cold lakes with no clothes on, then I can do this. I just have to focus."

As Ev'ren focused with his hands in the air, the clouds dissipated and allowed the sun to peak through. It was as if he was the master and the sun was his pupil. His eyes shimmered a golden yellow as the river began to heat up and create a grey mist around him.

A brownish red energy ball formed between Ev'ren's hands. He quickly aimed it towards some huge boulders across the river.

"*Red Giant*," he cried as he discarded the energy ball, and struck a huge boulder shattering it into the river. Ev'ren jumped for joy as he exited the river with his hands clutched into a fist of triumph.

He quickly returned to the cave, ready to tell his teacher what he accomplished. When he arrived at the cave, it was difficult for him to see. Ev'ren rubbed his eyes as they adjusted to the light in the cave.

As he glanced towards the fire, he saw Dr. Henzu sitting on a stool.

"Were you responsible for the loud boom I heard outside?" asks Dr. Henzu.

"Yes Sir. I was in the freezing river trying to overcome the cold. I felt the sun's energy flowing through me and before you know it, I created another energy attack," says Ev'ren with excitement!

"Ev'ren, are you crazy? You could have passed out. You know how weak you can get," says Dr. Henzu! "I could hear you shouting, not to mention the bright light that flashed through the entrance of the cave. You have to be more discreet, so we do not alert anyone," he says.

"Your right," says Ev'ren apologetically.

"Good son, but I am proud of you."

"I took a chance and it paid off. I was focused, powered up and withstood the cold. This solves our problem," says Ev'ren.

"It is amazing you are getting strong so quickly," says Dr. Henzu.

"I wonder if cold and darkness will continue to make me weak," asks Ev'ren.

"If you are absorbing the sun's rays, as you say, you should be fine in the dark," says Dr. Henzu, "now tell me how you developed your new energy wave."

"It's called "*Red Giant,*" says Ev'ren with excitement.

Ev'ren explained how he developed his new attack. Dr. Henzu listened with pride, but tried not to show him just how much. He did not want Ev'ren to become complacent or develop an ego.

After Ev'ren finished telling Dr. Henzu what happened, he told him it was time for dinner, and sent him out to get some wood for the fire. After a half hour of gathering wood, Ev'ren arrived back at the cave. As he walked into the cave's entrance he saw a paper Shinigami hanging at the entrance.

The cave was dark, for the exception of a dim glow in the distance. Ev'ren used the infrared vision to see where he was going. He called out, but there was no response.

Ev'ren called out to Dr. Henzu again, but there was no answer. He cautiously and quietly entered the den area where he saw a pig roasting over the fire. He smiled and rubbed his stomach in hunger, hoping that dinner would be ready soon. As he walked over to the pig to pull a piece of meat off and taste it, a man wearing a mask quietly emerged behind him. Ev'ren continued to stare at the pig and question whether he should sneak another piece or not, but he heard the unsheathing of a sword behind him. When he turned around, the attacker swung in his direction.

Ev'ren dodged the attack and prepared to defend himself.

"Stop," he says as he continued to dodge the attacker.

The masked man laughed insanely at Ev`ren, as he attacked him in every direction possible. Ev'ren recognized the voice of the attacker as he continued to defend himself.

"Doc is that you," he asks?

The attacker stopped laughing for a second, and raised his sword ready to bring it down on Ev'ren. When Ev'ren quickly dipped down and swept the attacker off of his feet, the masked man started to laugh hysterically.

His attacker took the mask off and bowed at Ev'ren in defeat. Dr. Henzu was impressed at Ev'ren's reaction to his surprise attack.

"Amazing, I wanted to make sure you had the courage to protect this house. You have learned so much, so fast, so I wanted to test you to see if you were worthy. You are now a member of The House of Honzo. Live with honor and die with honor," says Dr. Henzu!

"It's an honor, but I am not worthy. I feel like I still have so much to learn," replies Ev'ren.

"Ev'ren, yes you do, but you have mastered the wave techniques in a very short time. There are martial artists who have trained all of their lives, and have never mastered the wave technique. You are a light hearted soul with the strength of a colossus. You are getting stronger with each passing day, and your potential may be beyond my teachings, which is why you have earned this mask."

"Thank you Dr. Henzu," replies Ev'ren.

"This mask represents fierceness and the sword of protection. Carry this with honor and pride. It is time to celebrate," says Dr. Henzu.

Ev'ren smiled as he took the mask into his hands. He bowed and thanked Dr. Henzu for all he taught him, and promised to make him proud.

They celebrated with the roasted pig Dr. Henzu prepared. Ev'ren told him how he was first distracted by the pig just before he was attacked. Dr. Henzu laughed and admitted how he did that on purpose.

Despite the cold temperatures and night fall, Ev'ren showed little signs of fatigue. After they got ready for bed, Dr. Henzu slept with relief. For the first time in long time, he felt they had a fighting chance against Francisco and his army.

The next morning Ev'ren woke up tired but encouraged. He stumbled towards the table calling out to Dr. Henzu, but no one answered. He grabbed an apple and noticed a letter on the table with his name on it.

"Ev'ren by the time you wake I will be half way to Canada. I received an urgent message from a credible source that Willamina and her forces were under attack by Francisco's army. It was an attempt to bring you out of hiding, but I need you to stay hidden and do not follow me. The city of Stone Mountain will need your assistance after Hope strikes the planet. Don't worry about your family and friends, Willamina sent some of her soldiers to protect them from the asteroid and Francisco's forces. Your aunt is much better and they will be safe. I will come back for you once I have assisted Willamina. I have one more request. Take care of

yourself."

Ev'ren paced back and forth pondering what he should do. So much was going to happen today, because of Hope. His family and friends were all in danger.

"I hate this," he says!

He struggled with his decision, contemplating whether he should stay or leave. He did not want to sit around and do nothing. He thought about his parents, and the sacrifices they made for him. He decided at that point, instead of meditation, he needed prayer. So, he fell to his knees and prayed for a sign. Just as he finished his prayer, he heard a buzzing sound in the corner of the cave. He searched high and low to see if there was a bee in the cave, but to his avail, it was a dragonfly. The dragonfly flew out the cave. Ev'ren received the sign he needed, so he picked up his belongings and exited the cave. As he walked away, he glanced back one last time, and then headed towards the snowy mountains.

Chapter 18
"Faith over Hope"

After a few hours of walking, Ev'ren looked at his watch which read ten o'clock in the morning. As he approached the mountain range, he came across four old log cabins. An old man, with a rifle in his hands, was sitting on the front porch of one of the cabins. As Ev'ren approached, he pointed his gun towards him. Ev'ren slowly raised his hands up, and told the man about the asteroid. The man told him he knew about it, and demanded that he leave his property. Ev'ren stepped back, and continued toward the mountains.

"Shoot, only an hour and thirty minutes before millions of people die! This can't be happening," he says.

Ev'ren thought about his aunt and his friends. Then, out of nowhere he heard a high pitched sound in the air. Ev'ren screamed, as he attempted to cover his ears. When he looked into the sky, he saw glimmers of light. Four meteors appeared from the cold grey sky, and rapidly descended towards the earth. One landed half a mile away from where he stood. The force threw Ev'ren to the ground, causing cuts and bruises over his body.

As he recovered to his feet, he noticed the cuts and bruises began to heal. He was amazed at this miracle, though he was not sure how it was possible. He watched as a cloud of dust and ice dispersed from the meteor impact, and rose into the air

About a minute later, Ev'ren felt uneasiness in the air, and looked towards the sky at the second meteor. It was headed in his direction. He immediately ran towards the base of the mountain as fast as he could. The meteor landed a few feet away from him, and propelled him into the base of a mountain. Ev'ren screamed as he slammed into rocks and boulders. A few seconds later, he helplessly watched as a third meteor passed above him, and slammed into the area where the cabins were. He thought about the old man with his riffle as he cried out.

Just when he thought it couldn't get any worse, the largest of the four meteors flew towards him without warning. The meteor exploded in mid-air, sending a burst of energy towards him.

The intensity of the blast created superheated winds, and temperatures around Ev'ren that reached an upward of twenty-five hundred degrees. Wild fires broke out all over the once snowy landscape. The blast radius of the meteor stretched out for two miles. Ev'ren was burnt and tossed around like a mingled doll. He suffered burns to his entire body, and was in excruciating pain. He cried out in agony, as he attempted to rise to his feet, but fell to his back. He was on the verge of shock, until a sliver of sunlight appeared. He felt tingling all over his body, as he saw the burns slowly disappear. He was astonished by this miracle, and second chance.

Ev'ren rose from the ashes, and looked at his healed body. He felt a breeze of air on his back side and realized that, his clothes burned off of his body. He searched for something to cover up with, but nothing was around. Everything around him was burnt and barren, as wildfires continued to burn out control in the distance.

Ev'ren sighed as he quickly trekked back toward the cabins, in hopes to find the old man. As he felt the sun's ray, each of his steps grew stronger. Along the way, he saw remnants of his partially burnt back pack. He found his broken sword, his cracked mask, a pair of jogging pants and an under shirt with smut on it. He quickly grabbed his items, and threw on the jogging pants and under shirt. As he continued toward the cabins, his worst fears came true. He saw the damaged rifle of the old man, and realized that he needed to hurry.

As he rushed down the path, he saw all four cabins a blaze.

"NO," he shouts!

When he came closer, he saw the old man on fire. He saw a burnt plastic doll beside the old man, and realized more people may be in the cabins.

Ev'ren searched for survivors, but all he found were the remains of families who lived there. The sight of dead men, women and children made Ev'ren upset.

"I'm so sorry I couldn't save any of you! Why is this happening," he questions?

"Millions of people are about to die, and there is nothing I can do."

Ev'ren looked towards the dimming sunlight. He knew time was running out. He buried the dead, and continued towards the mountains. He began to rant and swear in anger.

"God, are you punishing me? I have lost almost everyone in my life, yet you still forsake me! Death and evil are all around me, and there is nothing I can do to stop it!"

As Ev'ren continued to yell at the heavens, a dark blue hue of light surrounded him. He didn't realize his anger was getting the best of him. He continued to yell at the heavens shaking his fist, as his breathing became sharp and quick. His ocean blue eyes crystalized and became iridescent as the earth started to tremble.

"Why," as his voice trembles with anger!

The ground continued to tremble beneath his feet, making people in nearby towns think Hope was about to land.

Ev'ren's anger consumed him like a raging storm, as he pounded his fist into the ground. Before long, blue flames engulfed Ev'ren, causing an explosion of energy around him. Anything within the area where he stood was destroyed. Rocks and bounders were pulverized by Ev'ren's intense energy. The surrounding mountain side collapsed as he started to lose control.

"Why did you take my parents away from me," yells Ev'ren!

Ev'ren's energy became so volatile, it radiated to the core of the Earth causing minor earthquakes.

"I'm tired of losing everything I love," he says with a stern face, "I'm tired of being alone."

Ev'ren held his head down as thoughts of his parents, his friends, and Mrs. Anderson ran through his mind.

His rage took control of him, just as Dr. Henzu warned. He was blinded by his fury and did not realized the magnitude of his anger. The Earth was on the brink of destruction, but Hope was no longer the executioner, Ev'ren was.

He looked up in the distance and saw the asteroid appear like a bright star in the sky.

"Damn you Hope, Damn you too hell," he says with anger as his eyes started to glow!

He held his hands towards the sky, and launched a massive energy wave towards the asteroid. The energy wave bounced off of the asteroid like it was nothing, but it was still strong enough to make matters worse. Hope slightly changed directions, and moved further south. Her new area of impact was Atlanta.

Ev'ren's anger had fully taken hold of him. He didn't realize what he was doing, or what he was becoming. His body was transforming. He grew a foot taller. His skin color changed to a burnt orange. The energy that flowed within, began to expel from every part of his body. He was about to explode.

Just as all hope was lost, something strange occurred and brought Ev'ren to silence. A beautiful young woman, with long red hair, and ocean blue eyes appeared in the midst of his anger.

Ev'ren shook his head in disbelief, as he spoke to the woman he longed for all of his life.

"Mom," he says.

The woman looked at him with a smile on her face and gently said, "Enough my son."

Ev'ren continued to shake his head in disbelief.

"I can't," he says, "it hurts too much."

"I know things have been painful for you, but you must overcome your anger, or you will destroy the very thing you were destined to protect."

Ev'ren fell to his knees.

"Mom, this is too much for me. I don't want this fate. All I want is to be with you and dad."

Ev'ren reached out his hand, but the spirit moved back.

"Please mom, take me with you."

"You will not see us for a very long time son, so you must put this pain and anger aside. We love you more than you will ever know. Ev'ren, do not fear my son. Don't lose faith. You have an amazing gift, and it must be used to protect those who cannot protect themselves. If you don't control your rage, you will destroy the very thing you hold dear. That is your fate son, whether you want it or not."

Tears began to flow from Ev'ren's eyes as his anger subsided.

"Yes ma'am," he says like an obedient child.

The spirit of his mother vanished into the dust, as quickly as she appeared. In the distance he could hear her voice humming a familiar lullaby.

"You are my sunshine my only sunshine, you make me happy when skies are grey...please don't take my sunshine away."

Ev'ren dried his tears as he calmed down and refocused. He realized he lost control, and went to a dark place he didn't know existed inside of him.

"I must protect what I love the most, and I will not fail," says Ev'ren.

Ev'ren was no longer in flames. His eyes changed, as the energy around him illuminated a yellow glow.

Ev'ren's rage changed to a calming meditation. He held his hands apart as all thoughts of negative energy left his mind. His meditation was so solace, a tiny spark of yellow light emerged between his hands. When Ev'ren realized what he created, he patiently waited for Hope to enter into the atmosphere.

A few minutes later, Hope slammed into the atmosphere at about forty thousand miles an hour and erupted into flames. People near and far screamed, as they braced for their deaths.

Ev'ren thrusted his hands forward towards Hope. As he released his energy wave, he named it *"Faith."* When he released Faith into the atmosphere, his powers increased.

Faith screamed through storm clouds, and towards the killer asteroid like an atomic missile. It slammed into Hope like a hammer, slowing it down and changing its trajectory. As Hope continued a downward descent, Ev'ren held his stance, and braced for impact as he attempt to stop it. He grunted and struggled with Hope. The ground under Ev'ren's feet began to crumble due to the tremendous pressure of the asteroid. As Hope continued to descend, Ev'ren continued to push back, which caused a huge crater beneath his feet.

He began to levitate from the ground. The power between Faith and Hope created massive amounts of thunder, and lightning that was seen around the world.

Ev'ren pushed Faith forward, and floated in mid- air while every ounce of his body throbbed with adrenaline.

Hope pushed against Faith with relentless fury, as their showdown continued. The asteroid was so close to the earth, impact was imminent.

"Come on," he cries as he struggled against Hope.

For a moment he thought all was lost, until he re-gained control of Faith, and sent Hope back into space like a shooting star.

The threat she once posed was no more.

When Ev'ren slowly descended back to the ground, he collapsed to his knees in exhaustion. He panted for air, as he thought about his mother and blew a kiss towards the heavens. He also asked for forgiveness, and prayed for the people who died that day around the world.

He was not sure of how he created such powerful energy, but felt he had some help from a higher power.

Ev'ren looked at the damage around him. Suddenly, he heard the screams of men, women and children in the distance. He looked west and realized it was coming from Stone Mountain about twenty-five miles away. He thought it might be from the remnants of the asteroid, but something did not feel right about their screams.

Ev'ren looked at his hands and feet in amazement of what

just transpired. He felt himself flying when he pushed his energy wave against Hope.

"I can't believe it. I can fly," he says.

With both hands towards the sky, Ev'ren pushed himself forward and flew towards Stone Mountain.

Chapter 19

Ev'ren vs. Vinares

After Ev'ren's epic tug of war with Hope, he briefly relished his ability to fly. He soared through the puffy grey clouds, twisting and racing amongst the birds, until he reached the sunny and blue skies. He suddenly felt a rush of energy as the warm sun recharged him. In the distance, he heard the cries of the people of Stone Mountain. He quickly headed towards Stone Mountain. When he arrived there, the city was near the brink of destruction. There were buildings on fire, looters vandalizing stores and the dead laying in the streets. Ev'ren quickly took shelter in a clothing store.

He became a teenage boy again, and once again naked due to his transformation. So, he immediately looked around for some clothes. After putting on a pair of blue jeans, black t-shirt, and a baseball cap he kept low and looked around the store for survivors. He came across two female employees, passed out on the floor.

He did not want to be seen if someone was in there, so he kept low to the ground and made his way towards them. They were breathing, but appeared to be unconscious. When he saw both ladies with bite marks on their necks and arms, a new fear arose inside of him. Suddenly, Ev'ren heard a woman's voice crying in one of the dressing rooms. He slowly and carefully walked over to the door and opened it. When the lady saw him, she jumped up swinging frantically, until she realized he was just a boy.

"I'm here to help, ma'am! Is everything ok," asks Ev'ren?

"I don't know," replies the woman as she looked around and moved back into the dressing room.

"It's okay. You can come out," says Ev'ren.

The woman came out of the dressing room as Ev'ren instructed.

"Are you one of them," she asks?

"Excuse me ma'am, but did you say one of them? Please tell me what happened in here, and to the ladies on the floor?"

"We were taking cover from the asteroid, when those things ran in and attacked the store clerks, biting and clawing them on their necks. They looked like normal human beings, but they act like wild animals."

"Sunstrokers," replies Ev'ren as he remembered Willamina's warning.

"Who and what are Sunstrokers? Are they aliens? Did they arrive on the asteroid," ask the woman?

"They are manmade machines that are half human, and half android. A friend told me, they feed off of human energy, draining a person within a matter of minutes."

"My God," replies the woman.

"Ma'am please be careful and listen to what I am saying. These things are very strong, but they are slow and the main weakness is their belly button. If you hit them there, they will shut down," says Ev'ren.

"They look so real. How will I be able to tell if they are human?"

"That's easy, they will chase you for your energy."

"That's great," replies the woman sarcastically.

"During the day time they are hard to see, but at night, you will see them glow."

"They glow?"

"Yes ma'am, they glow. Now we need to get these two ladies into a dressing room quickly, and hide them safely until they wake up," says Ev'ren.

"Are they dead?" asks the woman.

"No ma'am. They will be fine. I guess the Sunstrokers must have had their fill. "

Ev'ren and the women dragged the ladies into a dressing room, and Ev'ren told her to stay hidden.

"You should stay here with us boy," replies the woman.

"I will be fine, and you will be safe too, as long as you do not bring any attention to yourselves. Ma'am do you have a cell phone?"

"Yes."

"Is the volume of your cell phone ringer off?"

"Yes, do you want to use it?"

"No, but I would like for you to send a mass text message, to friends, family and as many people as possible?"

"I don't know if I can do that. My data plan is limited."

"I need you to try. Let as many people know, that if they encounter a Sunstroker, hit them in the stomach and they will shut down. Please spread the word."

"How do you know ?"

"A friend told me."

"What's your name son," asks the woman.

"My name is, Ev'ren."

"Thank you Ev'ren. My name is Zola," says the woman.

They smiled at each other and made eye contact for a moment longer. Zola stared at Ev'ren like they've met before, and just as she was about to speak, they heard a man cry for help in the distance, followed by the savaged roars of hungry Sunstrokers. He told her to stay hidden, and to send out the mass text message. Then, he ran off to see what was happening.

When he ran into the streets, two men sprinted towards him. The two men were being chased by six Sunstrokers. Hit them in the gut. It's your only chance," shouts Ev'ren!

Two Sunstrokers dragged one of the men to the ground and bit into him. The man screamed for help, as the Sunstrokers feasted on his energy.

The other man ran in fear as Ev'ren came to his aide. One by one he struck the Sunstrokers in the stomach with quickness and veracity. The man looked at Ev'ren with amazement.

The last two Sunstrokers growled and hissed as they stood

over the man they dragged to the ground. Ev'ren raised his energy level, so the Sunstrokers would attack him.

"Sir, when these monsters come after me, go and get your friend," says Ev'ren.

The Sunstrokers sensed Ev'ren's energy level, and charged towards him. The man ran towards his friend.

Ev'ren quickly finished the two Sunstrokers off with a kick to the stomach, and ran over to the two men.

"How is your friend?"

"My friend is weak, but alive. How did you know what to do in order to kill them," he asks?

"With all of the commotion, more Sunstrokers could be on the way! You saw what happened when I struck them in the stomach."

"Yeah, I saw it."

"Do you have somewhere safe to go?"

"My house was overrun by those things. We are going to the shelter. Come with us!"

"I have some unfinished business to handle. Spread the word about the weakness of the Sunstrokers at the shelter, and stay off of the street. Be careful."

"Okay kid. Thank you!"

As Ev'ren and the two men went their separate ways, Ev'ren heard their screams a few seconds later.

When he ran in their directions, he saw them laid out on the ground. He looked around for Sunstrokers, but he did not see any.

"What just happened to them?"

When he got closer, he saw a needle protruding from their chest and head area. Ev'ren quickly realized something else killed them.

Ev'ren heightened his senses and focused carefully on his surroundings to see if anyone was nearby. In the distance, he heard so many voices, such as crying and people whispering. Suddenly, Ev'ren heard the sound of an object cutting through the wind. He saw a shower of the needle like projectiles from above. He took off running and dodged each one while he took cover. He heard laughing in the distance from above. It was Vinares Vega laughing at Ev'ren's as he descended to the ground.

"You little runt, I enjoyed watching you run like a mouse trapped in a maze," laughs Vinares.

Vinares quickly vanished and reappeared behind Ev'ren, and tackled him. Ev'ren punched Vinares numerous times landing attacks on his face, chest, arms, and legs. They flew through the air knocking down barrels as Ev'ren's unrelenting attacks had no effect on Vinares.

"Stop tickling me boy," says Vinares as he laughed at Ev'ren.

Ev'ren assumed an open stance as a red glow surrounded him.

Vinares boastfully laughed at him and disappeared.

Ev'ren kept his stance as he felt Vinares' movement. Then he yelled out "*Red Giant*," and landed an attack on Vinares' chest. Thinking he destroyed Vinares, Ev'ren took a deep breath, but Vinares reappeared laughing at him and thanking him for the light show.

"My turn," he says with a sinister grin.

Vinares extended his right hand and began to fire needles at Ev'ren. Ev'ren easily dodged them, but when Vinares saw an opening, he grabbed Ev'ren and slammed him to the ground. Ev'ren recovered to his feet and attacked Vinares in the same manner, by picking him up and slamming him to the ground.

Vinares offered a combination of punches, kicks and his lethal needles. Ev'ren avoided most of them, until one landed in his arm.

In fear, Ev'ren ran and hid behind a wooden wall. He pulled the needle out of his arm and his wound begun to heal. Ev'ren realized Vinares had the advantage, because none of his attacks affected him.

"What happen to all that power you had boy? We know you sent that asteroid back into space. It must have taken a lot of power to do something like that. Maybe that is why your attacks are so weak. Maybe you used all of your little boy power to save a planet that will be ruled by us!"

Ev'ren continued to search around for a way out. He saw an opening in the wall big enough for him to squeeze through, and escaped into the forest.

Vinares continued to taunt and gloat, until he grew

impatient, and broke down the wall Ev'ren hid behind. When he saw that Ev'ren escaped, Vinares was furious. He made a fist and yelled, as small horns began to protrude from his back. A light fog began to expel from his horns and released poisonous gases that were so toxic, any plant, animal, or human being within five hundred feet of him would die. Vinares thought his gases would bring Ev'ren from hiding, but when he realized his plan did not work, he frowned and quickly took to the sky in pursuit of him.

In the forest, Ev'ren hid amongst some bushes. He began to itch, and quickly realized the bushes were poison ivy. He cringed as he remained silent and ignored the urge to scratch.

In the distance, he heard Vinares searching for him as he knocked down huge trees.

"Come out! Come out wherever you are!"

The forest fell silent, and suddenly, Ev'ren felt an intense energy coming from Vinares' direction. Vinares' bones cracked and skin popped, as the energy grew. Then suddenly, Vinares yelled out in anger, as Ev'ren wondered what he was doing.

When Ev'ren spotted Vinares, he looked different. Vinares transformed into some type of beast, with huge horns that emerged from his back, shoulders and knees. He also noticed a metallic breast plate was branded into his chest. Vinares looked hideous and terrifying which frightened Ev'ren.

"Come and feast your eyes on my new form. I have been waiting to show you what I am made of," says Vinares as he continues to search for Ev'ren.

Vinares became impatient and unleashed more poisonous gases from his horns. With all of the commotion going on, Ev'ren could hear people and heavy machinery in the distance. Unable to bare the itching any longer, he leaped out of the bushes.

Vinares spotted Ev'ren, and began to chase him through the woods. He grabbed fallen trees and hurled them.

One of the tree limbs hit Ev'ren on his back. He fell down, but quickly recovered to his feet and sped up, leaving Vinares behind.

When Ev'ren arrived at the edge of the forest, to his surprise, there was an army platoon with tanks pointed in his direction.

Ev'ren ran towards them hoping they were on his side.

"Help, something is after me," he says.

A few seconds later, one of the tanks shot towards him.

"What are you doing? Don't shoot at me! Shoot at him," says Ev'ren pointing at Vinares who finally caught up with him.

Vinares charged towards Ev'ren and threw him into the platoon of men. They watched in disbelief as Ev'ren attacked Vinares. Vinares picked Ev'ren up by his arms, and threw him into a tank, as he laughed hysterically.

The commander told the platoon to attack Vinares. They immediately waged war on Vinares, as the commander ran towards Ev'ren. Vinares was taken by surprise, so he quickly retreated to the forest.

"Are you okay son?" asks the commander with a southern accent.

"I think so Sir," says Ev'ren.

"What was that thing chasing you," asks the commander?

"His name is Vinares Vega, and he is a very dangerous man with superhuman powers."

"You mean the cousin of Francisco Vega, the billionaire," ask the commander?

"Yes sir," says Ev'ren.

"We are on our way to Stone Mountain to restore order; because I received a call that some human like machines were attacking the town. These things are all over the world. My sources also told me they were tied to Vega Powers. Now tell me son, why is Mr. Vega's cousin chasing you?"

"He wants me dead."

Ev'ren thought about Vinares' transformation and his strength. He knew Vinares had the strength of a hundred men, and feared what might happen to the platoon if he returned.

"Commander, please disengage your platoon and get them to safety. Vinares cannot be killed with bullets. He will be back soon, and ready to kill," warns Ev'ren.

"I have two hundred men here, and he will not bring us

down," replies the commander.

"Listen to me Sir. He will slaughter everyone here if you do not retreat commander."

The commander ignored Ev'ren's warning and urged his soldiers to press on into the forest. They proudly marched towards the woods where Vinares retreated.

Ev'ren stayed at the edge of the forest, and watched as they marched towards evil. A few minutes later, a thunderous explosions reined within the forest. He heard gun shots, and men screaming as bones snapped and projectiles flew in mid-air. Vinares laughed hysterically as he launched his projectiles at each soldier, killing all but one. The last soldier stood his ground to the bitter end, until Vinares delivered a devastating blow to the soldier vaporizing him, and illuminating the forest. The commander was in disbelief, of what just happened to his platoon in a matter of minutes.

In the distance, Ev'ren heard everything as shock and anger took hold.

"Why didn't the commander listen to me? I never should have allowed them to enter those woods, I shouldn't of involved them," says Ev'ren.

As effort rose in Ev'ren heart, he emerged from hiding. He ran past the weeping commander, who was filled with regret, and took flight in mid-air landing a swift kick to the side of Vinares' head.

"You monster," he cries!

The kick had no effect on Vinares. Vinares grabbed Ev'ren

347

by the head, and slammed him into a battered tank. Ev'ren was motionless for a few seconds. The commander saw Ev'ren laying there as he attempted to attack Vinares, but he was thrown towards the tank as well and passed out.

"Stop," screams Ev'ren!

"Did you like that boy? Now that I'm in my ultimate form, my fists have the power of a nuclear blast. As soon as I hit that toy soldier with my *Thunder Punch*, he blew up into pieces," boast Vinares!

He charged towards the commander to deliver the final blow, but Ev'ren blocked him. Vinares attempted to deliver a thunder punch to Ev'ren, but he dodged it causing Vinares to hit a military truck. The truck exploded, sending Ev'ren and the commander into the air. Ev'ren landed on the ground very hard, as Vinares slowly walked over to him laughing. He was about to strike Ev'ren, until a surprise attack landed a knife in his back. The commander stabbed Vinares in the back multiple times. Vinares turned around, and saw the battered commander behind him.

"I thought you were blown up with my *Thunder Punch*," he yells!

"Your blast threw me in the bushes," says the commander.

Ev'ren helplessly fell back to the ground, as Vinares took the blade from his back and bent it. He then joked with the commander, and called him a back stabber.

Vinares grabbed the commander and held him with a tight grip. He taunted the commander by telling him he was going to die a slow and painful death. He slowly squeezed the life out of the commander as he cried out in pain. With every squeeze, Ev'ren heard the cracking of the commander's bones. Finally, his cries were reduced to a gasp, as Vinares broke his spine and crushed his ribs. He dropped the commander to the ground like a paper doll, as he continued to gasp for air.

Ev'ren cried, "No," as he stumbled to his feet and walked over to the commander. Vinares watched with amusement, as Ev'ren kneeled beside the commander, and held his hand as he took his last breath. Ev'ren grieved for the commander and the soldiers.

As the sun began to set, Vinares called S.I.C. and told them to send down *the package*. Within minutes, two huge Sunstrokers emerged from the forest and handed Vinares a blue dagger. The Sunstrokers grabbed Ev'ren by the arms, and began to drain him of his energy.

"You are truly pathetic. You were strong enough to send an asteroid into space, yet too weak to fight me. You could have saved all of these men, but you chose to run," says Vinares.

"You didn't have to kill them Vinares."

"I didn't kill them. You did! I don't know where that incredible power went, but it will be all over soon."

"Somehow you will pay for this," says Ev'ren.

"You are in no position to make empty threats. I have afflicted a plague of death all around you. I killed all of these men; I took your parents away from you, and soon I will kill your friends and anyone else you love. They will all burn in hell, and I will enjoy watching them die a slow and painful death." says Vinares.

"You're an animal," shouts Ev'ren!

Vinares grabbed Ev'ren by the head and spat in his face.

"And you're dead. Do you see this blue dagger boy? It held fragments of a very special sword Francisco carries. Once I run this through you, you will die. Do you hear that! You will not be able to recover from this weapon," yells Vinares.

Vinares laughed, as he told the Sunstrokers to kneel Ev'ren down on the ground. He held the dagger over Ev'ren, ready to pierce it through his heart. Just as he brought his hands down, Ev'ren broke free of the Sunstrokers, and attempted to block the dagger with the last bit of energy he had. He and Vinares struggled, until the last ray of sunlight disappeared over the horizon. Ev'ren weakened as Vinares brought the dagger down with great force, and plunged it into Ev'ren's chest. Ev'ren yelped in pain, as an evil smile came upon Vinares' face. Tears filled his eyes, as he saw his own blood leaving his body.

"Die!" shouts Vinares as he watched Ev'ren become motionless.

Vinares and the Sunstrokers walked away from Ev'ren with complete gratification. Suddenly, an explosion of heat and energy expelled from Ev'ren's body and knocked them to the ground. Vinares was startled by the amount of energy expelled from Ev'ren. He thought he killed Ev'ren with the dagger, but he had underestimated his power.

Though Vinares and Ev'ren's power were the products of

nuclear energy, Ev'ren's power was biologically inherited from his father, whereas the Vega's were a result of a chemical accident. They thought the dagger would kill him, but soon Vinares realized the sword that killed his Billy, was not powerful enough to kill Ev'ren.

Ev'ren cried out in anger as his energy intensified. Vinares felt his energy and began to panic.

"What's going on here?"

Suddenly, Ev'ren exploded into blue flames, and vaporized the Sunstrokers. Vinares was thrown into a tree, as Ev'ren levitated off of the ground. Ev'ren's energy increased so rapidly, the sky lit up like it was mid-day. His intense heat cremated the dead soldiers around him, as the earth bubbled like magma beneath him. Ev'ren released several massive flares, which created wild fires around Vinares. He attempted to launch several projectiles at Ev'ren, but they turned to dust before they touched him.

"S.I.C," replies Vinares as he attempts to contact someone.

"What's going on," responds the S.I.C command station?

"I don't know. Something is wrong."

Vinares told S.I.C. to fire the plasma cannon at the precise coordinates where Ev'ren stood. Then, he quickly ran away from Ev'ren as several green rays of light flashed in his direction. The plasma cannon fired upon Ev'ren with pin point accuracy, but Ev'ren deflected the blast back towards S.I.C.

The state of the art super computer and space station raised its shield to protect itself. S.I.C.'s shield cushioned some of the fire, but the damage was extensive. All communication and weaponry were compromised. Vinares tried to reconnect with S.I.C., but there was no response.

"What have you done!" shouts Vinares as he turns toward Ev'ren.

He saw a cloud of smoke and dust surrounding Ev'ren. He could barely see, until the smoke and dust diminished. When he laid eyes upon Ev'ren, he was amazed at Ev'ren's transformation. He was surrounded by dark blue flames, with a small purple stone branded into his chest from the dagger. His eyes once again changed colors, and with an intense look, he descended to the chard ground.

"So you finally came out to play," says Vinares, "and just in the nick of time!"

"You are a monster Vinares," shouts Ev'ren!

"You are no match for my super strength. I can move mountains. All you can do is shoot off fireworks for the kiddies," laughs Vinares.

"What you and Francisco did to my family, friends, and to this entire world are inexcusable. You choose to use your gift for evil. I will use my gift to bring you down and protect the innocent."

Vinares charged at Ev'ren like a raging bull. Ev'ren extended his hands and suspended Vinares into mid-air, holding him in a gravitational lock. Surprised at Ev'ren's power, Vinares became angry and demanded Ev'ren to release him.

"Release me at once," shouts Vinares!

"As I said before, no more people will be hurt by you. I have a special place in mind to settle this score, without any more lives being lost," says Ev'ren.

Vinares continued to argue with Ev'ren, as he frantically twisted and turned to undermine Ev'ren's grip.

"Stop trying to break my hold. Or you will get wet," shouts Ev'ren!

"What do you mean, I will get wet?" replies Vinares.

Ev'ren smiled at Vinares and leveraged him over his head. Then, he took off into the sky with Vinares in his gravity hold. Vinares wasn't sure of what was happening, but he was scared of the outcome. Suddenly, Ev'ren took off into hyper-speed with Vinares, as they arrived a few minutes later on a deserted island in the South Pacific.

When they reached the deserted island, Ev'ren descended upon the beautiful pristine beach.

"Wow, this is more beautiful than I read in the books," he thought to himself.

The warm sun shined brightly, as the emerald and blue ocean rushed against the coast. In the distance, a lush rain forest ascended up a chain of green mountains.

"Do you feel that Vinares," says Ev'ren as he took a deep breath.

"Go to hell boy," yells Vinares!

Ev'ren looked at Vinares and nodded. He released his gravitational hold on Vinares, as he landed head first into the soft white sand.

Enraged and threatened, Vinares viciously leaped into the air to attack Ev'ren. Ev'ren laughed at him as he dodged each punch.

Finally Vinares thought about what Vaul taught him. *"Use more Ki,"* he thought to himself. He extended his arms and embraced the warmth of the sun. Suddenly, he began to spin his arms round and round in circled vigorously until it created two massive firey twisters. Ev'ren looked at Vinares' attack with astonishment as the twisters uprooted anything in it's path and burnt everything else.

Vinares laughed at his accomplishment calling it his *Firey Funnel Attack*, and sent them both in Ev'ren's direction.

Ev'ren had to do something quick, so he used his gravitational hold to slow them down. Then, he used his Red Giant attack causing a massive explosion of heat and fire on the island. Smoke and dust was everywhere, but when it settled, the twisters were gone.

Vinares yelled in frustration of Ev'ren's efforts and clapped his huge hands together creating a thunderous blast. Like a missile strike, the blast caused the island to shake. More smoke and sand went into the air, and created a dense fog that covered the island.

Vinares though the blasted affected Ev'ren, but he stood firm and unfazed.

Ev'ren stared defiantly at Vinares with the look of superiority on his face. Vinares became enraged and continued his attacks.

"You're like a roach. Every time I stomp on you, you keep moving. Stay down, and die dammit!" yells Vinares as he attacked Ev'ren.

Ev'ren stood in one spot, and dodged Vinares punches and kicks. As Vinares continued his attacks, Ev'ren became more and more confident.

"With all that strength you're fairly weak. Is this the best you can do?" taunts Ev'ren.

"Shut up," shouts Vinares as he continues to lose his cool!

Ev'ren clutched his fist and charged at Vinares like an unstoppable wrecking ball. He landed his fist in Vinares' face and knocked him to the ground. Vinares stumbled to his feet only to be bolded over again with a strike to his chest. Vinares cradled his chest and notice a dent in his breast plate. Enraged, Vinares swung wildly at Ev'ren without touching him. Ev'ren counterattacked with hyper speed punches and kicks which completely overwhelmed Vinares. He fell to one knee, clutching his chest as the dent widen. Vinares painful grunted, as he looked at his chest and began to laugh.

"What is so funny Vinares? It looks like your chest is starting to cave in."

"Quite the contrary boy, you can hit me as much as you want, but I will only heal in this environment," replies Vinares.

"How is that possible," ask Ev'ren?

"I'll tell you what, if you can defeat me in battle, which you won't, I will tell you everything you need to know about your powers," bargains Vinares.

"I don't care about your information or tall tales. All I care about is justice, and you are going to pay for your crimes," says Ev'ren.

"If you say so child. While we have been talking, my powers have been growing. I am now prepared to launch my ultimate attack against you."

Ev'ren was confused about Vinares' comment. When Vinares stood up, his body began to transform again. Black veins showed through his skin. His horns and eyes were blood red.

"You can change a million times old man, but I will crush you like the monster you are," says Ev'ren!

Vinares formed a black projectile about the size of a tank shell. He threw it high into the white clouds.

"*Diablo Tears*," shouts Vinares!

A thunderous explosion rattled the sky, and created small hair like follicles that drizzled like tear drops. Ev'ren did his best to dodge them, but they were all aimed in his direction. They attacked him ferociously, as he attempted to brush them off. Suddenly, they burst into blue flames all over him.

Ev'ren was on fire while Vinares prepared for another attack. He pulled each of his horns out of his body, and fused them together into a red javelin. Vinares smiled, as he prepared for his final attack.

"Now strike," yells Vinares!

Vinares moved back and threw the spear at Ev'ren. As it passed through the shower of projectiles, Ev'ren made a quick dash out of its way. The javelin redirected itself, like a heat seeking missile and came after Ev'ren again. Each direction Ev'ren went, the javelin followed him.

Unable to out run the javelin any longer Ev'ren took to the sky, and so did the javelin. It maneuvered and came at Ev'ren from above. On contact with Ev'ren, it exploded causing Ev'ren to let out a painful cry.

Vinares cheered in victory, as he attempted to contact S.I.C again.

"Well boy, now that you are finally dead, this ends your family legacy."

Vinares laughed profusely, until his laughter was changed to a painful cry, when a constricting force took over his body.

As the smoke from the explosion cleared, Ev'ren descended to the ground with clutched fists. He stood before Vinares, with a wave of energy that radiated from him. He used his gravity attack to immobilize Vinares, and apply enormous pressure to his body.

Ev'ren slowly ripped the metal from Vinares, causing him to scream out in pain. Blood poured from Vinares' like black soot, as Ev'ren twisted his fist in the air, like he was controlling a puppet. With every move Vinares made, Ev'ren's grip tightened. The breast plate on Vinares' chest began to crack, as he cried out for Ev'ren to stop torturing him.

Ev'ren looked at him with little to no remorse, and tore off

357

his breast plate. Vinares made a horrific sound as a part of his chest was ripped off.

"The end of a legacy you said," says Ev'ren, "you are right about that, but it will not be mine, it will be yours."

Ev'ren loosened his grip and struck Vinares in the face with several jabs, and a right hook to the jaw extracting a tooth. Vinares screamed, as Ev'ren kicked him high into the air.

His right hand turned a flaming red, as Vinares' mingled body was slammed to the ground over and over again.

"This is what happens to those who mess with my family and friends," he says as he stretches his arms out like a bird.

"*Rise of the Crimson Phoenix!*" shouts Ev'ren as he hits Vinares with a blazing upper cut.

Vinares erupted into flames and was sent into the air.

"*Red Giant!*" he shouts, releasing a huge fireball towards Vinares.

The energy thrusted Vinares into the air, as the pressure held him there. He could see and feel the huge fireball coming his way, but was unable to escape.

With all of his strength, Vinares tried to avoid Ev'ren's attack, but it was hopeless. At the last minute, Ev'ren guided his attack away from Vinares, and spared his life.

Vinares was in pain from the intense attacks of Ev'ren. His body was burned, as he crashed into the earth. Ev'ren rapidly descended over Vinares and placed his right knee into his stomach. Blood left his mouth, as he screamed in agony.

Vinares breathing was deep and rapid. He looked up at Ev'ren and smiled. Ev'ren continued kneeing Vinares in the stomach asking him "why" over and over again. Ev'ren continued to torture him until he was unrecognizable.

Then suddenly, his mouth moved as he uttered a word.

"Forced," he says.

Ev'ren stopped for a moment and asked him to repeat himself.

"I was forced," he says.

"Are you telling me you were forced to kill my family, after you just bragged about it," says Ev'ren.

"My pride and ego took a tremendous blow today, but my heart is now at ease," says Vinares as he grunts in pain.

"I know you are furious, and you have every right to be," says Vinares.

"You have no idea. I lost my parents, because of a chain of events you and your cousin created. This battle would have never occurred, but you took everyone's fate into your hands and destroyed it," shouts Ev'ren!

"Francisco isn't a bad person, he is misunderstood," says Vinares as his eyes shift from left to right.

"Did a misunderstanding murder my family in cold blood for no reason, and set out to kill me? You call that a misunderstanding," cries Ev'ren as he struggles to hold back his tears!

"Believe me when I say, I tried to convince him not to put a hit out on you and your family, but he forcefully threatened me," pleads Vinares.

"Everyone has a choice, and I would rather die, then to live as someone's lackey," says Ev'ren.

"Why didn't you finish me a few minutes ago with your energy blast?"

"I'm not a killer."

"You couldn't kill me if you tried," says Vinares with a smirk on his face.

"Don't tempt me Vinares."

"You don't understand kid. We are immortal."

"Immortal? That's a load of bull crap."

"It's true. When the accident occurred sixteen years ago, your father, Francisco, and I were exposed to some harmful chemicals. We should have died in that explosion, but we were blessed with these incredible powers and the ability to regenerate. Your father possessed super speed and invisibility. I have super strength and needle-like projectiles that can penetrate anything. Francisco has speed, strength and a multitude of other skills. But what really makes us immortal, is our ability to regenerate and heal. More impressively, in our ultimate form, no weapon known to man can hurt or kill us. We don't need air to breathe, and poisonous gases have no effect on us."

"This is impossible."

"Our only true weakness is extreme cold, darkness and the weapon I used against you earlier, which was plain old tin. Tin can drain us of our power. If penetrated by it, we can die. That is why Francisco destroyed ninety percent of the world's supply of tin."

"You're lying."

"It's the truth, but there is something else you need to know about Francisco. He was once a military soldier named Vaul. He is the world's greatest fighter, and he trained in the House of Honzo."

Ev'ren was surprised about Francisco's façade. He called him an eco-terrorist and a traitor.

"Don't take the information I am giving you for granted boy. Francisco is a master. His most lethal weapon is called the Sword of the Universe. It is a mystical sword that can unleash huge amounts of dark energy. If you are pierced by it in the heart, it will drain you of your energy and life for good."

"Doesn't that sword belongs to the Honzo family," ask Ev'ren?

"Yes. The metal came from a meteor in space. It has traces of tin embedded in it also. It is important you do not hesitate when you fight with Francisco. If you are going to take him out, do it," says Vinares as he runs out of breath.

"I am not a killer," replies Ev'ren.

"Then you are already dead. He will kill you and think nothing of it."

"I am not a killer," repeats Ev'ren, "hear me when I say that Vinares. I am not a killer!"

"Don't be foolish child. You will have to kill at some point, and it may even be me."

Vinares continued to share information about Francisco. He told Ev'ren that Willamina and her brother finally escaped Francisco's control, and were in hiding. He said it would only be a matter of time before Francisco found them again, and when he did, she would not survive.

Just as he was about to speak, a sword came out of nowhere and pierced Vinares in his heart. His eyes became widen with shock and fear, as he looked towards the sky.

"Vinares," cries Ev'ren!

"I am truly sorry for what I did to you and your family. Avenge your family by defeating mine," says Vinares as he took his last breath, and dies with his eyes towards the sky.

Ev'ren knew someone was behind him. He looked high into the overcast sky, and saw a tall individual dress in a black business suit with a red tie. He had on a red and black demonic mask that resembled the one Ev'ren saw before, but with different colors. The sky behind him was dark and ominous, as thunder echoed and the lightning raced behind him.

"It's him. He killed his own flesh and blood," says Ev'ren to himself, as he stands up and stares upon Francisco Vega.

Chapter 20

Ev'ren vs. Francisco: "The challenge of the sun"

Francisco descended to the ground stopping about fifty feet from Ev'ren. He took off his mask, and held an intense look on his face as he pointed at his cousin. His eyes were red and filled with hate.

"Behold boy, this will be your fate as well," he says.

"How could you murder your own cousin in cold blood," asks Ev'ren?

"Treachery is something I will not tolerate from anyone, not even my own flesh and blood," says Francisco.

"Vinares deserved to be punished, but he didn't deserve to die. Does life have any meaning to you?"

"Of course it does. Life has plenty of value to me boy."

"Then why did you murder my family," says Ev'ren?

"They didn't have any value to me."

"You are a bully and a monster!"

"Flattery will get you nowhere with me," says Francisco laughing.

"I wasn't giving you a complement!"

"Do you realize I can kill you right where you stand?"

"I would like to see you try!"

"It's still up for debate. Listen to me Ev'ren. I am going to say this slowly, so you can understand what I value. Your power and rage is what makes you who you are. There is something special about it that I can use. You and I are the last of our race, so join me as I rule this world as its king and you as its prince. What do you say?"

"I have a question for you Francisco? Are you high or something? This is not the fifteenth century when kings ruled the world and beheaded people? Also, the last time I checked, I was human. You must be off your meds pal."

"I don't have time for your petty insults. Join me in my quest to conquer the world or die!"

"You think I fell off the potato truck or something? I will never join you, and allow you to manipulate me like you have done to so many others. You lied to the world, by making them believe you cared about saving the environment and promoting world peace! You murdered my family and countless innocent people. You're truly dishonorable! I would rather burn in hell first! You are lower than scum!"

"Enough you little brat, no one talks to me like that and lives," shouts Francisco!

"You're right. I've had enough of your BS!"

"Do you wish to test me little boy?"

"I'm here to defeat you and restore justice," says Ev'ren.

He pointed at Francisco and stared as his eyes glowed.

"You have brought great shame to the House of Honzo and

364

that is why I must defeat you."

"So you are a member of the House Honzo," replies Francisco.

"And if I was…what's it to you?"

"I challenge you boy…in human form."

Ev'ren paused for a brief second and thought about Francisco's offer. He knew it could be a trick, but he felt like Francisco's ego might be clouding his judgment.

"Human form," he replies.

"Yes," says Francisco, "fight me man to man using our natural capabilities to win."

"I have nothing to prove to you. Besides, you were excommunicated, and that sword you have belongs to Dr. Henzu. He is the last of the Honzo clan."

"Dr. Henzu? He is nothing! Just because he is a part of their bloodline, doesn't mean he has earned anything. That sword is a part of me now, and there is nothing you can do about it, but if you are scared to fight me, I can use it to finish you off right now."

"I will fight you, but on one condition," says Ev'ren.

"Name it!"

"Once I defeat you, you will turn yourself into the law for the murders you orchestrated, and the other laundry list of crimes you have committed."

Francisco smirked at Ev'ren's naivety, but he agreed to

Ev'ren's terms, and gave him his terms if Ev'ren lost.

"When you lose son, and believe me you will, you must throw yourself upon my sword," says Francisco.

Ev'ren clinched his fist in anger, and agreed.

"Prepare yourself maggot, your salvation will be a slow and painful death. That I promise you, La muerte le aguarda Nino…death awaits you boy," shouts Francisco!

Francisco's hair changed from white to its natural black and silver color. He was now in his human form, and charged at Ev'ren! Ev'ren changed back to human form as well, and braced for Francisco's onslaught.

Francisco immediately attacked Ev'ren with a barrage of kicks and punches. He knocked Ev'ren to the ground, and Ev'ren quickly recovered to his feet. Francisco threw continuous kicks and punches knocking Ev'ren down each time. Francisco kicked Ev'ren on the side of his head, causing him to cry out in pain.

Francisco laughed as he taunted Ev'ren, and all the while, kicking him on the ground. Ev'ren rolled over in pain as Francisco looked at his sword turning black!

"You are no match for me boy! Human form or advance form you are still no match for me."

"This fight isn't over yet," says Ev'ren as he grunts.

"I thought Dr. Henzu taught you something, but look at you all rolled over from a little kick and a bloody nose. Do you want your mommy now," taunts Francisco, "then die and maybe you will get to see her."

Ev'ren smiled as Francisco continued the onslaught. He threw an energy wave at Ev'ren, then, Ev'ren quickly counterattacked with his own energy wave. Ev'ren slowly studied Francisco's moves, and began to react quicker to his attacks. Before long, Ev'ren was blocking some of Francisco's attacks which irritated him.

"You want to know what I learned," asks Ev'ren?

Francisco looked at him confused.

"Why do I care," he says with a snarl.

"He taught me patience, self-defense, and to never quit," says Ev'ren as he quickly leaps toward Francisco striking him twice in his face.

Francisco angrily retaliated with an open hand thrust to the chest and chin, which lifted Ev'ren off of his feet and knocked him to the ground.

"I had enough of this," yells Francisco.

He pointed in the direction of the setting sun and looked at Ev'ren.

"No one, and I mean no one strikes me in the face and lives," he shouts!

"Ignite!" yells Francisco as he leaped high into the air.

The winds picked up and the ocean behind him became violent. A supersonic wave of kinetic energy pulsed in every direction accompanied by blue, green and red lighting. Ev'ren knew something was horribly wrong, because he could feel Francisco's rising energy.

Ev'ren felt the evil power of Francisco getting stronger. As Francisco transformed, Ev'ren quickly ignited into flames and did the same.

"Fight fire with fire you said...you have no honor," says Ev'ren!

"Never make a deal without a signed contract boy."

Ev'ren's transformation was much easier this time, and more controlled. He was covered in flames as his eyes glowed.

Francisco had white hair, with dark empty eyes and scaly white skin that resembled armor. The transparency of his body made him resemble a phantom.

"You're pathetic Francisco. Two little punches from me and you lose control? You're not use to being hit. Remember I am just a pesky little boy?"

Ev'ren's fury increased as he ran towards Francisco to attack him. Francisco braced himself, as they clashed into each other. With each attack, a thunderous sound filled the desolate island. Lightning illuminated across the evening sky with colors of white and red. Francisco gained the upper hand by using various techniques, which threw Ev'ren off balance and kept him on the defense.

As the night progressed, they battled back and forth until the early morning.

Francisco was impressed with Ev'ren's speed and endurance.

"You are strong and fast, but it will take more to defeat me," he says.

"You're right," says Ev'ren as he disappears into thin air.

"Invisibility, I'm impressed. Your father had that ability," replies Francisco as he tries to locate Ev'ren like he was looking for a fly.

Without warning, Ev'ren appeared underneath Francisco. With his right hand, he surged at Francisco with a fiery uppercut he called *"Rise of the Crimson Phoenix"*. Francisco erupted into flames on contact, which sent him spinning high into the sky. He gasped, as he spun out of control.

"This is not invisibility," says Ev'ren, "this is hyper-speed."

Francisco was stunned and angered by Ev'ren's power. He gained control of his body and extinguished the flames.

"How dare you strike me," he shouts!

Francisco clasped his hands together, and when he opened it, a high burst of ultra-violet radiation appeared. Ev'ren was blinded momentarily, as Francisco used the opportunity to strike him with an elbow to the head. The hit stunned Ev'ren, and he began freefall from the sky.

Francisco grabbed him, and drove him into the soft beach sand head first. While Ev'ren's head was stuck in the sand, Francisco quickly created a black lightning sphere struck him with it. Ev'ren was amazed, when the dark sphere dissolved into his body without doing any harm.

"Now the conditions are perfect for my attack! This is the end for you boy! Now witness my greatest technique," he

369

shouts!

Francisco ascended higher and higher into the stormy sky laughing at his master piece.

Ev'ren braced himself, not knowing what to expect.

Francisco held out his hands, and summoned a sphere of lightning the size of a large beach ball.

While he preoccupied Ev'ren's attention, his lightning sphere gained more energy.

As static electricity engulfed Francisco, he gazed upon Ev'ren and saw the fear in his eyes.

"*Lightning Blast*!" he yells with a voice that thundered from the clouds.

The sphere accelerated towards Ev'ren in hyper sonic speed. Ev'ren could hear the crackle of lightning as it neared him. He quickly recovered to his feet, and miraculously caught the sphere with his gravitational powers. Ev'ren desperately tried to overpower the sphere, but suddenly lightning emerged from below and struck him.

He immediately fell to the ground and lost control of the lightning sphere. When it struck him, he began to convulse as his eyes rolled into the back of his head. He cried out in pain, because he could hear his rapidly beating heart.

Francisco's *Lightning Blast* was so powerful, it stretched for miles, and killed anything left on the island.

As the sand, smoke and fire started to dissipate, Francisco began his slow descent to the ground. He began to laugh.

"Bang is it over! All that power you possessed, what happened boy? What happened to you?"

Ev'ren laid on the ground motionless as Francisco continued to speak. He was back to his human form.

"I will tell you what happened. As you know, when I first arrived to this island, you probably noticed lightning above my head. I released a charge of my energy into the clouds, and allowed it to build in strength while we fought. When it was time, I hit you with a lightning sphere from above. Though you tried to stop it, that dark sphere inside of you and the sphere from above were destined to become one, and that sealed your fate."

Francisco looked at Ev'ren taunting him, as he remained on the ground unconscious.

"Vinares survived my attack because of his size, but it took him weeks to recover mentally. That hole in his chest never fully healed. He used that garbage can of a breast plate to protect his chest so he wouldn't be killed. However, unlike Vinares, you won't have time to recover. I am going to use my sword to finish you off."

Francisco drew his sword and held it over Ev'ren when suddenly, Ev'ren opened his eyes. He took a deep breath and jumped effortlessly to his feet while transforming.

"*Red Giant*," shouts Ev'ren!

Ev'ren's attack created a sonic blast of heat towards Francisco. Francisco desperately tried to flee, but was unable to escape the two story wide blast. He screamed out in pain as Ev'ren's attack burned his entire body, and knock

371

the sword out of his hands.

Francisco fell to a small island not too far from the one he and Ev'ren fought on. His entire body ached from the pain of Ev'ren's attack.

"This isn't over," he says furiously to himself.

He took a few minutes to rejuvenate himself, and then stormed back to what was left of the tiny island. He wondered, how Ev'ren could not only survive his lightning blast attack, but mount a massive counter attack. That gravity field of his must of protected him somehow.

"What a freak!" utters Francisco.

When he landed, he began searching for the one thing that could put an end to his battle with Ev'ren. He searched for the sword, but it was not on the island anymore. Francisco flew around the circumference of the island in hopes of find the sword.

He finally spotted the sword glimmering on the ocean's shallow floor, so he dove in to reclaim it. When he held the sword in his hands, he tipped the blade with his long black nails and smiled.

"Ev'ren!" shouts Francisco as he looked around desperately for him.

Francisco saw a blue hue of light in the distance, and flew off in that direction to find Ev'ren. When he saw Ev'ren, he quietly hid to spy on him. He saw blue flames emerging from Ev'ren's hands, as he looked in amazement. Though he appeared unaware, he felt Francisco's energy and knew he was nearby. When Francisco realized he was spotted, he quickly descended upon Ev'ren. An ultraviolet light emerged from Francisco, and blinded Ev'ren momentarily. This gave him enough time to draw his sword. Just as Francisco brought down the sword's tip, Ev'ren caught a glimpse of it, and caught the sword with both of his hands.

"Die!" shouts Francisco as he held the blade inches from Ev'ren's heart.

Francisco pressed down hard, as the blade inched a little closer to Ev'ren's chest. He laughed as Ev'ren struggled with the sword.

"I have greatly underestimated you boy. You are much stronger than I thought."

Ev'ren struggled with Francisco as he thought about ways to defeat him. He decided to use his gravitational hold to keep Francisco still. His eyes became yellow as Francisco struggled to break free. When he realized what Ev'ren was about to do to the sword, he demanded Ev'ren to stop.

"The sword boy, look at what you are doing," shouts Francisco!

Ev'ren continued to hold Francisco in place, as he redirected the sword towards him.

"How does it feel Francisco to know you are about to die," says Ev'ren.

Francisco's eyes widened with fear and anger. He could not escape Ev'ren's attack, and was unable to move.

"No Ev'ren, don't kill me," he shouts!

"How many people died by your hands with this sword. Did they beg and plead to you, as you mercilessly ended their lives?"

Francisco fell silent.

"Answer me," demands Ev'ren!

"Yes they begged, and I did it all for money and power. I would do it all over again if I had to," he says.

"Money and power can't help you when you're dead."

"If you kill me boy, you will have to live with it for the rest of your life. Can your conscience handle that," asks Francisco?

"Don't try using reverse psychology with me. I took that class last year."

"Fine then, I will see you in hell," shouts Francisco!

Francisco desperately struggled to break free of Ev'ren, as he hesitated about killing him. He struggled with the thought of killing someone, even if it was Francisco.

Francisco laughed at him, because he knew he planted doubt in Ev'ren's head.

"You don't have the balls to kill me boy, and that makes you weak."

"No it doesn't. It makes me human," replies Ev'ren.

Ev'ren stared at the sword as a glow began to surround it.

"A dark power such as this should not be controlled by

374

anyone," says Ev'ren.

"What are doing?" says Francisco with a puzzled look.

Ev'ren grabbed the blade of the sword and with all of his might, and broke it in half.

A bright white light emerged from the broken blade, as it raced into the heavens and then into Ev'ren.

"No," shouts Francisco!

The force of the energy caused Ev'ren to released Francisco, and stunned them both momentarily. Francisco was outraged, as he stormed towards Ev'ren and struck him across the face, knocking him to the ground. Francisco picked up the broken blade, and stabbed Ev'ren in his heart.

The blade shattered on impact.

"The sword had a lot had of dark energy, so I made a judgment call and destroyed it. It's over Francisco. You lost," says Ev'ren.

Francisco told Ev'ren it was not over, as he ran behind him and began to choke him.

"Stop," says Ev'ren gasping for air.

"Stop squirming," says Francisco, "I still have one more ace up my sleeve."

"What you are doing," ask Ev'ren?

A blue light consumed both of them as Francisco laughed. Then suddenly, they both disappeared.

Chapter 21
Farewell

Somewhere close to the coast of Antarctica, Ev'ren and Francisco reappeared. The conditions were brutal with temperatures of negative fifty degrees, and gale force winds. Fatigue began to conquer Francisco and Ev'ren.

"How and why did you bring us here," shouts Ev'ren!

"You possess the power of gravity, which is most impressive, but I possess the power of transporting. As long I'm in contact with an object, I along with that object can transport anywhere in the world."

"Why did you bring us out here? It is freezing," exclaims Ev'ren!

"You destroyed the sword; therefore, I can't kill you. So, I will do the next best thing, and send you into an induced deep freeze coma you will never wake up from," says Francisco laughing.

"We are immortal," says Ev'ren thinking Francisco's plan will not work.

"Immortal? We aren't immortal you stupid boy. Where did you get that idea from," he asks?

"Vinares," says Ev'ren shivering.

"You're as fool as he was," laughs Francisco!

"Then how can we die? Now that the sword is destroyed, what can kill us?"

"How gullible can you be? Look kid, I am a God. I could care less how long you live or die. All I know is that, it's time for you to take a long nap," says Francisco.

"You really are delusional."

Francisco turned away and began to leave Ev'ren in the cold frozen wilderness. Ev'ren grabbed him forcefully.

"Where are you going," he demands?

"Don't you ever touch me you filthy ingrate."

Francisco knocked Ev'ren to the ground.

Francisco knew intense cold temperatures made them weak, so he walked away, knowing Ev'ren was no longer a threat.

"Wait! Come back," yells Ev'ren!

Francisco stopped with his back still turned to Ev'ren.

"Give it a rest you weak and pathetic child. Go to sleep. I have won."

As Francisco continued to walk away, Ev'ren thought about the cold and how it affected him at the cave. He was angry Francisco brought them there. Ev'ren decided to make one last attempt on Francisco, so he charged at him landing a kick in the middle of Francisco's back. The two of them engaged in battle once again.

Both of them reverted to their superhuman form, however, with every attack, they became weaker. Francisco quickly gained the upper hand, and kicked Ev'ren to the ground, driving a thunderous elbow into his ribs. Ev'ren gasped for air after the wind was knocked out of him. As he laid there on the frozen field struggling to get up, the ground beneath him rumbled, and started to crack.

Francisco took a few steps back and laughed at Ev'ren's misfortune, as he struggled to stand on the slippery ice.

"My. My. My. Step on a crack and break your mother's back as they say in America."

Francisco laughed uncontrollably, as the crack beneath Ev'ren widen to expose a deep crevasse. Ev'ren shouted for Francisco to help him, as he slid further into the rift. While he held on, he looked down, saw an icy river below and began to panic.

Ev'ren tried to claw his way out, but the more he tried the further he slid. He continued to call out for Francisco to help him, but Francisco laughed and walked away.

"Please, help me," replies Ev'ren.

"Fall brat, fall to your dark icy hell where you will be frozen for eternity!"

Ev'ren was losing his grip on the ice. Francisco decided to walk back over towards him, and extended his hand. When Ev'ren reached out his hand to Francisco, he gave him a high five, which caused Ev'ren to fall into the icy river. Francisco watched in amusement as Ev'ren fought to stay afloat.

The current of the river was swift with huge chunks of ice. The icy water felt like a thousand needles piercing him all at once. Ev'ren continued to scream for Francisco's assistance, but he did not come to his aide.

Slowly, Ev'ren's yell for help became a faint whisper as he continued to lose his power. Francisco stared at him, as he was carried under the current.

"Have a nice trip," he says.

Underneath the river, Ev'ren drifted with the current. He was weak and nearly frozen as the river carried him crashing into an icy sea. Ev'ren's face was pale and blue, as he grabbed on to a slab of ice. In the distance, he saw a huge glacier, and thought how incredibly blue and beautiful it was. The glacier was the size of a small island. Suddenly, out of nowhere, Ev'ren felt something pulling him. He was caught in an icy whirlpool.

Ev'ren was so weak, he could not fight the current luring him closer every second. He started to reflect back on his life, family and friends. As he slipped out of consciousness, the word "PROTECT" echoed in his mind. Then, finally he mercilessly drifted into the whirlpool.

Meanwhile, Francisco walked through the icy wasteland, laughing and celebrating his victory as the supreme ruler of the world. He had a fortress and S.I.C. hideout nearby, that he used as a military base.

As he continued to walk, he thought about his next course of action, which included executing Mrs. Anderson and all of Ev'ren's friends, especially Willamina.

He felt the ground tremble a little and decided to pick up some speed on his journey to his hide out. When he arrived at his fortress, he took off his suit and changed into some warm clothes.

A few hours had elapsed. Francisco sat in the warmth of his fortress sipping on aged whiskey by the fire place, when the ground began to tremble again. He knew that area of the world was affected by global warming, which caused large amounts of ice to fall into the ocean and, occasionally create small tremors. But with each minute, the shaking intensified, until Francisco decided to walk outside to see what was going on.

As he squinted, he saw a huge iceberg in the distance. Slowly it progressed toward him, while he watched in curiosity. A gust of wind swept across the land where Francisco stood. He slowly moved to avoid potential cracks in the ice. There was an intense energy coming from the iceberg, as he shook his head in denial.

"It can't be," says Francisco.

The ground shook fiercely as huge cracks appeared. The river beneath the ground began to rise rapidly, and forced icy water to the surface. Water rushed towards him, as he took flight to avoid it. While in the air, he marveled at what he saw below.

Covered in ice from head to toe was Ev'ren, who transformed again. His eyes were grey and his skin was the color of ice blue with platinum curly hair. His body had jagged icicles attached to the back of his arms and legs.

Francisco was horrified at what he saw. He thought Ev'ren would be frozen for eternity, but never did he think Ev'ren would have absorbed the powers of the Antarctic.

"Impossible," he yells as Ev'ren looked at him without saying a word.

The anger and bitterness Ev'ren had for Francisco was beyond redemption.

Francisco fired an energy ball at Ev'ren, but it vanished before it touched him. Ev'ren threw the iceberg at Francisco, but he dodged it. He used his hyper speed to get behind Francisco, and threw him to the ground cracking the ice. Francisco yelled in pain as Ev'ren struck him in the face knocking a tooth out.

"No," he shouts, "you cannot do this to me!"

Ev'ren quickly formed an ice ball that started to glow.

"*Arctic Blast*," yells Ev'ren as he launched the frozen energy ball towards Francisco.

Unable to escape it, Francisco was struck. His body began to freeze from the neck down.

Ev'ren used his powers of gravity to push Francisco towards the iceberg he originally carried.

"How did you escape? How did you transform into this," asks Francisco?

"I don't know. All I know, is after all you have put me and my family through, my time wasn't up."

"Then finish me fool!"

"I am not going to kill you; however, I want you to stay here frozen and awake. You need to reflect on all of the evil things you have done to so many, and I pray you change into a better person. I have finally beaten you," says Ev'ren

"This isn't over Ev'ren Smalls. When I am free, I will come

for you and unleash a hell unlike anything this world has ever seen."

Ev'ren knew Francisco's threat could happen, but he ignored his warning and smiled.

He blew cold frigid air from his lips, and created a thick layer of ice over Francisco's face. He was silent, but his eyes were frozen open.

Ev'ren moved the iceberg to a remote part of the area so, it would blend in with the rest the surroundings.

Then, he remembered that Francisco mentioned having a S.I.C. base in the area. He used his infrared vision to pick up any signs of heat that was around. He saw a large heat source a few miles away, so he took off in that direction.

When he arrived at the base of a mountain, not far from where he first spotted Francisco. To his surprise, there was a cave with military officials inside from all over the world. He also saw a militia of Sunstrokers that were not activated yet.

Ev'ren decided to attack the base head on with multiple energy balls. The S.I.C. military officials ran out of the cave in a panic, as he told them to leave. Then, he formed a *"Red Giant"* to sink the base, and all things under it, into the icy sea.

Ev'ren took a deep breath of relief. He thought about Francisco's threat once more, but knew if he escaped, he would be ready for him. Then he thought about his family and knew they were probably worried about him.

He began to search for his way home. When he saw a break

in the clouds, he found his compass, the North Star, and flew towards Stone Mountain, Georgia.

As he left the Antarctic, he saw the sun in the distance and extended his fingers to become engulfed in flames. The icy frame he had, begun to melt away as he took off into hyper speed.

Before long, he was home. He quietly landed in his back yard behind a tree, and hid so he could transform back to normal.

Once again he was a teenage boy hiding behind a tree in the nude.

Ev'ren looked around to see what he could use to cover up with. He saw an old newspaper, so he used it to wrap around his lower body parts. He ran up to the front porch, and looked for the house key Mrs. Anderson kept underneath a flower pot. Just as he was about to open the door, it opened for him. Mrs. Anderson greeted him happily as he turned a shade of red from embarrassment. She looked like her usual self, but had a cane in her hand to keep her balanced. Megan and Tye stood behind her at the door, with their mouths wide open.

"Heaven sakes boy, where have you been and where is your clothing," yells Mrs. Anderson!

She took her scarf off and placed it around Ev'ren, then gave him another big hug. Megan ran up to him as well to hug him, but Mrs. Anderson told her it would be inappropriate. She smiled and blushed at him.

"I didn't know y'all were going to be home," replies Ev'ren.

"They released me out of the hospital after the asteroid scare. Your friend Willamina took all of us somewhere safe. We were worried sick about you, but Willamina assured us you would return," exclaims Mrs. Anderson!

"Tye, please get Ev'ren some clothes," says Mrs. Anderson.

A few seconds later Tye ran to the porch and tossed Ev'ren a pair of jeans and a t-shirt.

"Thanks Tye," says Ev'ren.

"Man where have you been," asks Tye?

"I don't remember. All I remember is waking up in the field of my aunt and uncles old farm. I walked home, and that was it," says Ev'ren.

"We were all worried about you. We thought you were killed in all of the chaos that happened around here."

Tye placed his arms around Ev'ren, as they walked towards the house.

"Hold it boys," says Megan walking up to Ev'ren and jabbing him in his stomach, "you idiot, we were worried sick about you! And showing up here naked, what do you expect us to think?"

"I lost my cell phone, and I can explain why I was naked," replies Ev'ren.

"Explain," says Megan with her arms folded!

"Oh, okay! I know I messed up, but what's important right now is that everyone is safe, and I am hungry," says Ev'ren.

"Hungry," shouts Megan!

"Yeah isn't it time to eat," asks Ev'ren?

Ev'ren, Megan and Tye walked into the house. Mrs. Anderson was still disturbed about Ev'ren being missing for so long. She began to cry, as she explained to him she no longer had cancer. The doctor couldn't explain why her cancer suddenly disappeared, but it was nothing short of a miracle.

Ev'ren hugged his aunt, and thanked God for saving her.

They all sat down at the dinner table, and ate in celebration of Mrs. Anderson and Ev'ren being home.

Several days later, Ev'ren had a surprise visit from Dr. Henzu. He told him about his battle with Francisco and Vinares. He also told him about the sword. Dr. Henzu felt relieved, and was pleased with Ev'ren's new abilities. They talked about Ev'ren's icy transformation, and how he showed up at home naked.

"How is Willamina and her brother," ask Ev'ren?

"They are safe, but in hiding. She was worried about you as well, when you suddenly disappeared," says Dr. Henzu.

"Why are they still hiding, when I just placed Francisco on ice," says Ev'ren.

"She is still at war with a small criminal organization. She found out Francisco had put a hit out on her, and her brother. She has a score to settle with them, so until then, she is incognito."

"I should go help her," replies Ev'ren.

"Trust me Ev'ren, she will be fine. These are personal demons she has to handle. If she needs our help, she will call."

Ev'ren and Dr. Henzu talked about his future, and the dangers that still exist in the world. They both knew Ev'ren's powers could not stay hidden for long, and he would have to protect his family at all cost.

Mrs. Anderson called for them to come in, and offered Dr. Henzu dessert and coffee. She laughed and flirted with Dr. Henzu, as he obliged and did the same. Dr. Henzu stopped by to offer Ev'ren, an opportunity to study physics abroad.

"Wow, where," says Mrs. Anderson?

"In Japan," answers Dr. Henzu.

"Is this what you want Ev'ren? You will be so far away from home."

"This is a great opportunity Auntie, and besides I can visit you guys anytime," says Ev'ren optimistically.

"Anytime Ev'ren? Japan is on the other side of the world, and plane tickets are not cheap," says Mrs. Anderson.

"I will take good care of your great-nephew," says Dr. Henzu, "he is an incredibly gifted young man. I feel the world could use someone with his talents, if given this opportunity."

"When would he leave," ask Mrs. Anderson?

"In a week," replies Dr. Henzu.

"A week! We just got him back," exclaims Mrs. Anderson!

She reluctantly agreed and allowed Ev'ren to leave, because deep down, she felt there was more to Ev'ren's life than Stone Mountain.

She cried and hugged him, as she told him how proud his parents would be, if they were alive. Megan and Tye decided to spend the night with Ev'ren. They promised him they would continue to look over Mrs. Anderson.

Megan and Ev'ren stared at each other for a split second, and wondered if they would ever have a real chance at love.

A week later a black limo pulled up in the yard. Dr. Henzu stepped out and asked Ev'ren if he was ready. With a look of certainty, he said he was.

He said goodbye to his aunt, Tye, and Megan. As he turned to walk away, Megan called his name and ran up to him. She kissed him on the lips which surprised him. Mrs. Anderson cleared her throat, and Dr. Henzu tapped on his watch to speed things along. They said goodbye one last time as Ev'ren got into the car.

When the car drove off, Ev'ren asked Dr. Henzu, if this was the end. Dr. Henzu laughed at Ev'ren.

"No son, this is not the end. This is just the beginning," he says.

"Of what," says Ev'ren.

"Of your unknown fate son…your unknown fate."

The End